PORTRAIT OF A DISCIPLINARIAN

Aishling Morgan

This book is a work of fiction.
In real life, make sure you practise safe, sane and
consensual sex.

First published in 2008 by
Nexus
Thames Wharf Studios
Rainville Rd
London W6 9HA

Copyright © Aishling Morgan 2008

The right of Aishling Morgan to be identified as the Author of
the Work has been asserted in accordance with the Copyright,
Designs and Patents Act 1988.

A catalogue record for this book is available from the
British Library.

www.nexus-books.com

Typeset by TW Typesetting, Plymouth, Devon
Printed and bound in Great Britain by CPI Bookmarque,
Croydon, CR0 4TD

Distributed in the USA by Macmillan, 175 Fifth Avenue,
New York, NY 10010, USA

ISBN 978 0 352 34179 2

The Random House Group Limited supports The Forest Stewardship Council (FSC),
the leading international forest certification organisation. All our titles that are
printed on Greenpeace approved FSC certified paper carry the FSC logo.
Our paper procurement policy can be found at *www.rbooks.co.uk/environment.*

1 3 5 7 9 10 8 6 4 2

PORTRAIT OF A DISCIPLINARIAN

Twisting violently round, Stephanie gaped in horror. In the doorway was her Aunt Gertrude, and she was not alone. A man stood beside her, a tall, solidly built man, who managed to project an air of pompous superiority even as he stared in open astonishment at her exposed rear. Aunt Lettice released Stephanie's wrist. Taken by surprise, she tumbled on to the floor, to lie for a moment with her legs splayed and any detail of her quim that the spectators might have missed while she was bottom up now available for inspection between her open thighs.

Immediately she jumped up, clutching her drawers, but tripped over them and sprawled forwards, straight into the arms of the man. He caught her, ducking down as he did so, and for an instant his hand cupped one hot bottom cheek before he hauled her up and set her on her feet.

Symbols key

 Corporal Punishment

 Female Domination

 Institution

 Medical

 Period Setting

 Restraint/Bondage

 Rubber/Leather

 Spanking

 Transvestism

 Underwear

 Uniforms

One

'I say, Stiffy,' Freddie Drake remarked.

'Don't be vulgar,' Stephanie Truscott replied, knowing full well that his remark was occasioned by the shape her bottom made under her dress as she leant out of the window. 'Just pass me the boathook. I think I can get one.'

'Right ho,' Freddie answered and, as Stephanie's hand reached back, something long and hard was pressed into her palm. 'Ah, one day, Stiffy . . .'

'Do be quiet, Freddie,' she told him. 'I'm trying to concentrate.'

A policeman was almost directly below her, a stoutish individual with three stripes on his sleeve indicating that he was no normal specimen but of sergeant's rank. His helmet would be a prize indeed, and would put Myrtle Finch-Farmiloe firmly in her place. A careful insertion of the boathook into his chinstrap, a quick jerk, a hasty retreat through the Dove to where her two-seater stood ready, and it would be done.

Unfortunately neither the Oxford nor the Cambridge crew were assisting. The two boats were so close together that the crowd were watching with rapt attention, either cheering for one side or the other or, like the police sergeant, watching with their mouths open in excitement. In most cases this would have been beneficial, as their attention was diverted from her careful manipulation of the boathook, but with the sergeant it meant that the chinstrap of his helmet had become

1

wedged between his second and third chins, making easy removal an impossibility. Yet a small gap remained where one reddish ear and a bulging cheek held the strap clear of his skin for a space of perhaps an inch.

Stephanie braced her feet apart and pursed her lips in concentration, moving the boathook gradually forward towards her target – only for the sergeant to step forward a pace as the man in front of him moved away. He had also closed his mouth, now apathetic as Oxford got into a tangle with their oars and began to lose way. The strap now dangled a good inch clear of his chin, yet he was no longer within reach of the boathook, and leaning any further out of the window risked a drop of some twelve feet on to granite cobbles.

'Hold on to me, Freddie,' she instructed.

'Rather,' he replied, full of enthusiasm for the task.

His hands closed on her hips, holding her firmly in place, but he had also moved directly behind her, in such a way that he was pressed firmly against her bottom. Something suspiciously long and hard was nudging between her cheeks, causing her eyes to widen and her mouth to open in a little O of shock and surprise before she managed to collect herself.

'Freddie!' she protested.

'Too tight?' he enquired politely.

'No, but . . .' she began, and trailed off, unsure how to point out to him, without resorting to improper language that it was the height of bad manners to wedge his erect penis between the cheeks of her bottom.

'Just stop it!' she hissed, a poor choice of words, as he immediately let go.

For one awful moment she felt her body begin to topple forward, only for his grip to tighten once again.

'Better hold on, don't you think?' he suggested.

'Yes!' she answered. 'But could you . . . will you . . . just behave yourself, Freddie Drake!'

'Right ho,' he answered, and immediately pressed himself to her bottom, exactly as before.

2

Stephanie said a word she had once heard used by her grandfather's pigman when he had inadvertently rolled a cart laden with several hundredweight of mangel-wurzels over his foot, but she said it under her breath. The boats were now well past, and much of the crowd had moved on up river, reducing the noise level so that it was possible that the police sergeant might hear her. Although he appeared to have fallen into a reverie as he looked out across the river, there was every chance he would turn round. The deed had to be done without delay. Inching the boathook forward, she braced herself for the adroit flick that would secure her prize. Just then, Freddie began kneading her buttocks with his thumbs.

'Will you stop that!' she demanded in a fierce whisper, twisting round as she spoke.

'Be a sport, Stiffy old thing,' he answered, pressing closer still to her body. 'You have such a darling little bottom and, I mean to say, what's a chap supposed to do?'

'Freddie!' Stephanie hissed, urgent now as he began to rub himself between her cheeks. 'Must you be so beastly!'

Freddie's answer was a low moan, then to lower the window on to her back, carefully, so as not to hurt her, but leaving her unable to move.

'Freddie!' she repeated, in rising consternation as the rubbing grew faster.

He didn't reply, and she began to wriggle, but only succeeded in rubbing her bottom against him, which he took for a sign of encouragement. Not daring to call out, for fear of alerting the policeman to her intentions, she could only stay as she was, pinned helpless by the waist as he amused himself with her bottom, now fondling her cheeks as he rubbed himself in her crease with rising excitement.

'Oh, do hurry up then, if you really must!' she snapped. 'But you really are an utter beast!'

She was not at all sure he could hear her, but in any case the remark was made more to soothe her own ruffled feelings than for him, as he clearly had no intention of stopping until he had finished his business. Tucking the boathook between her tummy and the window ledge, she braced her hands against the brickwork. Her tiny mouth set in a petulant grimace, then slackened as she realised that he would be unable to see her disapproval. Besides, what he was doing to her felt both deliciously naughty and deliciously nice.

But when he suddenly began to tug up her dress she did react, wriggling frantically in a vain effort to escape, terrified that she was about to have her virginity taken, maybe even be left pregnant, or perhaps have his cock inserted up her bottom instead of between her cheeks. He disregarded her struggles and quickly jerked up her dress, exposing the seat of the American union suit that was all she had on beneath. Both her consternation and her struggles grew fiercer still as she was unbuttoned behind, leaving her bare bottom sticking out of the hole in her union suit.

She felt his cock, naked and hot, as he once more pressed it between her cheeks, not against either of the vulnerable little holes between, but upright as before. He squeezed her cheeks together, folding the meaty little hemispheres around his burning erection, then again began to rut in her slit, now fast and urgent. Stephanie opened her mouth wide, unable to control her feelings, half wishing the thick cock between her cheeks were inside her instead, whatever the consequences. The other half of her wanted him suspended by his feet and dipped into the Thames for an extended period, head first, but she had no choice in the matter and could do no more than gasp out her feelings and clutch the rough bricks of the wall as her bottom was abused. Her body had begun to rock back and forth to his thrusts, rolling the shaft of the boathook between her tummy and the window ledge, faster and faster still, until he gave one last hard shove.

Stephanie Truscott felt something warm and wet splash on to the small of her back, just in the V where her cheeks opened out. She cried out in disgust as she realised what he'd done, and jerked round. The boathook shot free of the window ledge, to fall in a slow arc that terminated on the helmet of the policeman below. Stephanie tried to pull back, but the window held her firmly in place, and Freddie was too busy wiping his own helmet on her bottom to notice as the sergeant turned around.

'A five-pound fine or seven days in the jug,' Stephanie admitted.

Her mother drew a sigh.

'Really, Stephanie, the day will come when I will leave you to spend a week in gaol. Perhaps that would teach you a lesson?'

Stephanie hung her head, biting her lip and fidgeting as she stared at the toes of her shoes and waited for the inevitable summons.

'Meanwhile,' Lady Truscott went on, not unkindly, 'you had better come here and we'll have that naughty bottom of yours smacked, shall we?'

Stephanie walked forward, not even thinking of resistance or protest, despite the presence of a parlour-maid in one corner of the room, industriously polishing a walnut table from which every blemish had already been removed. The maid continued to work as Stephanie draped herself across her mother's lap, but she moved to the far side of the table to make sure she got the best possible view of the spanking.

Resigned to her ignominious fate, Stephanie lifted her hips to allow her dress to be pulled up, then settled herself across her mother's knees, her bottom now the highest part of her body. Her union suit was a little small, stretching between the buttons to leave slender ovals of milky white flesh visible, and the silk was both taut and thin, offering little or no protection to her bottom. That did not prevent her mother from unfastening the garment, undoing the buttons from the lowest up to the small of Stephanie's back, to leave her small, rounded cheeks sticking out between the open sides of the union suit.

Stephanie grimaced, thinking of the show she was making of herself both to her mother and, more importantly, to the parlour-maid, her bottom quite bare and the lips of her quim showing between her thighs as well. Not that it was the first time, by a very long way, but it was still horribly embarrassing to have it done, and a thousand times worse when it was in front of the servants.

She pursed her lips as her mother began to spank, determined not to make more of an exhibition of herself than was necessary. Fortunately her mother believed in chastisement for its own sake and didn't spank particularly hard, allowing Stephanie to retain at least some of her modesty. She still wriggled a little when the slaps caught her thighs or made her cheeks open to provide peeks of her bottom hole to the ever-attentive parlour-maid, but she managed to stop herself throwing a tantrum or even crying, save for a single tear that drew a long black line of mascara down her cheek.

Finally she was allowed to stand up. She turned to face her mother.

'Go to the corner,' Lady Truscott ordered, 'and you can think about your behaviour for a while.'

Stephanie went, holding her dress up, because she knew only too well that when she was told to go to the corner she was to stand with her nose pressed into the angle of the walls and her bare red bottom showing to the room. She even adjusted her union suit to make sure she showed properly from behind, hoping that her mother would mistake the gesture for contrition, but Lady Truscott had picked up the novel she'd been reading and took no notice. Only the parlour-maid was watching, with a nasty little smirk on her face. After a moment Stephanie plucked up the courage to stick out her tongue.

Turning back into the corner, she hung her head, feeling every bit as rueful as her mother might have hoped, but far from repentant. Her principal emotion was irritation, because it was all so grossly unfair. It wasn't her fault at all, but she was sure that the beastly Freddie Drake wouldn't be standing in his living room with a hot red bottom on show to the world. Admittedly, once he'd realised what was happening he had done his best to help her escape, and it wasn't his fault that the alley he'd suggested she nip down had had two constables coming along it the other way in response to their sergeant's whistle. That had just been bad luck, and it had also been bad luck that the inspector at the police station had recognised her from the time before.

So she'd been pinched, and Freddie had not only got away but had the immortal crust to come to the magistrates' court and pay her fine, passing a few choice remarks about delinquency in the modern girl to the very sergeant he'd so narrowly avoided in the alleys of Hammersmith. He hadn't even been particularly sympathetic, giving her the briefest of hugs before making an unpardonably rude joke about what she'd have to do to pay him back the five pounds, and going on to describe how Cambridge had won the boat race by ten lengths to secure their fifth victory in succession.

At the memory of his behaviour her lips moulded into the same petulant expression she had worn while having his penis rubbed between her bottom cheeks. Then they softened again. Despite her very genuine resentment at his cavalier treatment, it was impossible not to feel a thrill, a deliciously naughty, thoroughly improper thrill. They had misbehaved, in a way that would have utterly scandalised their friends and relatives, and that felt wonderful. So, she was forced to admit to herself, had his cock, as he rubbed it so energetically up and down in her bottom slit.

Besides all that, she seemed to have earned the worst fate of all: being sent down to the country, where she would be unable to prevent Myrtle Finch-Farmiloe either from securing the coveted position of club secretary for Gaspers or from forcing her beastly attentions upon Freddie. He, Stephanie was certain, would be unable to resist, as among Myrtle's numerous faults were a dark, slumberous beauty and a nasty habit of appearing coy yet mysterious whenever men were around. Then, too, Myrtle didn't get spanked and never had been, which had always provoked a sharp sense of inferiority in Stephanie. If the committee at Gaspers found out that Stephanie not only still got spanked but did so frequently, her chances would become slimmer still. It was essential to be in London.

'That's long enough, I think,' Lady Truscott stated, closing her novel with a snap. 'You may come out of the corner now, Stephanie, and first thing tomorrow morning you will go down to Devon, where you will stay until further notice.'

Stephanie's first move on being given permission to come out of the corner had been to reach for the buttons of her union suit, intending to put her bottom away first so that she could hide it from the attention of the parlour-maid, which was suspiciously intense. At her mother's words she froze, then opened her mouth wide in protest.

'Mother!'

'I'll have no nonsense,' Lady Truscott replied, suddenly stern.

'Yes, but Mother –,' Stephanie blustered.

'Stephanie Amelia!' Lady Truscott snapped.

Stephanie winced, painfully aware of the implication of having both her Christian names used. Another word and the parlour-maid was likely to be told to fetch a cane, and maybe even to hold Stephanie while she was beaten, a prospect far more painful and humiliating than a simple spanking. She made a face, but remained silent as her mother went on.

'You will go to Devon, and remain there until further notice, as I have said. To Driscoll's, I think.'

'Driscoll's?' Stephanie echoed. 'But Mother, please . . .'

'To Driscoll's,' Lady Truscott said firmly.

'Why not Stukely Hall?' Stephanie demanded.

'Your great-grandmother is ninety-five,' Lady Truscott explained patiently, 'and your grandmother has requested absolute calm, something that seems to be an impossibility with you about. You are going to Driscoll's.'

'How many of my aunts are there?' Stephanie asked.

'Only two,' her mother replied. 'Three if you count your Great-aunt Victoria. Lavinia, Edith and Rosalie are at Beare.'

After a moment of calculation Stephanie winced again. Three aunts could mean only one thing: more spankings. Possibly the cane, too.

'I want you well away from bad influences,' Lady Truscott went on, 'and that dreadful club of yours. I suppose you were with that awful flapper Myrtle and Roberta Drake?'

'Not at all,' Stephanie replied. 'I was escorted by Mr Frederick Drake.'

Her mother gave a cluck that indicated as low an opinion of one Drake as of the other.

'Your sister is at Driscoll's, of course,' she continued, 'so I will be sending Vera to keep an eye on you.'

Stephanie's face grew sulkier still and she cast a dirty look at the parlour-maid, who now looked the picture of dutiful service as she curtsied to Lady Truscott.

'May I at least take the two-seater?' Stephanie asked.

'I suppose so,' her mother answered. 'It's only getting in the way here.'

'I don't mind doing without a maid,' Stephanie volunteered, made bold by her mother's acquiescence.

'Vera will go with you,' Lady Truscott said firmly. 'And Vera, if Miss Stephanie doesn't behave herself, I think you know what to do.'

9

'Mother!' Stephanie exclaimed in horror.

'Yes, Lady Truscott,' Vera supplied, her voice thoroughly smug. Stephanie wondered if there was to be *any* female member of the household who was not allowed access to her bottom.

The two-seater took the brow of Shapely Down at very nearly sixty miles per hour and, as the view of Dartmoor spread out before her, Stephanie's mouth curved into a satisfied smile. It had been a good journey, and a fast one. She'd had the car up to seventy-five on the long straight outside Salisbury and, more importantly, she was on her own. It was, she felt, jolly clever of her to wait until her father was in but her mother was out, and then insist on taking so much luggage that the maid was obliged to follow by train. Her father had indulged her, as always, and the awful Vera had been left with no choice but to comply. The consequences were likely to be both painful and humiliating in the long run, but Vera obviously intended to make full use of her permission to smack Stephanie's bottom anyway, so it made little difference what excuse was used.

The thought did nothing to remove her smile. This was her own land, and it was impossible not to enjoy the breeze in her hair as she tried to take the two-seater over the seventy mark again along the straight past the Warren House Inn. Every detail of the vast sweep of Dartmoor was familiar, each tor familiar by name and the site of many a childhood expedition, while many of the places within view related to a family history that went back before records were kept.

It was in Postbridge, where she was forced to slow down owing to some fool who had stopped his cart almost in the centre of the road so that he could unload thatch, that a direct ancestor known as Devil John had wooed and won Alice Eden, after disposing of a rival suitor by inserting a fox's brush up the unfortunate man's bottom and giving him a quarter-mile start on the hounds. Then, invisible beyond the shoulder of White Tor, there were the ruins of the Pargade House, where Arabela, a great-aunt, had shot a man for compromising her sister's honour.

Stephanie wasn't sure of the details of either event, having had the stories related to her by her grandfather when he'd had considerably too much to drink, but she heartily approved. She couldn't see Devil John or Arabela putting up with the likes of Vera Clapshott, although she didn't suppose Devil John or Arabela had had to put up with five widowed aunts either. It was jolly inconsiderate, she felt, for all five of their husbands to have managed to get themselves killed during the war. One or two, perhaps, would have been understandable, but five began to look like clumsiness.

As she accelerated up the long slope out of Postbridge she was earnestly wishing that she didn't stand just four feet and eleven inches in her stockings and that she had rather fewer aunts. The five widows were bad enough, but Great-aunt Victoria was the worst of all, one minute as jolly as anything and the next flying into a temper over something as trivial as letting one of the dogs take a bite from a teacake. After all, the silly old woman should have seen a bite had been taken out of it before putting it in her own mouth, and there really hadn't been all that much drool on it.

She put her foot down on the accelerator at the memory of the incident. Victoria Truscott had exceeded all bounds, dishing out a bare-bottom spanking in front of not only an assortment of aunts but Stephanie's grandparents, her little sister Hermione, a maid, the butler and a local farmer who'd come to see about purchasing some seed turnips. Among the embarrassing moments of Stephanie's life it ranked seventh: worse than what Freddie Drake had done to her, but hardly to be compared with being unexpectedly mounted by George Hamilton Gordon, when only the fortunate interposition of a pair of stout flannel pyjamas had prevented her virginity being taken in a manner that didn't bear thinking about.

Now feeling distinctly cross, she kept her foot down as she passed along the slope of Bellever Tor, reaching sixty miles per hour as the bridge over the Cherrybrook came into view. A heavily laden dray had stopped there, so that the driver could relieve himself into the stream. Stephanie jammed her foot on the brake, felt the wheels lose their purchase and shut her eyes tight as the car hit the wall, burst through it, bucked violently on the rough chunks of granite and slithered sideways down the slope into the Cherrybrook, depositing her – really quite gently – in the deepest part of the stream.

Slowly, Stephanie stood up, and spat out a newt that seemed intent on making a new home of her mouth. She removed her driving goggles and opened her eyes. Above her, the drayman was looking down, his weather-beaten face set in astonishment, his fly unbuttoned, a large, brownish penis held in one hand with a single yellow drop hanging from the tip. Their eyes met.

'You want to be careful, Miss,' the drayman advised.

Temporarily bereft of speech, Stephanie could only shake some water from her hair and retrieve her hat before it floated away downstream. The drayman, apparently keen to make conversation, put his penis away and went on.

'Terrible dangerous corner, this one. You're lucky not to be scat all abroad to flibbits. Why, it can't be no more than seven, maybe eight year ago that fellow from Princetown gaol, doctor he was, and should've known better –'

'Please could you help me out, if you don't mind?' Stephanie interrupted.

'Why, certainly, Miss,' he offered, and began to make his way down the bank.

Stephanie took his hand and allowed herself to be pulled from the water. She had lost a shoe and was drenched to the skin, but her first concern was for the state of the car. It lay sideways, half under water, the front crumpled from her impact with the stone wall, which fortunately had been partially demolished by some earlier accident. It wasn't as bad as it might have been, and there had already been several dents in the fender, so with the services of a good mechanic she might even get away with it altogether, as long as she could get the car out of the river and back to Postbridge. She noticed that two powerful Shire horses were harnessed to the dray.

'Would you be a sweetie and pull my car out?' she asked, aiming at the drayman a smile few men had ever been able to resist. 'Your horses look terribly strong, and I'm sure they could pull my little car up the bank, and maybe you'd be kind enough to take me into Postbridge?

He nodded thoughtfully.

'I dare say.'

'Would you?' Stephanie ventured after a pause. 'I'd be awfully grateful.'

'I dare say,' he repeated, then paused as if reflecting on some deep matter. 'But how grateful, that's the question, ain't it?'

'Ever so,' Stephanie promised, then she paused too.

She'd had a bite of lobster at the Crown in Sherborne and filled the tank in Moretonhamstead, which left her with very little money until she got to Driscoll's. In any case, the thought of telling her aunts what had happened made her lip twitch and her bottom cheeks tighten. Retrieving her bag, which had somehow been thrown out of the car and come to rest beside a large cowpat, she dug inside. There was a half-crown, a threepenny bit and a handful of copper. Also a five-pound note, but she would need that for the repair.

'Would um . . . three shillings and tuppence-farthing be all right?' she asked.

'Three shillings tuppence-farthing?'

'It's all I have on me, I'm afraid.'

Again he was quiet for a moment, but this time his eyes were fixed on where her dress was plastered to her chest, showing the low half-egg mounds of her breasts, each topped by a largish nipple made protuberant by the cold. She bit her lip, all too aware of the quality of his attention and hoping that his thoughts weren't going in the direction they seemed to be.

'I wouldn't say it's all you have,' he remarked, his voice now sly.

'I really can't image what you mean,' she replied sulkily.

'Well, my dear,' he went on, bolder now, 'you've a fine little pair of devil's dumplings up front, for one, and I'll bet you've a nice round sit-upon behind and all.'

Her worst fears confirmed, Stephanie made a face, wondering just how beastly the drayman wanted to be, and whether she should make an offer or wait for him to propose something. Judging from the behaviour of both Freddie Drake and George Hamilton Gordon, men liked to rub their cocks between a girl's bottom cheeks, but she couldn't bring herself to say the words, especially as the drayman might not keep to the agreement, but push it up her instead. He spoke again before she could find her tongue.

'So how about you show me them,' he suggested. 'And while you're at it, you could take John Thomas here and pop him in that pretty mouth of yours.'

There was no mistaking his meaning, as he had taken hold of his cock through his trousers, squeezing it to show off the long, thick bulge it made in the coarse wool. Stephanie felt her face colour. She could not believe that any man would expect a girl to take his penis inside her mouth. The act was so blatantly obscene that it beggared belief.

'What a horrid suggestion!' she exclaimed. 'How could you!'

'No trouble at all,' he assured her. 'I'll just pop him

inside, and you can pretend like you're sucking on a lollipop.'

'I don't imagine it would taste like a lollipop,' Stephanie retorted, thinking of the single yellow drop she'd seen hanging from the tip just minutes before, 'and besides, I'm not at all sure it would fit.'

'Oh, he'd fit, ' he answered, 'just the same as he'd fit up that little cunt of yours, if I were to push hard enough.'

'Why, you filthy . . .' Stephanie began, the blood rushing to her cheeks.

She stopped, thinking of the caning she would undoubtedly get if her aunts discovered that she had crashed the car. That it hadn't been her fault would make no difference, it would be up with her dress and off with her union suit, for the application of maybe as many as two dozen strokes of Great-aunt Victoria's whalebone cane on her naked bottom cheeks. The cane burned like fire and would leave her unable to sit comfortably for a week or more, while if she consented to the drayman's horrid suggestion it would all be over quite soon, presumably in much the same time as it had taken Freddie Drake to do it all over her bottom, three or four minutes at most, only it would be in her mouth. She bit her lip in consternation and indecision. At school, Myrtle French-Farmiloe had once made her put a slug in her mouth. Could it be any nastier?

'Wind's getting up,' the drayman remarked reflectively. 'Could be rain.'

'Nonsense,' Stephanie retorted, glancing around at the unbroken blue of the Dartmoor sky.

'You never can tell with the moor,' the drayman went on. 'Mist can come up out of the ground as easy as winking –'

'Oh, do be quiet!' Stephanie snapped. 'I'm trying to think about your beastly proposition.'

He paused a moment before speaking again, carefully, as if each word had been chosen only after considerable reflection.

'Seems to me, seeing as how you want to think about it, that maybe you're not so very prim and proper as you might be. And seeing as how you can manage to think about it, you might as well do it. Seems so.'

Stephanie threw him an angry glance, unable to dispute what he was saying because he was right. He responded with a dirty grin, as if reading her mind, then spoke again.

'Done it before, have you?'

'No, I have not!' she answered him.

'How do you know it's so bad then?' he asked.

Again Stephanie made a face, not knowing what to say.

'A lot of girls like it,' he went on. 'Very keen, my missus used to be, back when we were courting. Used to rub him between her dumplings and all, she did. Nice, that was. Shame you're not so generous in your hamper, but I do like small ones . . .'

Stephanie put her hands to her breasts, conscious of how their shape showed through her wet dress.

'That's right,' he said, 'give them a little rub. Make you feel better about it.'

'I am not . . .' Stephanie began in outrage, and stopped.

Despite the bright spring sunshine she was starting to feel cold, and badly needed to take off her clothes to let them dry. The drayman obviously wasn't going to go away. At the thought of taking her clothes off in front of him she began to blush again, and, as she turned away, she spotted her lost shoe, lying at the water's edge beneath the bridge. She went to fetch it and slipped her foot inside, only to discover that it was full of mud, which squashed up between her toes and around her ankle, soiling her stocking. It seemed that fate was against her.

'So what's it to be?' he demanded. 'If you're going to be missish about it, I'd best be getting along.'

'I am not being missish!' Stephanie snapped. 'You're being a beast!'

He merely shrugged and began to walk towards his dray. Stephanie watched, her mouth working in indecision as she thought of the ignominious arrival at Driscoll's without her car, the shamefaced interview with Great-aunt Victoria and the others, the exposure of her bottom in the drawing room, the bite of the cane into her tender flesh . . .

'Oh, very well!' she spat. 'But I'd like you to know that you're a horrid pig, and no gentleman.'

'I don't recall saying I was a gentleman,' he answered, leering as he turned to her once more. 'Let's get the business done, then, and my girls'll have you out of there in a trifle.'

Across the road was a small quarry, perhaps used in the construction of the bridge, which looked as if it might provide suitable concealment. Feeling thoroughly put upon but nevertheless acutely conscious of the intimacy of what she was about to do, Stephanie took the drayman by the hand and led him across the road, her feet squelching in her muddy shoes. He followed, suddenly pliable now that he'd got his way, and she found herself within a ring of cut granite, open only at one side, and that grown over with gorse and brambles. It was obvious that nobody had worked the place for years. At least nobody would see her disgrace herself.

Several chunks of granite lay among the soft grass on the quarry floor. The drayman went over to the largest of them, unfastened his trousers, pushed them to his ankles and sat down. Beneath, he had coarse woollen longjohns of a greyish-yellow hue, with buttons at the front, two of which he unfastened to allow him to flop out the large dun-coloured penis she had seen before, along with a set of large dun-coloured balls.

'Off with your clothes then, my love,' he ordered as he began to stroke himself, 'and I dare say if you spread them out on the rocks they'll be dry in a moment.'

Her face set in an angry scowl, Stephanie obeyed, peeling her dress up and off, then starting on the buttons of her union suit. He watched, his eyes feasting on her body as it was revealed, one big dirty hand moving slowly back and forth on his already swollen cock shaft. She spread out her dress to dry, but when she put her fingers to the shoulder straps of her union suit she felt suddenly far more vulnerable, so that it took all her willpower to do as she'd agreed and shrug it down, then off. She stepped free, to stand naked but for her shoes, stockings, hat and gloves.

She'd begun to shiver, not from cold but from being naked in front of him, and, although it made no sense, she knew that if she stripped off completely she would feel more vulnerable still. Besides, his cock was now a rigid pole in his hand, with a fat, purple helmet popping in and out of his leathery foreskin as he played with himself. It obviously needed sucking, but the thought of taking it in her mouth was barely tolerable. She hesitated, unsure whether she should complete her strip, go down on her knees and take the awful thing in her mouth, as she had promised, or run.

'Turn around,' he said. 'Let's see that little sit-upon.'

Stephanie did as she was told, grateful for the delay, turning slowly round to show him her bare bottom and back. He began to pull faster, rolling his foreskin vigorously back and forth over a helmet now so swollen it looked fit to burst. Wondering if she could make him do it in his hand and so spare herself the supreme indignity, Stephanie repeated the manoeuvre, this time sticking her bottom out a little, the way Freddie was always trying to persuade her to.

'Oh, you little angel,' the drayman grunted, now hammering at his cock. 'Do that again ... only more ... show that little cunt ...'

Her face feeling as if it was about to catch fire, Stephanie obeyed, pulling her back in and pushing her bottom out to let him peek at the rear view of her quim.

Her cheeks were open wide, showing off the tight little hole between. He grunted, apparently no longer able to speak. His face was the same rich purple as his straining helmet. Stephanie smiled, batted her eyelids and gave a little wiggle of her bottom, but saw that he was beckoning frantically at her.

She said a rude word under her breath, but it was all too easy to imagine him refusing to help if she didn't go through with it. She stepped close and dropped to her knees in the warm, soft grass in front of him. She caught the scent of his cock, intensely masculine but more like a bull or a boar pig than any of the men she knew, rich and musky and horribly strong, but also compelling. Before she knew it she was leaning forward, her mouth agape, and as he pushed down his cock she took it in her mouth.

Something inside her seemed to give. The tears welled from her eyes and began to trickle down her face even as she sucked earnestly on his erection, doing her best to pleasure him though she didn't understand why. For the first time in her life she had a man's penis in her mouth, something she had never even imagined doing, something so rude, so utterly unsuitable that it made her whole body burn with shame. What made it infinitely worse was her desperate need to touch herself between her thighs.

Sobbing and gulping on the drayman's penis, her body shivering until her tits shook and her bottom cheeks quivered, the tears streaming hot and angry down her face, Stephanie sucked. One hand went to his balls, a gesture she had never intended, the other to his shaft, and she was fondling the bulbous wrinkly sack and tugging on him at the same time, barely conscious of what she was doing, appalled by her own behaviour, but performing with ever-rising enthusiasm, until the drayman at last gave a deep groan and jammed himself deep.

Stephanie's eyes popped and her cheeks bulged as his enormous, bloated helmet was rammed down her gullet.

She felt his stuff explode into the back of her throat, which went into violent, uncontrollable contractions. A great gout of come and mucus erupted from her nose, and more from her mouth when she finally managed to pull back. It dribbled down her tits and belly as she knelt panting in the grass, unable to speak. The drayman gave a long, contented sigh.

'Now who's a little liar?' he said happily. 'If you've not done that before, then I'm a monkey's uncle.'

Stephanie said nothing, partly through sheer outrage, partly because she still felt the awful need to rub her quim, but mainly because she was still coughing up a mixture of come and saliva on to the grass between her knees. He got up, tugged his trousers high and patted her on top of her hat as he walked past. Only then did he put his cock and balls away. Through eyes blurred with tears Stephanie watched him go, then climbed slowly to her feet.

Her thoughts were a muddle, with several strong emotions vying for her attention, but the most compelling was a warm, urgent arousal, which she was determined to ignore. To have stripped off and taken a man's cock in her mouth until he came was bad enough, but she could at least save some face if she could pretend she'd had no choice; to get excited over it was unthinkable.

To avoid having to admit her true feelings she busied herself with her clothes, kicking her shoes away and peeling off her stockings and gloves to go stark naked but for her hat, which was already dry. She went to sit on a rock but soon began to feel silly, while the granite was uncomfortably rough against her bare bottom. Moving to the entrance of the quarry, she peered cautiously out, to find the road empty and the drayman busy with his horses.

She was quite alone. It would have been so easy to slip a hand between her thighs and play with the sensitive little bump of flesh that formed the very heart

20

of her quim until she achieved that exquisite sensation that exceeded every other pleasure she knew. Yet it would be the drayman's cock she was thinking of when it happened, and somehow that was a worse disgrace than what she had already done. So she watched him work instead, her arms folded across her chest and her mouth set in a tight, determined line.

Finally he managed to haul the two-seater out of the stream and back on to the road. The interior was sodden and muddy, the paint scratched and the front bumper badly dented. Still, she reflected as she pulled on her now merely damp clothes, she might still escape retribution. As long as the mechanics could get the car going again, and she arrived after dark, she could put it in the garage and take it out again first thing in the morning. There was a big garage in Okehampton that would make the necessary repairs, and she would have evaded the cane.

As they drove back to Postbridge with the two-seater hitched to the back of the dray, Stephanie grew increasingly confident. All that really mattered was getting the car going; the rest could wait. She had driven so fast that she wouldn't be expected for hours anyway. It was all going to work.

The mechanic came out as they reached the garage, rubbing his hands on an oily rag and contemplating the wreck with what Stephanie felt was an insolent lack of surprise.

'Hairy Hands get you?' he enquired, grinning.

'No,' Stephanie answered, indicating the drayman. 'This idiot was parked in the middle of the bridge. Do you think you could get me back on the road, please?'

The mechanic paused to suck in air between his front teeth, then shook his head.

'No chance of that, I'm afraid, Miss,' he said, pointing to the trail of oily spots running from beneath the car and back along the road. 'You've cracked your sump, you have. Be a week, maybe more, it will.'

21

'But I have to get to Bidlake Village,' Stephanie insisted, 'near Lydford.'

'I know Bidlake,' the drayman told her, pausing from his efforts to load an ancient and badly stained pipe with fresh tobacco. 'I'll give you a lift if you don't mind taking your time, and perhaps . . .'

Stephanie Truscott wiped the last trace of the drayman's come from her lower lip. He had taken her as far as the Okehampton Road before insisting on having his cock sucked for the second time, and punishing her for calling him names by deliberately wiping a blob of come on her nose while he held her firmly by the hair. All of which had left her feeling more chagrined than ever, and also more in need of the touch of her hand between her thighs.

The episode had demoted what Freddie had done to her to ninth place among the most embarrassing incidents of her life, or possibly tenth if it counted as two, but she was unsure how it ranked in comparison to the teacake incident, because, while it had been utterly disgusting, or so she kept telling herself, it had been neither painful nor done in front of witnesses. George Hamilton Gordon still held sixth place.

By the time she got to Driscoll's it was dark, and had been for some time. The lights of both dining room and drawing room were on, suggesting that dinner had reached the stage when the ladies retired to leave the gentlemen to their port, while rhythmic, fleshy smacks punctuated by heartfelt squeals suggested that her little sister was being spanked. Stephanie bit her lip, wondering whether she would suffer the same fate as soon as Hermione had been finished with, assuming she entered the drawing room at all. A much better plan was to go in by the tradesmen's entrance, where she would find Catchpole the butler, who was a kindly soul and could be relied on for a badly needed sandwich.

She had already decided on her story, concocted during the long slow drive across the moor, with the driver prattling of this and that, either unaware of or indifferent to her sulky expression and terse answers. If she admitted she had crashed it would mean the cane for certain, but if she claimed she had run out of petrol they were unlikely to do more than smack her bottom for being a silly girl, maybe not even that. Or so she had thought, but now, with Hermione already spanked, they would be in the mood for chastisement. If they'd had rather too much wine, they might do something really awful, like pass her around from lap to lap, taking turns with her bottom, which seemed to be what was happening to her sister. Maybe they would accept her story and ask her to take her turn with Hermione, but probably not.

It was much less risky to slip upstairs and pretend she'd arrived after everybody but the servants had gone to bed, then blame the garage for the time it took to get the car back. That presented another problem, because the bill was likely to eat up so much of what remained of her allowance that she would be unable to sneak back to London for the Gaspers election, as she was determined to do. For the time being, though, all that mattered was getting safely upstairs to bed with her bottom still in pristine condition.

Catchpole was everything she had hoped and more, a dispenser of not only sympathy and sandwiches but bottled beer, two kinds of pie and a kitchen-maid to act as look-out while Stephanie nipped up the servants' staircase to the Blue Room, which had already been prepared for her. Exhausted, she undressed, risked a quick visit to the bathroom while the aunts who lived at Beare House were being put into a car, slipped into the short cotton nightgown that had been laid out for her, and collapsed into bed.

Her eyes closed, only to open again in irritation. Whoever had chosen the nightgown must have thought she was about six, or eight at the outside. As Vera didn't seem to have arrived, presumably it had been Mrs

Catchpole, who kept house. On her previous birthday she had presented Stephanie with a golliwog and set of bricks. The woman was plainly dotty but had been with the family for ever and was the soul of kindness, so it was pointless to complain.

She rolled on to her front, telling herself she would just have to put up with it, but the new position was even worse. The nightie had been made at the height of the war, when economy was considered the prime virtue, and had been short then. Now it was hopelessly inadequate and didn't even cover her bottom, leaving her acutely conscious of the way her bare cheeks stuck out below the hem, even though there was nobody to see. She felt vulnerable, as if she was due to be spanked, and rude, as if Freddie Drake or perhaps the drayman, whom she knew only as Lias, had made her lift her dress to show off her bottom.

Again she turned over and tugged the nightie down, but the moment she reached up to cuddle her pillow in her favourite sleeping position the garment rode up again, showing her quim. The urge to touch was almost overwhelming, preferably with her legs spread in the position she knew she would be obliged to adopt on her wedding night but was not supposed to think about until then. Yet again she rolled on to her front, but it only made matters worse, tempting her to stick her bottom up in an even ruder position, to caress her cheeks and slip a finger between them to find her hole, which badly needed a tickle.

She turned on to her side, pushing the disturbing thoughts away, and began to count sheep, but they turned into rams, each with a pendulous purple-headed cock swinging from its woolly underside. She pulled the nightie right up, so that at least the lace trim wouldn't tickle her bottom and thighs, but that made her feel more vulnerable still.

Finally she gave in, kicking the sheets down and rolling on to her back. Her thighs came up and open

24

and she spread her quim to the cool night air as she imagined how one day she would offer herself to a man whose hard cock was ready to puncture the taut knot of flesh that blocked her virgin opening. She knew he'd probably want to see her breasts too, just as Lias the drayman had done, and she quickly pulled the nightie all the way up to her neck, baring her chest.

With her eyes lightly closed she began to explore her body, thinking of Freddie Drake and how rude he'd been with her bottom. She ran her finger over the low mounds of her breasts, pausing to tease her nipples to erection before moving lower, across the gentle bulge of her tummy and around her thighs to the swell of her bottom cheeks. One long fingernail found her bottom hole and she sighed in pleasure as she gave the tiny, wrinkled opening a much needed tickle. She began to giggle at how naughty she was being, imaging what Freddie would think if he saw her as she was, how rude he'd think her and what he'd want to do with her. At the least he'd make her suck his penis, as the drayman had done, and when she remembered how it had felt to kneel naked but for her stockings and shoes and hat and take an erect cock in her mouth she gave in completely. Spreading her thighs as wide as they would go, she began to stroke her quim, touching the plump fleshy lips and the moist folds between, at the same time teasing one nipple, while she struggled to think of Freddie Drake instead of the lecherous drayman.

It was no good. She gave in with a resigned sigh and her mind was filled with memories of the taste and smell and feel of his big dark cock. She began to masturbate. He'd been such a beast to her, making her strip, making her suck, but he was really no worse than Freddie, rubbing himself on her bottom until he did it all over her. Men were like that, utter beasts, doing rude things to girls with their horrible ugly cocks, cocks which she wanted to suck and lick and hold, to rub on her breasts and between the cheeks of her bottom, to have thrust up her virgin quim and into the rude little hole behind.

Her back arched in pleasure as she found herself wishing the drayman had taken her, and Freddie too, maybe the mechanic as well, and his mate, all four of them making utter pigs of themselves with her helpless body, using her in her mouth and her quim at the same time, maybe up her bottom as well, taking turns with her, but Freddie first, taking her virginity as the others clapped and cheered their approval, then making her suck her own maiden blood from his penis while the others filled her up between her thighs.

Stephanie bit her lip as the exquisite sensation hit her, determined not to repeat the fifth most embarrassing moment of her life, when she had been doing exactly the same thing and cried out in her ecstasy. Great-aunt Victoria had come into the room just in time to catch her grand-niece at the supreme moment of climax, spread-eagled naked on the bed with a small candle up her bottom.

Two

Stephanie Truscott awoke to bright sunshine filtering through a crack in the curtains and an assortment of thoughts, good and bad. For a while she lay still, considering each and putting it in its proper place. On the bad side she had been exiled to Devon, but on the good she was in Devon. On the bad side she had crashed the car, but on the good none of her relatives knew. On the bad side she had been made to suck a man's penis, but on the good side she had really rather enjoyed it. On the bad side she had Vera Clapshott as her personal maid and no less fewer than six aunts all of whom seemed to consider a day wasted unless it involved the application of a hand to her bare bottom. On the good side she hadn't actually been spanked yet.

Unfortunately there were also Freddie Drake and Myrtle Finch-Farmiloe, which left her ledger heavier on the debit side, and she was frowning as she got up. The air was a little cold and she hurried to wash, hoping nobody would be about as she scampered across the corridor, her bare bottom showing beneath the hem of her abbreviated nightie. Reaching the bathroom door, she quickly pushed it open, entered and locked it behind her, glad she had not been seen – only to turn around and discover a man standing at the washbasin, a rotund, elderly man with a moustache so abundant that he appeared to be staring out from above a quickset hedge, while his notably corpulent body was clad in pyjamas of a stupefying mauve.

27

Stephanie stopped, staring at this unexpected apparition, which she recognised as Sir Murgatroyd Drake, Freddie's father and a neighbouring landowner. He was no less surprised than she, his small protuberant eyes moving from her face down to the neat naked V between her thighs, whereupon she remembered just how much she was showing and fled, treating him to a display of her bottom cheeks as well.

Telling herself that the incident wasn't even worthy of her top ten most embarrassing moments did nothing to abate her blushes, and she cursed Sir Murgatroyd, Mrs Catchpole and Vera Clapshott indiscriminately as she hurriedly put on her clothes. Still pink-cheeked, she completed her ablutions in a different bathroom and made her way downstairs, listening for prowling aunts as she approached the morning-room.

None were present, only Hermione, who glanced up from a plate of kedgeree, her freckled face immediately breaking into a broad smile.

'Hi, Stiffy! Catchpole said you were down. Have you got the car?'

'No,' Stephanie admitted. She paused to kiss her sister and made her way to the row of tureens on the sideboard. 'Actually, you might be able to help me with that, but anyway, what's old Murgatroyd Drake doing here? I met him in the bathroom, looking positively foul in mauve pyjamas.'

'He was here for dinner,' Hermione explained. 'He got so beastly drunk last night he couldn't drive his car home.'

'Yes, but why was he here at all?' Stephanie demanded. 'The last time I was down, Grandpapa was threatening to shoot him if he came near the place.'

'They want to buy each other's pigs,' Hermione went on, 'so they've called a sort of truce while they offer each other more and more money.'

'Grandpapa would never sell the Emperor,' Stephanie said with conviction, 'but that's good news, because now he won't kick so much when I tell him I'm engaged to Freddie.'

'You're engaged!' Hermione exclaimed.

'As good as,' Stephanie answered. 'We haven't actually named the day, but ... well, he has to marry me.'

'You didn't!' Hermione shrieked, and immediately put a hand over her mouth.

There was a moment of silence while both sisters looked apprehensively towards the door, before Stephanie continued.

'Not that, no, but nearly.'

'Tell me!' Hermione demanded in an urgent whisper.

Stephanie merely smiled, preferring to remain mysterious than to explain the truth, which she knew would only make her sister laugh. Instead, she began to investigate the contents of the tureens, which contained, in order of progression along the sideboard, bacon, fried eggs, kedgeree, kippers and a peculiar American substance with the consistency and flavour of cardboard, favoured by her Aunt Lettice, who was vegetarian. She helped herself to bacon and eggs and went to sit opposite her sister. Bright sunlight was streaming through the window. The gardens, the wooded slope of Burley Down and the hills and moors beyond were a patchwork of yellow and vivid greens, a scene at once so familiar and beautiful that she found herself smiling happily as she tucked into her breakfast. Hermione did not seem to share her enthusiasm, her face now sulky, and yet there was an odd trace of pride in her voice as she spoke.

'I got spanked last night.'

'I know,' Stephanie replied. 'I heard. That's why I didn't come in. I thought they'd do me too.'

'Quite likely,' Hermione agreed. 'They were very cross, and all because I put a toad in Aunt Lettice's salad.'

Stephanie chuckled.

'It was a really good one, big and fat, with lots of wattles. I couldn't waste it.'

'Of course not,' Stephanie agreed.

'I mean, it's not every day you find a toad like that,' Hermione went on, 'and I was going to put it down Sir Murgatroyd's bed, but there was the salad, sitting on the sideboard, and it was just too tempting. She really screamed.'

'I bet she did,' Stephanie replied, 'but I'm not surprised they spanked you.'

'It was hardly fair,' Hermione protested. 'Just Aunt Lettice, yes, but upstairs in my room, in private, not in the drawing room where Grandpapa and Sir Murgatroyd could hear through the door, and they took turns with me as well, and on the bare. Great-aunt Victoria used a hairbrush.'

'Ouch,' said Stephanie sympathetically.

'Ouch is about right,' Hermione agreed. 'I'm still sore this morning. Look.'

She got up and, after a brief silence to listen for anybody approaching, lifted her dress and quickly unbuttoned the union suit she was wearing underneath, displaying two round bottom cheeks, still meaty with puppy fat, each topped by a smudge of purple bruising. Stephanie took a moment to appraise her sister's bottom before delivering her considered opinion.

'That's not too bad.'

'I was red all over last night,' Hermione pointed out.

'I'd put your bottom away if I were you,' Stephanie advised, 'or you'll be red all over this morning too, at both ends if Sir Murgatroyd comes down while you're being done.'

Hermione nodded, covered herself up and then sat down again, wincing slightly as her bottom settled on to the chair. Stephanie grimaced in sympathy, spent a moment carefully piling bacon and egg on to her fork, ate them, then spoke again.

'Anyway, what's the QV?'

'I suspect Aunt Lettice is still cross about the toad,' Hermione informed her, 'and you know what Great-aunt Victoria's like. Aunt Gertrude's taken up political campaigning again. She says the new bill to let women under thirty vote is all wrong. Apparently we're irresponsible.'

'She's only thirty-five,' Stephanie pointed out. 'But I suppose it keeps her out of the house?'

'Not really, it mainly means she's always bringing the most frightful stiffs here.'

'Oh. What about the Beare mob?'

'Be careful of Aunt Lavinia. One of the critics in London slated her latest collection of poems, a fellow named Roland Bassinger –'

'I know Roly Bassinger,' Stephanie interrupted. 'He's a good egg. What did he say?'

'He called it stearine bilge,' Hermione explained. 'I had to look "stearine" up, and it means a fatty precipitate in oil.'

'That sounds like Aunt Lavinia's poetry.'

'Aunt Edith has found a new illness to have, and takes mustard rubs every day, then goes in a patent steam bath she's bought. Aunt Rosalie's still trying to breed zebra-striped cats, but a ginger Tom got in a few weeks ago and has ruined the experiment, so she's a bit cross too.'

Stephanie gave a thoughtful nod, wondering which of her relatives would be best to touch for the extra money she needed. None of them seemed particularly promising, although if her Aunt Edith was enjoying a new illness she might prove a soft touch, and feigning an interest in Aunt Gertrude's political causes, while risky, had been known to produce modest results. The best bet was certainly her grandfather, who at least was unlikely to whip her across his knee and dish out a bare-bottom spanking at the first mention of pounds, shillings and pence.

Escaping from the house before the aunts could converge on the breakfast table, Stephanie made her way across the lawn and past the lake to where the old icehouse had been converted into a sty for her grandfather's pig, the Emperor of Driscoll's. For any other pig the accommodation would have been positively palatial, but so vast was the Emperor that he was generally touching the sides in at least two places.

Her grandfather had left the breakfast table even before Hermione had arrived, so it seemed likely that he would have wandered down to the sty. Unfortunately he wasn't there, only the bucolic pigman, Cyril Wonnacott, and the Emperor himself. The first greeted her with a gap-toothed grin and a wink so suggestive that she found herself checking that her dress wasn't tucked into the flaps of her union suit; the second with a noise not dissimilar to the one she had made when expelling the drayman's spunk through her nose.

Cyril Wonnacott went back to preparing a mash of old seed potatoes and mangel-wurzels, while the Emperor ambled across his sty, grunting hopefully. Clearly he recognised Stephanie, but she had often wondered if it was as a friend and occasional provider of such *bonne-bouches* as over-ripe apples and bacon rinds, or as a potential addition to the menu. Certainly the way he snuffled at her legs when she approached the well-made wrought-iron fence that prevented his escape suggested a more than purely social interest.

She had brought a stick, and began to tickle him behind one ear, a process that never failed to provide satisfaction. This occasion was no exception, and she soon had him grunting and snuffling in delight, while doing his best to press himself closer to her through the bars. She continued to tickle him, amused by how easy it was to provide so much pleasure, and was not aware of her grandfather's presence until she heard the pigman's respectful greeting.

'Morning, Sir Richard.'

'Good morning, Cyril,' Richard Truscott responded. 'Ah, and you too, Stephanie. Catchpole said you'd arrived. Don't agitate the Emperor, my dear, it's the Okehampton show in two weeks and I daren't risk him losing so much as an ounce. What does he weigh in at this morning, Cyril?'

'Ninety-four seven, sir,' Cyril replied.

'Splendid!'

'A fine weight, sir,' Cyril agreed, 'but Jan says Sir Murgatroyd's animal is pushing the hundred-stone mark, and like to be more before the show.'

'Mere propaganda, I expect,' Richard Truscott replied, but he looked worried. 'Still, we must take every precaution. A little more linseed oil in his mash, perhaps?'

As the two men began to discuss pigs Stephanie considered the animal itself. The Emperor was so vast that it was hard to imagine an animal larger still, and yet for the last four years the huge boar had taken only silver medals at the Okehampton and Tavistock shows, the golds going to Sir Murgatroyd Drake's still more monstrous creature. But the gap had been closing, pound by pound, which presumably explained why Sir Murgatroyd was keen to buy the Emperor.

'. . . three thousand pounds the fellow offered me,' her grandfather was saying, 'and d'you know, he had the nerve to suggest I needed the money, blast him!'

'Speaking of money, Grandpapa,' Stephanie put in quickly, 'I don't suppose you'd be a sport and advance me ten pounds until my allowance comes through?'

'I'd love to oblige, my dear,' he answered, 'but you're supposed to be in disgrace and you know what Vicky's like. I'd never hear the end of it. How d'you manage to get pinched anyway? Bit of a silly thing to do, wasn't it?'

'I was trying to get a policeman's helmet,' Stephanie explained, knowing that it was safe to make the confession to him.

'Silly ass,' he responded. 'I suppose you made the classic mistake of trying to grab it from the front? That's not the way at all. You have to come up behind

33

the fellow and give the helmet a sudden push. That way you dislodge the chinstrap, his helmet falls forward and you're up and running before he really knows what's happened.'

'I know that, grandfather, but I'm too small. I tried to get it with a boathook, from a window in this room Freddie Drake had hired in the Dove.'

'Ingenious,' her grandfather admitted, 'but whatever were you doing with that young gumboil Drake? I suppose it was him who got you pinched?'

'In a way, yes,' she admitted, 'but speaking of Freddie Drake, grandfather . . .'

'Don't,' he interrupted, 'or if you must, do so beyond the range of my hearing. So he ran off and left you to face the fury of the law, did he? Just the sort of behaviour I'd expect from a Drake. Bad blood, the lot of them, although I suppose young Bobbie's not a bad sort.'

Stephanie pursed her lips. It was clearly not a good moment to mention that she intended to marry Freddie.

'He did pay my fine,' she said, 'but the thing is, Grandpapa, that I needed the helmet as a trophy for my club, the Gaspers, so I could stand for secretary. If I don't get back to London soon, and with something pretty special for a trophy, then Myrtle Finch-Farmiloe gets the post by default. That's why I need the money, you see.'

'Myrtle Finch-Farmiloe?' he responded, evading the point. 'She was your Protector when you first went to Teigngrace, wasn't she? Showed you the ropes and all that?'

'Yes, Grandpapa,' Stephanie said, reflecting not for the first time that Myrtle had had some extremely peculiar ideas about what the role of Protector should involve. 'But now I'm up against her in this election, which is why I urgently need some money and to get back to London before the end of the month.'

'Can't be done, I'm afraid, my dear,' he answered.

34

'Vicky would blow a gasket, to say nothing of your mother and the girls. They'd make my life unbearable, and you know how badly the Emperor reacts when I'm out of sorts. It puts him right off his feed. Sorry, but there it is. You are in disgrace and in disgrace you had better stay.'

Returning to the house, Stephanie found that Vera Clapshott had finally arrived. A dray had brought both maid and Stephanie's luggage from the station and was being unloaded in the stable yard. Great-aunt Victoria was supervising, and slowing the process down considerably by attempting to instruct the stable lads and berate the maid simultaneously. Vera Clapshott accepted the admonition with her head bowed, looking thoroughly sorry for herself, a sight that Stephanie took a moment to enjoy before moving closer.

She gave her brightest, most girlish smile as she approached, while hastily running over her story in her head. Great-aunt Victoria noticed her, frowning in a way that set Stephanie's stomach churning and her bottom cheeks twitching, but she held her smile and managed a bright, breezy tone as she spoke.

'Good morning, Great-aunt Victoria.'

'There you are, Stephanie. I have been looking everywhere for you.'

'I was visiting the Emperor,' Stephanie explained. 'Sorry.'

'Wherever is your car?' Great-aunt Victoria demanded. 'And why do you look as if you have slept in your clothes?'

'I ran out of petrol,' Stephanie hastened to explain, 'so I had to leave the car at a garage in Postbridge, which was why I was so late, and because Vera hadn't arrived I haven't a thing to wear.'

Great-aunt Victoria gave a derisive sniff and turned once more to the maid, who began to babble her explanation.

'I . . . I'm most awfully sorry, Miss Truscott . . . Miss Stephanie. I mistook my connection at Exeter, and it was the very last train, so I had to come on in the morning.'

'Silly girl,' Great-aunt Victoria snapped, 'and the same applies to you, Stephanie. Really, does your car not have a gauge to indicate the level of petrol? And could you not have used the telephone to have Gurney or Annaferd collect you?'

'I didn't want to give any trouble,' Stephanie explained.

Great-aunt Victoria responded with another sniff and turned her attention to the stable lads, who had managed to drop one of Stephanie's trunks.

'I would like to change, Clapshott,' Stephanie announced, doing her best to imitate her great-aunt's imperious tone. 'You may bring my small valise up to the Blue Room.'

'Yes, Miss Stephanie,' the maid answered, her tone mild and obedient but a flash of her eyes sending a very different message.

Stephanie stuck her nose in the air, sure that Vera wouldn't dare risk Victoria Truscott's wrath, and made for the house. Vera followed, struggling with the valise, which was only small in the sense of being less large than its two companions or the travelling trunk. Indoors, Stephanie felt a little less sure of herself, wondering if her mother and Great-aunt Victoria had communicated on the telephone and, if so, exactly what had been said. By the time she had reached the Blue Room she had decided it was better to be safe than sorry, and therefore to adopt a less haughty attitude towards her maid.

'Thank you, Clapshott . . . Vera,' she said.

'That's no trouble at all, Miss Stephanie,' the maid answered, but the tone of her voice was no longer obsequious.

'I'll, er . . . I'll let you unpack then,' Stephanie said hastily, backing from the room.

'Don't you want to change, Miss?' the maid enquired innocently.

'In a while,' Stephanie replied, and made her exit.

It had been what her father would have called a strategic retreat, she told herself as she made her way back downstairs. Possibly her mother had told Great-aunt Victoria that Vera had permission to discipline Stephanie, possibly not, and possibly Vera might have taken matters into her own hands anyway. In any case Stephanie would have ended up over Vera's knee, which would have been bad enough at the best of times, but unendurable when the stable lads would shortly be bringing up the rest of her luggage. Both were young, lively men, as full as themselves as they were physically attractive, and just the thought of being spanked bare-bottom in front of them made her blush to the roots of her hair.

Congratulating herself on having escaped an embarrassing episode that might well have been a contender for her top ten, she made for the library. It seemed as safe a haven as any, since not even Great-aunt Victoria could object to her reading a book, while it would also provide the peace she needed to consider schemes for getting together some money and returning to London before the Gaspers election. Entering the room, she discovered that Hermione had made the same decision and was seated at the big table, studying an atlas.

'Hello, H., avoiding the aunts?' Stephanie greeted her sister.

'Yes,' Hermione replied. 'Aunt Lettice wants to take me to Lydford slaughterhouse to lecture me about eating meat, but Catchpole warned me in time.'

'The best of butlers,' Stephanie said. 'What are you up to?'

'This is where Papa fought,' Hermione answered, turning the atlas around.

'Don't be morbid,' Stephanie responded automatically,

37

then paused, wondering what her father would have made of her predicament.

Colonel Sir John Truscott seldom spoke of the war at all, but sometimes, when some of his old comrades had been to dinner and done themselves well on the port, they would discuss tactics and how matters might have been improved. As a small girl she had frequently listened from the top of the stairs, at once horrified and fascinated, while the even smaller Hermione hid in the shadows behind her.

Turning the pages back from Northern France to South-West England, she considered the map. She needed to reach London within two weeks, bearing some trophy so magnificent that it would put whatever Myrtle Finch-Farmiloe had secured firmly in the shade. That represented the objective, and in order to attain it she needed a strategy.

'You're making faces,' Hermione pointed out.

'I'm thinking,' Stephanie replied, 'about how best to sort out the stuff I told you this morning.'

'You're going to get spanked,' Hermione stated.

'That must be considered an acceptable risk,' Stephanie answered bravely, ignoring the sudden tightening of her bottom cheeks.

'You're going to get caned,' Hermione went on, in what Stephanie considered an unreasonably smug tone of voice.

'Shut up and help,' she said. 'I'm trying to work out what Papa would do in my place.'

'Shoot Myrtle Finch-Farmiloe?' Hermione suggested.

'Don't tempt me,' Stephanie replied. 'Seriously, help me. I have to get myself and a really good trophy to London by the last day of the month.'

'All right, you're the one who's going to get into trouble. How about old Sir Murgatroyd's pig?'

'Sir Murgatroyd's pig? What about it?'

'It would make a jolly good trophy.'

'It weighs a hundred stone!' Stephanie exclaimed. 'And it would probably cause comment on the train.'

'Not if you sent it by freight,' Hermione pointed out.

Stephanie began to answer, but stopped. She could think of a dozen objections to the scheme, but all seemed as nothing when set against the image of her entering the smoking room at Gaspers with a one-hundred-stone pig. Unless Myrtle had somehow managed to procure a hippopotamus, or perhaps the statue from the top of Nelson's Column, both of which seemed unlikely, Stephanie's election would be guaranteed. So, unfortunately, would the state of her bottom once her mother and probably the full complement of aunts had finished with her. Talking of acceptable risks was all very well, but she could already imagine herself holding tightly to her ankles with her dress flipped up and her union suit pinned open at the back as a queue of aunts flexed their muscles and discussed techniques for inflicting the most agonising welts on her unfortunate bottom.

'And think how pleased Grandpapa would be if old Sir Murgatroyd's pig went missing before the Okehampton show,' Hermione pointed out. 'You could probably touch him for fifty quid, maybe even more.'

'That would mean stealing the pig well in advance,' Stephanie said thoughtfully, 'so we'd have to keep it somewhere, maybe for as much as a week, and the police would be spreading dragnets and all that sort of thing.'

'We could keep it in the wood at Stukely Hall,' Hermione suggested, using the first person plural in her rising enthusiasm. 'Great-Grandmama scarcely goes out at all, and Grandmama and the housekeeper seldom go far, not down to the woods anyway.'

'You're going to help me, then?' Stephanie demanded.

'Um . . .' Hermione answered, suddenly cautious. 'I'll help you plan.'

'Come along, H.,' Stephanie urged, 'I need you to be my lieutenant. Please?'

Hermione made a face.

'I'll take you out in my two-seater,' Stephanie promised, 'anywhere you like, and I'll stand you a slap-up lunch, as soon as I've got the money.'

'Teach me to drive,' Hermione asked.

Stephanie hesitated only a moment before extending a hand to grasp her sister's. Bending together over the atlas, they began to plot, and continued to do so until the gong went for lunch.

Sir Richard Truscott had no sympathy whatsoever for his daughter Lettice's vegetarianism, considering it a pointless fad which she would no doubt get over in time and with sufficient exposure to the sight and scent of delicacies. Lunch for the rest of the family therefore consisted of the last of the season's pheasants, which had been hung until their tail feathers dropped out and then somewhat longer for good measure. The result was a meat so rich and tender that Stephanie found herself savouring every forkful, while even Great-aunt Victoria was rendered silent by her determination to do justice to the dish. For fully a quarter of an hour only Aunt Lettice spoke, remarking on the bad effects of meat on the large bowel while she picked at a green salad, having first investigated it with knife and fork to ensure that it contained no toads or other fauna.

The burgundy selected by Catchpole to accompany the pheasant was also above reproach, and Stephanie took full advantage of his generous hand, with her grandfather's approval for her hearty appetite. The pheasant was followed by a steamed pudding so rich and so liberally smothered with clotted cream that, out of concern for her figure, Stephanie insisted on taking no more than a taste, although she allowed Catchpole to refill her glass with Sauternes no fewer than five times. When she left the table she was feeling pleasantly tipsy, so much so that when she and Hermione returned to the library to continue plotting she confessed what Freddie Drake had done, to her sister's giggling horror.

The imparted secret served to seal their compact more firmly, and to reinforce what had always been a very close relationship. An hour later they had completed their discussion, creating a plan at once so mischievous and so satisfying that neither girl could look at the other without bursting into giggles. It was also extremely daring, but Stephanie was so full of burgundy and Sauternes that she felt equal to any number of irate landowners, giant pigs, rivals in love and even aunts.

'Watch me, H.,' she declared, pushing her chair back. 'This is Aunt Lettice.'

Hermione laughed and Stephanie cleared her throat, then went on, making her cheeks hollow in mockery of her aunt's lean face and speaking in a high, affected voice.

'Medical specialists have shown that the consumption of meat causes congestion in the large bowel, leading to dyspepsia, flatulence and irritation of the mucous membranes. Furthermore . . .'

She began to pace up and down, taking exaggeratedly large steps and with one finger raised in the air as if to illustrate the points she was making, until Hermione was laughing so hard that she was having trouble staying on her chair. Encouraged, Stephanie allowed the tone of her voice to rise to something close to hysteria and began to stab the air with her forefinger.

'. . . it has also been repeatedly proven that those of a carnivorous habit are prone to every form of vice known to mankind, including cannibalism, Catholicism, carpentry, being German, socialism, self-abuse and penis sucking . . .'

Her voice trailed off on the final word. Hermione had stopped laughing and was staring, past Stephanie in wide-eyed horror.

'Oh no,' Stephanie said weakly.

'Oh yes,' came Aunt Lettice's voice from directly behind her.

A bony hand closed on Stephanie's wrist even before she could turn around. One sharp jerk, and her arm was twisted into the small of her back; another, and she was pulled down across her aunt's knee on the chair she had vacated before, bottom up, then bottom bare as the blue summer dress and the light, silk drawers she had changed into before lunch were flipped up and down respectively.

Stephanie was facing Hermione and caught her sister's expression of shock and pity a moment before the spanking began, so hard and fast that she immediately lost control, thrashing in her aunt's grip and kicking her legs wildly about in her half-dropped drawers as the slaps rained down on her defenceless cheeks. It never even occurred to her to protest or try and beg off the punishment, because she knew it was hopeless. At first Aunt Lettice seemed to be too angry even to speak, and she did not find her voice until Stephanie's bottom was hot and pink all over.

'Disgusting!' she snapped. 'To use gutter language, and in front of your little sister! Disgusting! Disgusting! Disgusting!'

With each word she planted a fresh smack on Stephanie's glowing bottom, delivered full across both cheeks, a hard, methodical punishment that quickly turned to faster smacks as her temper overcame her once more. Stephanie burst into tears, blubbering uncontrollably across her aunt's knee with her hair in wild disarray and snot running from her nose. The stinging pain in her bottom was so severe that she could not keep her thighs together and avoid showing off her quim from behind.

'Disgusting little brat,' Aunt Lettice raved, still belabouring Stephanie's bottom with every ounce of her strength. 'To think that you could say such words . . . that you could even know such words! And as for . . .'

Her words were lost in another barrage of furious smacks that sent Stephanie into a full-blown, helpless tantrum. Her thighs pumped furiously in her pain and her bottom bucked up and down, showing off not just her quim but her bottom hole too. The display only served to encourage her aunt, who began to smack the backs of Stephanie's thighs, which hurt even more. Then she stopped, as suddenly as she had begun.

Stephanie collapsed across her aunt's lap, panting, her head down, snot hanging from the tip of her nose, her legs spread as far as her drawers would permit, her exposed quim and bottom slit strangely cool between her blazing cheeks and heated thighs. Relief that it was over began to well up, until her aunt spoke.

'I do beg your pardon, Gertrude, Mr Attwater, but I have had to spank Stephanie and she is being rather noisy about it.'

Twisting violently round, Stephanie gaped in horror. In the doorway was her Aunt Gertrude, and she was not alone. A man stood beside her, a tall, solidly built man, who managed to project an air of pompous superiority even as he stared in open astonishment at her exposed rear. Aunt Lettice released Stephanie's wrist. Taken by surprise, she tumbled on to the floor, to lie for a moment with her legs splayed and any detail of her quim that the spectators might have missed while she was bottom up now available for inspection between her open thighs.

Immediately she jumped up, clutching her drawers, but tripped over them and sprawled forwards, straight into the arms of the man. He caught her, ducking down as he did so, and for an instant his hand cupped one hot bottom cheek before he hauled her up and set her on her feet.

'Go straight to your bedroom, Stephanie,' Aunt Lettice ordered.

Stephanie didn't need to be told. She ran, clutching her hot bottom, tears streaming down her face, her drawers flapping around one ankle, only to come off completely halfway up the stairs. She didn't bother to retrieve them, too full of embarrassment and self-pity to care. Once she was safely inside the Blue Room she slammed the door behind her and was about to throw herself on to the bed and cry out her feelings into the pillow, when she realised she was not alone.

Vera Clapshott was still unpacking. Stephanie's travel trunk lay open on the floor by the bed, and the chest of drawers was arranged so that everything could be put away neatly and in its proper place. For a moment the two women stood looking at each other, Vera mildly surprised, Stephanie with her lower lip trembling violently as she struggled to blink the tears from her eyes.

'I've just been spanked,' Stephanie snivelled, desperate for sympathy, even though Vera seemed about the least likely person to provide any.

To her surprise the maid responded with a rueful smile, yet even in her distraught state Stephanie thought she noticed a cunning edge to the maid's voice.

'Well, I dare say it was needed,' Vera said, but softly, her voice so kind and gentle that Stephanie felt new tears well up in her eyes. 'Let me see.'

Too full of emotion to think of doing otherwise, Stephanie turned and lifted her dress, showing off her reddened cheeks and thighs.

'It hurt dreadfully,' she whined.

'I'm sure it did,' Vera agreed. 'Perhaps I can make it better for you?'

Stephanie's mouth worked in indecision. She wondered if her suspicions about the maid's personal preferences were about to be confirmed. Meanwhile, in the back of her mind were nagging memories of Myrtle Finch-Farmiloe's behaviour as a Protector. Yet the need to be held and comforted was too strong to resist, and her bottom had that hot glow which only ever came after a really hard spanking and always left her feeling pliable and sensitive. She nodded.

Vera put down the pile of carefully folded stockings she had been holding and stepped close, to place one cool hand on Stephanie's burning cheeks. Stephanie shut her eyes as the maid began to rub gently, full of shame for the little shocks of pleasure provoked by Vera's touch, but also feeling gratitude and a sense of absolute helplessness.

'You're ever so hot,' the maid remarked, now with both hands cupped round Stephanie's bottom cheeks. 'I think I know just what you need.'

Stephanie nodded, unsure what Vera meant, but too far gone in surrender to complain. As long as the maid held her and comforted her she didn't mind, even if Vera turned out to play the same rather beastly tricks as Myrtle. She let herself be taken by the hand and eased down on to the bed, side by side with Vera, who put an arm round her shoulder.

'There, there,' the maid said softly, and kissed Stephanie's hair.

Her body limp, Stephanie allowed herself to be held. For a minute or more Vera stayed as she was, gently stroking Stephanie's hair and whispering to her in a soothing tone, before tightening her grip. Stephanie squeaked as she was pulled down, but did not find her voice until she had been placed gently but firmly across Vera's knees.

'No, Vera, please,' she snivelled. 'That's not fair! I've just had it once, and I didn't mean to be bossy . . . don't spank me . . . please, I beg you!'

'Shh,' Vera said gently. 'Don't be such a baby. I'm not going to spank you.'

'No?' Stephanie queried, highly surprised.

The maid had just lifted one knee, bringing Stephanie's bottom into prime spanking position, raised and with the cheeks a little parted.

'I may have to spank you sometimes,' Vera said quietly, 'but at the moment that's not what you need.'

Stephanie swallowed, fairly sure that, considering the position she was in, there was only one thing Vera was likely to do with her, or rather a variety of things, all of them highly improper and extremely shameful. Not that she could stop it, too far gone to resist, and anyway the maid had a tight, no-nonsense grip round her waist. So she contented herself with trying to pretend she had no choice about what was happening as Vera leant back to rummage in the travelling trunk and extracted a large china pot labelled with the word Sootho.

'It's a patent preparation for the relief of nappy rash,' she explained, 'but there's nothing better for a smacked bottom.'

Cold, slippery cream was applied to Stephanie's cheeks, a large blob on top of each, which Vera then began to rub in. Stephanie closed her eyes, unable to resist the sensations of having her bottom gently caressed, although every excited contraction of her quim brought her new shame. Worse still, there was an awful and yet familiar intimacy about the maid's touch, the gentle fingers not merely rubbing the nappy cream into Stephanie's hurt skin but stroking and pausing occasionally to squeeze a handful of soft bottom flesh or simply cup a cheek. Only when Vera's fingers burrowed between her cheeks to cream her bottom hole did she find the will to protest.

'I wasn't smacked there,' she croaked.

Vera merely tightened her grip and began to tickle Stephanie's anus, using one finger tip to tease the little bumps and creases around the hole. At first Stephanie tried to resist, squeezing her cheeks on Vera's hand, but she got a little smack for her trouble and with that she gave in, pushing her bottom up for more. It felt too nice, too naughty, and she knew that her maid would stand no nonsense and would discipline her if she didn't give in.

As Stephanie's cheeks spread to her caresses, Vera gave a knowing chuckle. Her fondling grew more intimate still. Two fingers spread Stephanie's bottom hole open for inspection, then moved lower, to her quim. Another, louder sob escaped Stephanie's mouth as the lips of her quim were gently eased apart to show off her virgin hole. Vera gave a little tut, which might have been approval or amusement but proved to be disappointment.

'What a shame,' she said. 'I had hoped to put something inside you, but it would be wrong of me to ruin you for the sake of a moment's fun.'

Stephanie gave an earnest nod, then a gasp as Vera's attention turned back to her anus, this time not to tickle but to probe, and a soft moan escaped her lips as the tight little hole opened to the maid's finger.

'Not there, not up my bottom,' she managed, but she didn't mean it.

Vera took no notice anyway, but slid her finger deep into Stephanie's bottom hole and began to wiggle it about inside.

'I'm going to enjoy you, Miss Stephanie,' the maid announced as Stephanie began to wriggle helplessly on her intruding finger.

The words were a near echo of what Myrtle Finch-Farmiloe had said the first time she had coaxed Stephanie into an almost identical position, the only real difference being that Vera hadn't been the one to do the spanking. Stephanie felt her bottom hole tighten on Vera's finger at the memory and tried to get up, only to be eased back into position.

'Oh, no, you don't,' the maid said. 'I have something to show you before we're finished.'

As she spoke she extracted her finger from Stephanie's rectum and her hand moved back down, cupping the plump, sensitive quim, with one long finger between the lips. She began to rub and, as she did so, to spank, masturbating Stephanie with one hand and smacking her cheeks with the other. Stephanie hung her head, powerful sobs racking her body as she realised she was going to be brought off across the maid's lap.

'I don't suppose you've done this before?' Vera remarked. 'Not a well-brought-up girl like you.'

Stephanie didn't bother to contradict the maid. Her quim had already begun to squeeze and she was

47

squirming her bottom in helpless abandoned ecstasy under the slaps, which now brought only pleasure. She stuck her bottom up higher, spreading herself to both the smacks and the fondling of her sex, now too far gone to be anything but eager. Vera laughed and began to rub harder, her finger bumping over the little hot point between Stephanie's sex lips with practised skill as she spanked cheek and cheek about, ever harder. Stephanie cried out, wriggling her bottom for more and gasping as she started to come, her head dizzy with the same blend of ecstasy and shame that Myrtle had first taught her – feelings she had resented ever since, she reflected, even as her body shook in the ecstasy of orgasm.

Three

For the next two days Stephanie divided most of her time between plotting with her sister and trying to be well behaved in order to avoid the disciplinary attentions of her aunts, while surrendering her bottom each evening to the erotic attentions of her maid. To be tipped over Vera's knee, exposed and fondled brought Stephanie immense chagrin, but the pleasure made it impossible to resist, as did the maid's firm, no-nonsense manner. It had been much the same with Myrtle Finch-Farmiloe, which made the experience more humiliating still, as did the likelihood that the maid would soon expect rather more.

Only on the third day did Stephanie and Hermione manage to get to Postbridge, claiming that they wished to go into Tavistock for some new handkerchiefs and declining the offer of a lift in favour of the public omnibus. Arriving at the garage, Stephanie stood pondering the dented and scratched front portion of the two-seater somewhat ruefully, although considerably less ruefully than she had been pondering Phase One of the battle campaign: the extraction of the giant pig from its sty on Sir Murgatroyd Drake's estate at Combebow and its transport to Stukely Hall.

The principal difficulty in pinching the pig was its sheer bulk, one hundred stone of mobile bacon and chops being so far beyond their capacity for heavy lifting that the thing might as well have been Haytor

Rocks. The answer was bribery, in the form of ripe apples, which she felt sure could be guaranteed to lure the boar from his sty and on to the stout dray which was also an essential element of the plan, and also required bribery. Unfortunately she only knew one bribable drayman, and he was unlikely to be impressed by ripe apples, unless the term could be applied to her small, neatly formed breasts.

Another difficulty was Jan Wonnacott, pigman to Sir Murgatroyd Drake and brother of Cyril. He lived in a cottage adjacent to the sty. The operation seemed sure to be noisy, and although Jan was said to be in the habit of consuming as many as a dozen pints of cider in one or another of the local inns each evening, his absences came at times when the road was too busy for the safe removal of the pig. They would have to act in the dead hours of the night.

With the pig pinched, they would be able to move on to Phase Two, touching her grandfather for a sum large enough to carry out the remainder of the operation while avoiding the attention of assorted aunts. If the pig theft failed to soften the old man, things would be difficult. It was essential to get the car back as soon as possible, but the repair bill was going to eat up all but the last few shillings of what remained of her allowance.

'I'll come to collect it next week then,' she said with a sigh as the mechanic completed his assessment of what needed to be done and how long it would take. 'One other thing. Do you happen to know the full name and address of the drayman who helped me? I'd like to thank him, and I was too shaken to think to ask where he lived. I only know him as Lias.'

'Elias Snell. He lives to Princetown, last house on the Yelverton Road,' the mechanic answered promptly.

'Thank you,' Stephanie replied, and hastened across the road. What might be the only omnibus of the day was approaching. She and Hermione signalled to the driver, climbed in and paid their fares, responding to the curious looks of the other passengers with polite smiles as they took their seats. Stephanie was earnestly wishing she had her car back. All her life she had taken little or no notice of the general population, regarding them simply as part of the Devon background. Like tin mines, horses or clotted cream, they were always there and had always served their purpose, but they had never engaged more than her casual attention.

Since her experience with the drayman things had changed. Never had she imagined that a working man could be so lacking in respect, or so blatantly lecherous. The behaviour of Elias Snell had proved otherwise, likewise that of Vera Clapshott, and Stephanie now found herself suspecting every other passenger of harbouring similarly lewd intentions. The driver himself bore a suspicious resemblance to the drayman, and she was sure he would have preferred to have his penis sucked rather than accept her fare, perhaps sharing her with the conductor, a lean, ugly man who kept glancing at her with what she felt was a knowing leer; or, worse, making her kneel side by side with her sister while they received the same rude treatment.

The two large red-faced women who sat together at the very back seemed to disapprove of her, though their expressions suggested that they disapproved of everybody and everything. That didn't stop her imagining them singling her out for an impromptu spanking, delivered bare bottom in front of Hermione and the other passengers. An equally large but jolly woman, who had brought a small pig on to the omnibus, seemed less likely to feel the need to dish out discipline, but might very well do it for fun and enjoy a good feel at the same time.

The men were worse. A trio of farmers debating the price of wool appeared to be indifferent to her, but when they spoke quietly she wondered if they were discussing how amusing it would be to share her between them, using her mouth, quim and bottom hole simultaneously, while Hermione was made to watch. The lone man in a high-collared suit was presumably a clerk of some sort and definitely a pervert. It showed in his nervous manner and the small, piggy eyes that looked everywhere but at his fellow passengers, revealing his guilt at wanting to make Stephanie and her sister indulge him in unspeakable practices.

At length they reached Princetown and got down from the omnibus outside the Plume of Feathers. Stephanie's head was swimming with frightening yet compelling fantasies. What had seemed so straightforward when discussed over a decanter of Warre '08 kindly provided by Catchpole was now terrifying, yet to show her feelings in front of her little sister was unthinkable. As they came in sight of the final line of granite-built cottages, a solution occurred to her.

'I think you should do it this time, H.,' she stated.

Her sister's eyes rounded in shock before she replied. 'What, suck his . . . his thingy?'

'Of course that is what I mean,' Stephanie replied.

'Why me?' Hermione demanded.

'As Papa says,' Stephanie pointed out, 'on a campaign everybody should share the discomforts equally.'

'No,' Hermione replied, 'he says it's a good thing for an officer to share the discomforts of his men. You're in charge, so you should be the one doing the sharing.'

'I've already done it twice,' Stephanie pointed out, changing tack, 'so it's your turn.'

'No, it isn't,' Hermione answered.

'Yes, it is,' Stephanie insisted. 'I won't teach you to drive if you aren't a little bit more helpful, H.'

'But I don't want to suck his beastly thingy!' Hermione whined.

'I did, so you should have to do it too.'

'Why?'

'Why not?'

'It's disgusting!'

'You thought it was jolly funny that he'd made me do it!'

Hermione's face had begun to grow obstinate, and Stephanie again changed tack.

'Come on, H., please? For me? And just think, when I marry Freddie I'll be able to afford another car, maybe a Lagonda or something, and you can have the two-seater, but only if you're helpful.'

'I am being helpful,' Hermione replied. 'I came up with most of the ideas.'

'Exactly,' Stephanie said quickly, 'such as paying for the dray by sucking Lias Snell's penis. As Papa says, you should never make a plan you wouldn't be prepared to carry out yourself.'

Hermione made to speak, then fell silent, her face sulky. Stephanie pressed her advantage.

'I *will* give you my car, I promise, and sucking a penis isn't that bad, not really. In fact, it's rather nice, in a funny sort of way. It makes me feel like when ... you know ...'

She trailed off. Hermione was looking at her suspiciously.

'It is, really,' she insisted. 'Please, H.? Think of having your own car, and it really is only fair, and ... and I promise I won't spank you any more, even if the aunts are passing you around and I'm supposed to. Not hard, anyway.'

Hermione made a face, then gave a shy, nervous nod.

'Thank you,' Stephanie said, and quickly turned away to hide the smug look she could feel stealing over her face.

They had reached the end of the line of cottages and, despite Hermione's promise, it still took all Stephanie's courage to walk in at the garden gate and down between two neatly laid-out patches of spring vegetables. She was fighting the urge to bite her lip as she knocked at the smartly painted door, filled with sudden guilt for bullying her sister into sucking cock for the awful man who was about to confront her.

Except that he didn't. As the door swung wide, she remembered Lias mentioning a wife, although, looking at the woman who stood framed in the doorway, Stephanie felt that the drayman would have been justified in mentioning two wives, or even three. The drayman's wife was simply the largest woman Stephanie had ever set eyes on, from the substantial feet crammed into carpet slippers to the mass of greying hair on her head. Between were all the usual features, but painted with a broad brush: a head somewhat reminiscent of the pumpkin her grandfather had contributed to the previous year's harvest festival; a thick bull neck set on broad shoulders, from which depended arms that would have put many a railway navvy to shame; breasts each of which would have outdone Sir Richard's pumpkin with ease; a thick waist barely constrained by a creaking corset; massive hips; and legs that, though concealed beneath voluminous old-fashioned skirts, were presumably of similar proportions. Stephanie's face was on a level with the colossal breasts.

'Mrs Snell, I presume?' she managed, looking up.

'Mrs Endicott,' the woman corrected her. 'Anne Snell's my sister. How may I help you, Miss?'

'Miss Myrtle Finch-Farmiloe,' Stephanie lied, remembering their decision to use false names and choosing the first that came into her head. 'We had hoped to hire your brother-in-law's dray.'

'No difficulty there,' the woman answered. 'Come along inside.'

Stephanie and Hermione entered the house, where they were shown into a small but comfortably furnished parlour. The big woman disappeared and the two girls began to inspect the room. It looked out over a back garden as carefully tended as the front and also given over entirely to vegetables, while beyond the granite walls stretched the moor, with woods and fields in the distance and the dark smudge of Plymouth and the dull green of the sea visible even further away. The room contained several chairs, two tables and a sideboard, on which stood a photograph of a man she recognised as

Elias Snell, although it had been taken perhaps twenty years ago. He wore a somewhat ill-fitting suit and beside him was a woman in a wedding dress, presumably Mrs Snell, every bit as large and formidable as her sister, who now returned.

'If you'd just write down the details here,' Mrs Endicott said, offering Stephanie a ledger.

Taking the book, Stephanie hesitated a moment, then wrote a request for the drayman to come to the gates of Stukely Hall the following afternoon. That would allow her to make the real appointment without arousing suspicion, to show Lias Snell where he was supposed to take the pig, and to make – or rather let Hermione make – the appropriate payment.

Mrs Endicott took the ledger and a small deposit, provided a glass of cider that felt like sandpaper as it went down, and showed the girls back on to the road. The station was no great distance away and they decided to catch a train. They talked in low voices as they went along.

'Imagine being spanked by her,' Hermione said.

Stephanie grimaced. The thought had already occurred to her, although with Mrs Snell rather than Mrs Endicott attending to her bottom, which was no doubt the least she could expect if the woman discovered what had happened with her husband.

The following morning Stephanie rose early. Somewhat to her surprise, Vera Clapshott had not taken advantage of the intimacy between them, and was proving an excellent lady's maid. Stephanie's clothes, which were already laid out, had been chosen both to create a stylish effect and to suit what promised to be a warm day. Once dressed, she made her way down to breakfast, already nervous at the prospect of what was to come.

Hermione was not yet down, but Aunt Lettice was, and somewhat spoiled breakfast with a long monologue on the effects of too much protein on the intestinal tract.

Recalling her spanking, Stephanie responded with careful politeness and even forced herself to eat some of the American cereal. Aunt Gertrude joined them, and then her grandfather, allowing her to make the opening gambit of the day's elaborate plans.

'Hermione and I shall visit Great-grandmama Nell today,' she announced.

'That's unusually thoughtful of you, Stephanie,' her Aunt Gertrude responded, 'although Mr Attwater is lunching here, and he was keen to speak with you.'

'Mr Attwater?' Stephanie replied. 'Why ever would he want to speak to me?'

'The fellow probably wants you to join his Brown Drawers or whatever they call themselves,' Sir Richard put in.

'There's no need to be vulgar, father,' Gertrude responded. 'You know perfectly well that Mr Attwater's organisation is called the Brown Shorts.'

'Be that as it may,' Sir Richard replied, 'it's a load of nonsense, prancing around in footer bags, although some of the girls look deuced attractive.'

'They look positively indecent,' Lettice supplied. 'They might as well be running around in their underwear.'

'As I say, deuced attractive,' Sir Richard replied, and chuckled as both daughters gave him dark looks.

'I thought Mr Attwater disapproved of women?' Stephanie asked cautiously.

'Certainly Mr Attwater approves of women,' Gertrude responded. 'He simply realises that progress must be tempered with common sense, and therefore opposes this absurd extension of the franchise . . .'

Stephanie returned her attention to her American cereal, hoping it might prove more palatable than her aunt's political lecture. It didn't, but with Aunt Lettice regarding her from the corner of one eye she was forced to finish. It sat like a lead ball in her stomach. Not at all keen to renew the acquaintance of a man who had last seen her with her bare bottom sticking up in the air as she was disciplined, she left the house and climbed Burley Down to the old folly at the summit, where she sat admiring the view.

The western flank of Dartmoor occupied most of the horizon, verdant green sprinkled with the grey of rocks, and below the darker greens of woods and hedgerows, among which a scattering of buildings stood out: farms, the churches at Lydford and Sourton, and the squat towers of Stukely Hall. If there was a giant pig to conceal, the woodland around the hall was undoubtedly the place to do it, and she found her confidence growing as she looked back towards the house.

It seemed like a toy from so high up, and yet clear in the morning sunlight. The tiny figures emerging from the French windows were her Aunt Gertrude and Claude Attwater, while Hermione had just come out from the stable block, her bright red dress unmistakable, although the tall, apparently dapper young man was unfamiliar – or perhaps not. Stephanie narrowed her eyes, excitement welling up inside her as she realised that the man was Freddie Drake. Immediately she began to run back down the hill, less because she wanted to see him than because she was worried about what her sister might say.

By the time she reached the bottom, he and Hermione were approaching the pigsty. Stephanie ran straight to them and threw herself into his arms. After a moment of surprise he responded well, catching her up and kissing her, then holding her briefly at arm's length before setting her back down on the ground. Only then did she remember all the circumstances of their last meeting.

'I'm surprised you're so friendly,' she said, doing her best to sound haughty. 'I would have expected you to adopt a rather more apologetic attitude. Grovelling, even?'

'Oh, don't worry about that,' he said casually. 'H. has explained everything.'

Stephanie went scarlet and threw an accusing glance at Hermione, who was shaking her head and making urgent hand gestures to indicate that it wasn't true.

'So I know you're not really cross with me,' Freddie went on, 'and dammit, I did bail you out.'

'Very well,' Stephanie said, tilting her nose to indicate scorn, 'but next time you wish to cover my face with burning kisses I shall expect you to say something first.'

'I'd rather cover your bottom with burning kisses,' Freddie replied.

Hermione burst into giggles. Stephanie, who had been angling for either an apology or a proposal, hit him. Freddie merely chuckled and linked arms with both girls as he continued towards the sty.

'Beast,' Stephanie remarked.

'Absolutely,' he agreed. 'With girls like you about, a fellow's bound to be a bit of a beast. And speaking of beasts, I hear your grandfather thinks his animal is capable of beating the Porker at Okehampton.'

'Is that its name? Your father's pig?' Stephanie enquired. 'I thought it was something Latin.'

'It is,' he told her. 'In full, Singularis Porcus, meaning the singular or extraordinary pig, as any Teigngrace-educated girl should know, although from what Myrtle tells me you spent most of your time throwing ink darts and pulling each other's hair. Anyhow, what of the Emperor's form? Cyril Wonnacott's playing his cards close to his chest, as usual. Five pints we stood him last night and he still wouldn't spill the beans, and H. wouldn't tell even when I threatened to tickle her.'

Stephanie had begun to go red at the mention of Myrtle and Teigngrace, but quickly rallied.

'You'd hardly expect me to tell you,' she said. 'Why do you want to know, anyway?'

'Benjy Porthwell is running a book,' Freddie informed her. 'Rather appropriate, that, don't you think, one porker taking bets on some others? There are five runners in the fat pig class, but it's hard to establish form. The Porker's over the hundred stone, but the Emperor's been creeping up year by year, which is why I was hoping for a tip from the stable.'

'What are the odds?' Stephanie asked.

'The Porker's favourite at two to one,' Freddie told her, 'with the Emperor at five, which may be where the clever money is. Squire Cunnigham's animal is a no-hoper, a hundred to one and no takers, and the same for Farmer Beston. Farmer Urferd has threatened to shoot anyone who sets foot on his land, so he's up at a cautious ten to one. His pig, that is, not old Urferd.'

'I see,' Stephanie said cautiously.

'What's Porker Porthwell doing running a book?' Hermione asked with a trace of irritation in her voice. 'He's the curate at Bridestowe!'

'Yes,' Freddie explained, 'but that doesn't seem to dampen his sporting spirit, or his avaricious nature, although I dare say old Tredegar would play merry hell if he found out. We've quite a little party, as it goes, with you two down here, and Roly Bassinger and Eggy White at my place, and Myrtle of course –'

'Myrtle's down in Devon?' Stephanie interrupted.

'Rather,' Freddie admitted, somewhat embarrassed. 'You know how it is . . .'

'Yes, I do,' Stephanie answered, 'and I'd prefer it if you didn't speak to her.'

'Tricky, that,' he said. 'She's staying at the hall. Now about that pig . . .'

'My lips are sealed,' Stephanie replied haughtily before returning to the earlier subject. 'Is Bobbie coming down?'

'No, no,' Freddie replied, 'no baby sis. She would have come, but she's determined to get into Gaspers and felt she ought to stay in London.'

'Nobody would blackball Bobbie,' Stephanie replied with conviction.

'Never,' he agreed, 'but you know how she is, always has to be best at everything.'

Stephanie nodded. She had been Bobbie's Protector at Teigngrace, and had watched in awe as the tall, athletic girl went through the school like a whirlwind, to end as headgirl and captain of every available sport. Even Myrtle was friendly to Bobbie, despite being two years older, and had never dared persecute her. Stephanie frowned, reflecting how useful it would have been to have Bobbie about.

When they reached the sty, Cyril Wonnacott took one look at Freddie Drake and closed the door in a pointed manner.

'Bother,' Freddie remarked. 'Oh well, care for a stroll, old thing?'

'I shall stay and tickle the pig,' Hermione said tactfully, and detached herself from Freddie's arm.

'Shall we climb the down?' Freddie suggested.

Stephanie acquiesced and once more started up the long zigzag path through the thick ancient woods that cloaked the slope of Burley Down. Freddie spoke of this and that, but she wasn't really listening. It was a nasty shock to discover that Myrtle had managed to insinuate herself at Combebow, where she would be able to monopolise Freddie's company even more effectively than in London. It was also a highly romantic setting, with a river walk and not one but two rustic rose gardens. Desperate measures were called for.

'I've a little trick to show you,' she announced as they reached the folly. 'Come inside and sit down.'

Freddie obeyed in his usual insouciant manner, regarding her with polite enquiry as he lowered himself on to one of the marble benches inside the folly. Stephanie was feeling anything but insouciant. Her heart was hammering and the blood was hot in her face as she got down on her knees on the hard floor. Freddie's eyes widened, then his mouth, as she put her hands on his fly.

'I say, Stiffy!' he gasped as the first button popped open.

60

'Shh,' she said gently. 'This is jolly hard for me, so please don't say anything.'

'*I*'ll be jolly hard for you in a moment,' Freddie told her.

'Shut up,' Stephanie replied, and hauled his cock out of his underwear.

It was big, perhaps even bigger than Lias Snell's, but pale and smooth, with only a faint waft of male smell, accompanied by some expensive and equally masculine scent: very much a gentleman's cock. She still needed to pluck up her courage before taking it in her mouth, but once she was sucking it was easy. He had relaxed, his eyes closed in bliss and his mouth agape, and he just sighed occasionally as she moved her lips up and down his rapidly thickening shaft and licked the underside of his foreskin, a technique recommended by Elias Snell the second time she had sucked him off.

As he grew hard in her mouth she thought about how the same fine cock had felt between the cheeks of her bottom, and wished she could take him inside her properly, surrendering her virginity then and there, in the warm spring air with the countryside spread out all round them. Yet she held back, determined to reserve the moment for her wedding night, but pleased that she had learnt to appreciate men's cocks beforehand, and excited enough to want to touch herself even before he was fully erect.

She tried to hold back and to concentrate on his pleasure rather than her own. Grateful for Lias Snell's brief but practical lesson in the art of sucking a penis, she began to try out recommended techniques, first sucking on his helmet in imitation of a lollipop while she masturbated him into her mouth, then nibbling at the fleshy mass of his foreskin where it had peeled back down his shaft, lastly pulling out his balls to lick them with the tip of her tongue. He had opened his eyes and was watching in ecstasy and astonishment as she worked on his cock, and she gave him a little smile before popping him into her mouth once more.

He closed his eyes again, and the urge to play with herself was now too strong to be ignored. With no more than a touch of embarrassment, she reached down between her thighs and eased a hand into the slit of her union suit. Her quim was already puffy and open, the centre wet and sensitive to her fingers. She took his cock in her other hand and pulled it from her mouth, tugging up and down on the shaft, licking and kissing the tip as she masturbated them both. Little shocks were already running through her body, and she began to rub harder, lost to all thoughts of decency as she pressed his cock against her face, bumping it over her nose and lips while still tugging furiously at the shaft.

She was going to come; her quim and bottom hole were already in contraction. The feelings in her head were almost worshipful: she could not get enough of his cock, alternately sucking and rubbing it on her face, then licking his balls as she pulled on his shaft, which made him come. It was sudden and unexpected, a great gout of thick white spunk erupting from the tip of his cock, full in her face. A thrill of ecstasy ran through her as the sticky mess splashed across her nose and one cheek, and again as the second spurt caught her full in the mouth. She deliberately swallowed it, adding a delicious, dirty thrill to her climax as she rode it, and continued to milk his cock into her mouth and over her face, leaving her smeared with mingled come and saliva. Her excitement finally began to fade.

'Sorry about that, old thing,' Freddie gasped. 'Couldn't help it. Have a handkerchief.'

Stephanie accepted the handkerchief and began to clean up. Her knees were sore from the hard marble and even as she got up one leg wouldn't stop shaking, but she felt triumphant. Freddie was looking at her in awe, his mouth open like that of an expectant goldfish, an expression he usually reserved only for the tensest of cricket matches. As she put her make-up to rights she was sure he was only waiting for the moment to ask her to marry him. He failed to come up to scratch, though, contenting himself with taking her hand as they walked back down the slope, until she was forced to drop a hint.

'You do understand,' she said coyly, 'that I would never do such a thing for any ordinary man?'

'Oh, absolutely,' he assured her.

'Only for a man I could really trust,' she went on.

'Oh absolutely.'

'Only for a man I love . . .'

'Oh, absolutely.'

'. . . and who loves me.'

'Oh, absolutely.'

'My soulmate, my life's companion.'

'Oh, absolutely.'

'A man with whom I could walk down the aisle of any church in the land and say to myself, "Stiffy, this is the one, my love eternal, my knight on a snow-white charger, the lodestar of my life and the only plum in the pudding."'

'Oh, absolutely.'

'Frederick George Stanislaus Drake, if you don't stop saying "Oh, absolutely" in that infuriating manner and ask me to marry you this instant I shall do something very unladylike with the tip of my parasol.'

'Ah.'

'What do you mean, "Ah"?'

'Just "Ah".'

'No, not just "Ah". Why not?'

'Well, er . . . it's like this,' Freddie stammered, his face now the colour of beetroot. 'Naturally there's nothing in the world I'd like more than to marry you, Stiffy old bean, and I must say that after that splendid treat I shall still be kicking myself on the day I hand in my dinner-pail, but the thing is . . . the thing is, you see, that I sort of . . . inadvertently, you understand, got engaged last night to Myrtle Finch-Farmiloe.'

* * *

'He let me, and then he told me he was engaged to Myrtle!' Stephanie stormed. 'He let me suck his beastly penis, and then he told me he was engaged to Myrtle Finch-flipping-Farmiloe!'

'You should have kicked him,' Hermione answered with sympathy.

'I did,' Stephanie assured her, 'several times, and I hit him with my parasol, but however soothing these things are, they don't solve anything.'

'I don't suppose he'd have the nerve to tell her it's off?'

'No, he wouldn't, and anyway, I suggested that and he just started going on about the code of the Drakes. We'll have to get Myrtle to break it off herself, which won't be easy. She's been trying to get her claws into him for simply ages.'

'You could tell her he made you suck his thingy,' Hermione suggested.

'It wouldn't work,' Stephanie pointed out. 'She'd just pretend to forgive him and then use it as ammunition every time they had an argument for the next fifty years.'

She didn't mention the revenge that Myrtle would take on her, but contented herself with a delicate shudder and went back to brooding on Freddie's behaviour. They were on their way to Stukely Hall, walking between high, primrose-strewn banks with the woods and Dartmoor rising beyond the end of the lane, but neither the beauty of the place nor the prospect of once again meeting the rather less beautiful Elias Snell could do much to reduce her anger.

'How about this book Porker's making?' Hermione asked. 'We could clean up.'

'I was thinking the same,' Stephanie admitted, 'before Freddie ... never mind. If we get our money on the Emperor, ante-post at five to one, and Singularis Porcus goes missing, we'd do well, but we'd do better still if we leak the Emperor's true weight first, then get in when the odds are long.'

'Won't Porker scratch the bets?' Hermione queried.

'Why should he?' Stephanie answered. 'All the straight money will be on Singularis Porcus, and he can lower the odds on the Emperor when he takes over as favourite.'

'That's true,' Hermione admitted, 'but we'd need to put the money on before we pinch the pig, and you won't be able to touch Grandpapa until afterwards.'

'I'll borrow it from Freddie,' Stephanie stated. 'After this morning he wouldn't have the nerve to refuse.'

They had reached the Okehampton Road, and the towers of Stukely Hall were visible among the trees a little way to the south. Having telephoned ahead to say that they would be coming for lunch, they let themselves in at the tall wrought-iron gates and were presently making polite conversation with their grandmother and great-grandmother. Each of the old ladies seemed determined to outdo the other in spoiling the girls, convinced that both Stephanie and Hermione, who was still carrying enough puppyfat for a litter of Great Danes, needed feeding up.

After her third helping of plum duff with clotted cream Stephanie realised that politeness was no longer an option, and that she had a simple choice between refusing a fourth helping and being violently sick. Her stomach was a hard, round ball beneath her dress, and she wasn't at all sure if, when the time came to get up and leave the table, she would be able to do so.

After a game of cribbage, and some more polite conversation, they were able to leave on the pretext of taking a walk on the moors to aid their digestion. Leaving the hall by the moor gate, they looped round through the woods and once more came to the road, just in time to see Elias Snell and his dray approaching. There was a wide point in the road beside the low bridge where it spanned the river Lyd, and they signalled to him to pull in. There was no mistaking the nature of his grin as he jumped down to the ground.

'Afternoon,' he greeted them, his eyes flicking from Stephanie's chest to Hermione's and back. 'Myrtle, is it?'

Remembering the name she had given in Princetown, Stephanie bit back the hot retort that came to her lips at being mistaken for Myrtle Finch-Farmiloe.

'Myrtle, yes,' she replied instead, 'and this is my sister —'

'Jane,' Hermione said quickly. 'Pleased to meet you, Mr Snell.'

'No more pleased than I am to meet you, my dear,' he answered, casting another thoughtful glance at her chest. 'I hear you want to hire my dray?'

'We do,' Stephanie confirmed, 'but only if we can be assured of your absolute discretion.'

Lias made a face, then answered slowly.

'Expensive thing, discretion.'

'We realise that,' Stephanie said, struggling to keep her voice formal, 'and I feel that what we, er ... my sister, that is, is offering as remuneration will be fully commensurate with your requirements.'

'Beg pardon, Miss?' Lias responded.

Stephanie tried again.

'We are able to offer ample payment, but only in kind rather than in any financial sense.'

Lias nodded, but with no real understanding.

'She means that if you help us I have to suck your thingy,' Hermione said glumly.

'Now that I understand,' he replied, grinning. 'So what's on your mind?'

'Can we be sure of your discretion?' Stephanie insisted.

'Look at it this way, my dear,' he answered her. 'If my Anne were to find out what you and I got up to up along Postbridge way she wouldn't be best pleased, and nor would your father, I dare say. So yes, I'll keep tight-lipped. So what is it? Surely a couple of nice young ladies like you look to be wouldn't be thinking of going against the law?'

'Hardly that,' Stephanie answered, and attempted an airy laugh. 'It's just a little prank we want to play on a neighbour. What we need to do . . .'

She began to explain. His eyebrows gradually rose as he listened, and when she had finished he remained silent for a long time before giving his reply.

'So, if I'm straight, you want me to help you steal a prize pig from Sir Murgatroyd Drake, who's magistrate to Tavistock court, and bring him here in my dray, then help you with him again as far Okehampton Station?'

'Yes,' Stephanie admitted, 'although "steal" is really too strong a word.'

'Steal is steal,' he insisted. 'I'm not saying I won't do it, mind, and no offence to you, Miss Jane, because you're as pretty as a picture, but it's a fearful risk to be taking for a chew of my bone.'

'Perhaps one now and one on the night then?' Stephanie suggested. 'You don't mind, do you, Her . . . Jane?'

'Not at all,' Hermione assured her, 'as long as you're the one doing the sucking the second time, or better still, both times.'

'You agreed to do it!'

'Once!'

'Girls, girls,' Lias interrupted. 'There's no cause for you to argue, seeing as the least I'll be wanting is to have the pair of you together, twice at the least, and afters to keep my mouth shut, extras too.'

'Together?' Stephanie demanded.

'What sort of extras?' Hermione asked suspiciously.

'Much of what Myrtle gave me,' he explained, 'a show of your dumplings and sit-upons, maybe a peep of your cunts and arseholes, a bit of dirty play even.'

'Dirty play?' both girls exclaimed together.

'Rubbing each other and that,' Lias explained. 'Maybe a bit of cunt licking, and don't going playing the innocent with me. I know how you squire's daughters keep yourselves for your husbands. By pleasuring each other, ain't it so?'

Both Stephanie had Hermione had gone bright red and neither was able to speak, but Lias had no such difficulties.

'I've always wanted to see that, I have, a couple of pert little strumpets like yourselves stroking each other's titties and backsides and, best of all, licking cunt.'

He said the last word with a click of his tongue, his voice thick with anticipation. His hand had gone to his trousers, to adjust his cock, and Stephanie finally found her voice.

'Why, you filthy old goat!'

Lias merely shrugged, produced his ancient and blackened pipe from the recesses of his clothing and began to fill it. The state of his cock, which was making a long bulge in the front of his trousers, suggested that his indifference was largely feigned. Stephanie swallowed and forced herself to continue the negotiation.

'I don't think you realise how precious what we are offering is –'

'To you, maybe,' he interrupted, never taking his eyes from the tobacco he was packing into his pipe.

'And how often, pray, are you offered such . . . such delights?' Stephanie asked.

'About as often as I risk coming up before the magistrate for stealing his prize pig,' Lias responded.

'Yes, well,' she responded, 'if you do as you're told, that needn't be a concern. I . . . my sister and I will . . . will use our mouths on you as often as you like, until I leave for London with the pig.'

'Speak for yourself!' Hermione interrupted.

'Don't be difficult,' Stephanie answered. 'At least I'm not giving in to what he expected.'

'I'd rather cuddle with you than suck his horrid thingy,' Hermione responded.

Stephanie had thought her face could get no hotter, but abruptly discovered that she had been wrong. Lias laughed, struck a match and sucked the flame into his pipe as once more Stephanie was left struggling to find words with which to express herself.

'I think he has rather more than a cuddle in mind,' she finally managed.

Lias nodded earnestly. Hermione gave a single, sulky shrug. Stephanie grimaced in frustration and, for a moment, considered abandoning the entire project, only to remember that Myrtle Finch-Farmiloe was now engaged to Freddie Drake. The secretary's position at Gaspers was far less important, but to lose both would be intolerable. Trying to reconcile herself to what he was suggesting, she thought back to the fourth most embarrassing incident of her life, when she had been caught by her grandmother while demonstrating to Hermione some of the less cruel tricks she had been taught by Myrtle. Just the thought sent her face flaring red once more, and she realised that if she did as Lias was suggesting, the incident would rapidly be demoted. Whatever Hermione might think, it was far worse than sucking a penis.

'Perhaps,' she suggested, 'if I were to do the sucking part, Herm ... Jane might show off for you, as you made me do before?'

'Now you're tempting me,' Lias replied. 'Leastways, that would make a nice start, and we can see how we go on from there.'

Stephanie glanced at her sister, who was looking sulkier than ever but made no objection.

'Bare arse, mind you,' Lias remarked, 'and a good jiggle of those fat little dumplings.'

Hermione made a face and without another word started towards the wood. Stephanie swallowed hard. What had been a highly embarrassing but essentially detached negotiation had suddenly become a very immediate reality, and she could think of no reason to delay things, or at least no reason that Lias Snell was likely to accept.

He had moved to where his horses were standing patiently beside the road, and was puffing on his pipe as he fitted feedbags over their heads and did complicated things with bits of harness, with no sign of hurry save the occasional adjustment of his cock within his trousers. Hermione had already climbed the low stone wall that bordered the wood, and Stephanie followed, walking a little way in among the trees to join her. They shared a single, resigned glance before taking each other's hands and walking deeper in.

Both of them had played in the woods as children, and without needing to confer they made for the same place, a flat area of rock beside the river, which was scoured clean each time it rained heavily and was ideal for picnics, building a fire or, as in this case, showing off to a dirty old man. Reaching the rock, they waited for Lias to catch up before Hermione spoke.

'I shall perform a tableau entitled "Girl Bathing in the Belief that she is in Private".'

'You perform what you like, my dear,' he said graciously, 'just so long as there's plenty of flesh on show.'

'I shall go naked,' Hermione assured him. 'Anything less would mean a loss of artistic verisimilitude.'

Stephanie gave a wry smile, knowing that her sister was simply trying to come to terms with what she had to do, although it seemed curiously out of character, sulky resignation being more typical. She was also wishing she had thought of something similar, but unfortunately the idea of creating a tableau entitled 'Girl Sucking the Penis of a Lecherous Old Drayman' made little difference to the reality, and she decided to keep her eyes shut and pretend it was Freddie in her mouth rather than Lias.

He had made himself comfortable on a moss-covered boulder, still puffing on his pipe as he fiddled with the fastenings of his trousers. Stephanie watched in both fascination and revulsion as he dug within whatever undergarment he was wearing to flop out a now all too familiar set of cock and balls, dark-skinned and hairy, his shaft half stiff, so that the tip of his purple helmet showed where his foreskin had begun to roll back.

It would be, she told herself as she got down on her knees, the fourth occasion on which she had sucked a man's penis, and she seemed to be doing it with depressing frequency. She also recalled, as she took the fat, heavy shaft in her hand, that Hermione had offered to do it next time, or at least had been persuaded that it would be her turn. Finally, as she flopped the hideous thing into her mouth and began to suck on it, she accepted that it was really rather nice – not that she intended to admit any such thing to Lias Snell. As she worked on his cock she made sure to keep her eyes tight shut and her face screwed up in feigned revulsion. He took not the slightest notice, and after a moment she realised that he wasn't even watching her but concentrating on Hermione, who had begun to undress.

'. . . silk combinations,' he was saying, 'and don't they cover your little sit-upon ever so nice and tight. That's the way, my dear, nice and slow with the buttons . . .'

He continued to relish every detail of Hermione's striptease and ignore Stephanie, to her immense chagrin. It was bad enough to be made to suck his penis, without him ignoring her in favour of her little sister, and the sound of his lascivious drawl made it impossible to imagine that it was Freddie's cock in her mouth. She began to try some of the techniques he'd taught her, licking at the underside of his foreskin and sucking his helmet between her lips, determined to make him pay attention, which he finally did, but not quite in the way she had anticipated.

'Quite the darling, your sister,' he said, addressing Hermione. 'Best cocksucker this side of Exeter, I wouldn't be surprised. Now, how about a peep of cunt?'

Hermione was clearly nude, a thought that gave Stephanie a sudden twinge of shame. She'd made her little sister strip for a dirty old man and show her quim; perhaps even now her bottom was stuck out so that the soft, sweetly bulging lips pouted between her thighs, which would mean her bottom hole was showing too. A lump had begun to grow in Stephanie's throat, yet still she sucked, eager to make him come and end her sister's humiliation.

Remembering how he liked it, she tried to take him deeper, but the moment the bulbous helmet pushed into her throat she began to choke. He groaned in ecstasy and put his hand on top of her hat, pushing her head down once more. Stephanie struggled to take it, gagging on his cock as it was forced down her throat. Again he groaned, his cock jerked, spunk erupted against the back of her throat, her stomach gave a single, violent lurch, and her mouth was full not only of cock, spunk and saliva but regurgitated plum duff with clotted cream.

Though a novice in the art of fellatio, she was certain that it would be considered the height of bad manners to be sick over a man's cock, so she swallowed bravely. Her face screwed up in a revulsion that was anything but feigned as the contents of her mouth slithered back down her throat, and it took all her will power to keep them there. When she finally managed to open her eyes it was to find Lias looking down at his dirty, slippery cock in disapproval.

'I do wish you wouldn't do that,' he chided. 'Now be a dear and suck me clean.'

Stephanie made a face, but she was in the same state of helpless acquiescence as after a good spanking, and leant meekly forward to take his cock in her mouth once more, drawing back with her lips pursed to leave his shaft merely wet. From behind her Hermione gave a nervous and disgusted giggle.

'Yuck, Stiffy! Are you finished then, Mr Snell?'

'Quite finished, thank you, my dear,' he answered, 'and very nice too, if I may say so, especially when you went down on all fours like that, ever so pretty that was.'

Stephanie turned around, to find Hermione still on all fours, stark naked, her knees apart and her bottom lifted to provide not just the requested peep of her quim but a full show, including the wrinkled pink pit of her anus.

'You dirty girl!' Stephanie exclaimed. 'You're showing everything!'

'The human body is beautiful,' Hermione responded, 'and we should not be ashamed to show what God gave us, and besides, as I said, the pose was demanded by artistic verisimilitude.'

'Who told you all that?' Stephanie demanded. 'No, never mind. I'll talk to you later. Mr Snell, are we in agreement?'

'Call me Lias,' he answered as she finished buttoning his fly. 'I think you could say we're in agreement, yes, so long as you're willing to give me some more of the same before we steal the pig, and after.'

'If we must, we must,' Stephanie answered. 'Please listen carefully while I explain what we want you to do.'

Lias had kept his pipe in his mouth for most of the time Stephanie had been sucking his cock, removing it only briefly when he came, and he continued to puff, filling the air with evil-smelling smoke as Stephanie talked.

'Sir Murgatroyd Drake lives at Combebow, but his pig is kept in a sty next to the cottage where his pigman lives, on the main road. Nobody else lives close, but the pigman, Jan Wonnacott, needs to be out of the way . . .'

'Give him a suck,' Lias suggested, 'and after, he can help me get his pig on to my dray.'

'That is not a practical suggestion,' Stephanie said in her coldest voice. 'Mr Wonnacott knows us, for one thing, and also while I am prepared to accept your dirty habits out of necessity –'

'Jan Wonnacott's brother to Cyril, who lives at Bidlake, ain't he?' Lias interrupted.

'Yes,' said Stephanie.

'I knew you weren't Myrtle whatever-the-name-was,' he went on. 'You're Sir Richard Truscott's grand-daughters, or I'm a monkey's uncle.'

'Yes,' Stephanie admitted, making a face.

'Thought so, the way you couldn't remember your own sister's name,' he continued. 'Best be open, if we're to be stealing pigs together.'

'I'm Miss Stephanie Truscott,' Stephanie said, 'and this is my sister, Hermione.'

'Pleased to make your acquaintance, I'm sure,' he responded, 'and don't worry, I won't be telling anyone, not even my Anne. Least of all my Anne, as it goes.'

'Thank you,' Stephanie responded. 'Now, this pig. We can't pinch him –'

'Boar pig, is it?' Lias interrupted.

'Yes, and we can't pinch him while Jan Wonnacott is drinking, because people might be passing on the road, so we must wait until the early hours of the morning. What we have decided to do, so as not to risk awakening Jan Wonnacott, is to put Singularis Porcus in a muzzle and lure him down the road with ripe apples, as far as the gate into Sir Murgatroyd's water meadows, where you will be parked with your dray, Mr Snell ... Lias. All you need then do is help us get him on to the dray and drive here, which frankly seems very little for what you are demanding in return.'

'Not when it's a stolen pig,' Lias retorted. 'For a stolen pig, Miss Truscott, I'll be wanting to see you down on your sister's cunt.'

Four

The following day they returned to the woods in order to assess their suitability as temporary accommodation for stolen pigs. It was a part of the operation they had meant to perform the day before, but, given Lias Snell's propensity for demanding that his cock be attended to as soon as his balls were recharged, Stephanie had made her excuses, left and returned to Driscoll's. She had also been uncomfortably moist between her thighs, and had gone straight to her room to masturbate, only to find Vera Clapshott changing the flowers Stephanie had ordered placed on her bedside table. After a few not too subtle hints Stephanie had quickly found herself back across the maid's lap, her bare bottom pushed up as her quim was skilfully manipulated. Her climax had been rather nice, although Stephanie was unsure whether the insertion of a daffodil into her anus had been strictly necessary.

It was hard to fault the wood for the purpose. The ancient gate could be opened without too much difficulty and there was room for Lias to back his dray against it, while the wall was high enough and the wood thick enough to ensure that there was little chance of Singularis Porcus being seen from the road. An investigation of a tumbledown shack where some long-disappeared gamekeeper had once kept the tools of his trade, and more recently the sisters had played together, showed that it would make an adequate pigsty.

'How shall we feed him enough?' Hermione queried as they continued on up the river bank. 'If he's anything like the Emperor he eats an awful lot.'

'Once I've got my car back it shouldn't be too difficult to bring over the occasional sack of apples or something,' Stephanie responded. 'Meanwhile, he can grub for roots and acorns and things. It will do him good to diet for a while, and with any luck the Emperor will overtake him.'

'He certainly won't starve,' Hermione admitted.

They had reached the border of the wood, where the river Lyd entered the trees at the end of a steep valley which opened to the sunlit beauty of Dartmoor, the horizon made up of a line of tors, grey against the blue of the sky. For a while they walked in silence, enjoying the sunshine and solitude. There was no house and no other human being in sight, and the only sounds were the gentle murmur of water and the occasional snatch of birdsong. As they turned back towards Driscoll's, a question that had been nagging at the back of Stephanie's mind since the day before suddenly thrust itself to the front.

'Yesterday,' she said, 'you gave quite a performance in front of Mr Snell, didn't you?'

'I had to,' Hermione answered.

'Oh, no, you didn't,' Stephanie pointed out, 'not going down on all fours like that.'

Hermione merely shrugged.

'What have you been up to, H.?' Stephanie demanded.

'Nothing,' Hermione answered, rather too quickly.

'Oh, yes, you have, you rude little beast,' Stephanie insisted. 'What's all this about tableaux, and not being ashamed to show what God gave us, and showing your bottom off for the sake of artistic verisimilitude?'

Hermione made a face.

'Tell me,' Stephanie asked.

'I'd rather not,' Hermione replied.

'Tell me, H.,' Stephanie insisted.

'No, I won't.'

'I want to know.'

'I don't care.'

Stephanie fell silent, wondering if she should threaten to spank the truth out of her sister and then remembering that she'd promised not to, at least after a fashion. They continued to walk, now across a piece of open common that bordered the moor, while Stephanie's curiosity grew ever stronger. They came to a stile set in a wall, the lower step a convenient height for sitting on.

'Please tell me,' Stephanie said.

'No.'

'Please, H.'

'No.'

'If you don't tell me, I shall be cross.'

'I don't care.'

'You will if I have to spank it out of you.'

Hermione didn't answer, but threw Stephanie a worried look. Stephanie allowed her mouth to curve up into a small, satisfied style.

'Tell me, H., or I will spank you. I mean it.'

'No, you don't.'

'Oh, yes, I do. Now tell me or I'm going to take you across my knee and have that fat little bottom bare and smack it, right here.'

'But you said you wouldn't,' Hermione answered, her sulky tone starting to give way to panic, 'not any more.'

'I said I wouldn't when the aunts pass you around,' Stephanie said. 'This is different. Now come here.'

She reached out as she spoke and caught her sister by the wrist. Hermione tried to pull away but Stephanie held on, hauling her now pleading victim forward towards the stile.

'You can stop this any time you like, little sister,' Stephanie said as her calves bumped against the hard wood of the stile. 'Just tell my why you've suddenly gone all arty.'

'Please, Stephanie!' Hermione begged, now close to tears.

'Well, if you're going to be obstinate,' Stephanie replied.

She pulled, intending to haul her sister down across her knee and sit down at the same time, but Hermione pulled back.

'Get over my knee, you little beast!' Stephanie snapped.

'You're the beast!' Hermione yelled back.

Again Stephanie pulled. Still she couldn't get her sister off balance, and Hermione had begun to smile. With a horrible sinking feeling Stephanie realised that she was no longer the stronger of the two. Her cruelty turned to fear as she realised that Hermione not only wasn't trying to get away but was intent on turning the tables.

'Oh, no, you don't!' she spat, determined to exert her authority.

The two of them closed, grappling at each other's bodies, tearing at clothes and pulling hair, each determined to get the other down across her lap. Stephanie fought with the strength of her rising panic, determined not to suffer the unbearable indignity of a spanking from her baby sister. It did her no good. Hermione was heavier, stronger and just as determined.

An awful sick feeling welled up in Stephanie's throat as she realised she was going to lose, and she made a final desperate effort to throw Hermione down over the stile. It nearly worked; both of them were off balance for a moment, but Hermione managed to twist round and land with her bottom on the step of the stile, pulling her sister down with her. Hermione had a good grip and Stephanie was hauled slowly down in a flurry of wildly kicking feet and flailing arms, her brain seething with consternation as she was placed into spanking position across her little sister's knee, still yelling threats but begging at the same time.

'No, you beast! I'll get you back, Hermione! Let me go, you pig . . . you horrid fat pig, let me go! Please, H., I beg you . . . please, no, not this . . . please . . . you horrid little witch, you . . . I'll have Vera hold you down and I'll use my hairbrush on you, I will! Oh, you beast! Beast! Beast! Beast!'

Her dress had been hauled up in the middle of her tirade, exposing her bare thighs and the seat of her union suit to the cool moorland air. The field they were in was visible to the entire western face of Dartmoor, so that anyone out walking would get a prime view of her spanking, even if they were too far away to see exactly who was getting her bottom attended to. There was also a good chance of somebody coming along the path, and then there would be no doubt at all, at which thought her struggles redoubled and her protests turned to wordless shrieks.

'Do stop making that awful noise,' Hermione said calmly as she tightened her grip. 'Do you want somebody to see you getting it?'

'No!' Stephanie squealed. 'But they're bound to, if –'

'Then be quiet,' Hermione interrupted. 'I can't see anybody at all. Now do try not to be such a baby. It's only a spanking.'

'A spanking from you!' Stephanie gasped.

'Why shouldn't I spank you?' Hermione asked. 'You spank me.'

'Not for ages!'

'That's hardly the point, is it?'

'I'm older than you!' Stephanie howled. 'I had to spank you, sometimes.'

'And today I have to spank you,' Hermione told her, 'so at least try and take it like a lady.'

Stephanie scowled as she remembered all the times she'd used exactly the same phrase to her sister. She'd stopped struggling, exhausted and knowing it was useless, but she hadn't given up completely.

'I was only pretending, H.,' Stephanie lied. 'I wasn't really going to do you, I promise.'

'What utter nonsense!' Hermione said with a laugh. 'And just for being such a liar, I shall do you bare.'

'As if you wouldn't anyway,' Stephanie said sulkily. 'Come on, H., please let me up. You've proved you can do it, this is ever so much more humiliating for me than it would be for you, and . . .'

'I have my hairbrush in my bag,' Hermione said, 'and if you don't shut up I shall use it. The more fuss you make, the longer this is going to take.'

It was another of her favourite phrases, inherited from her Great-aunt Victoria. Stephanie shut up. She grimaced in horror as her union suit was opened, deliberately slowly, so that she could experience every moment of her exposure. As the recipient of so many spankings herself, Hermione knew exactly what to do to play upon her victim's feelings. She started at the top. Stephanie felt the air on her skin as the button over the small of her back was opened to reveal no more than a small diamond of flesh, down to where the next button closed the suit at the top of her bottom crease. That too came open and she had a little slit showing; then the next, and soon her cheeks were almost entirely on view as her union suit fell open.

'Properly bare, of course,' Hermione said complacently, and her hand burrowed between her sister's thighs.

As the button over her quim was tweaked open Stephanie let out a weak sob. She was now showing from the small of her back downwards, with only the flaps of her union suit to preserve a last scrap of modesty, which she knew was about to be stripped away. Sure enough, Hermione's thumbs dug into the split of the union suit, stayed as they were for a long moment to allow Stephanie to appreciate her exposure, and hauled wide.

Fully unveiled, Stephanie felt huge behind, her bottom a fat ball of girlflesh thrust out to the moor in a taut circle of white silk and lacy trim. Worse still, the tension of her open suit had made her cheeks part, adding to her woes the exposure of her bottom hole, while her quim was also on full, vulgar display. Hermione gave a low chuckle at the sight and settled one hand on to Stephanie's bottom, gently.

'It is an absolute disgrace, the frequency with which you require spanking, Stephanie,' Hermione lectured in a near-perfect imitation of their great-aunt's voice, 'but what must be done must be done.'

As she spoke she began to spank, applying a single, firm swat across the meat of her sister's cheeks. Stephanie gave a broken wail as Hermione's hand landed, not at the pain but at the raw emotion of having her bottom smacked by her own baby sister. A second smack followed, a third, and any hope of pretending it hadn't happened was gone. She hadn't just been smacked on the bottom, she was being spanked properly, held down over the knee, with her sister's palm applied to her naked cheeks as punishment.

She gave in, defeated, but as her bottom began to bounce and wobble under the slaps she couldn't help reflecting that had she not attempted to do exactly the same to Hermione, she would never have ended up in this undignified position. Her mouth set in a sulky pout, broken only occasionally when a harder slap made her squeak, or a low shot sent a jolt to her quim and pushed an involuntary sob from between her lips.

'Naughty, naughty, Stephanie!' Hermione chided, her voice full of laughter as she applied her hand to her sister's bottom. 'What a bad girl, to have to be put over her own sister's knee! What a bad, bad girl!'

Stephanie's scowl intensified, but she held her peace, knowing that anything she said would only make it worse; but then the spanking stopped and her sister's hand settled gently on her bottom, feeling the hot skin.

'Ooh, you're all warm and rosy!' Hermione said, laughing. 'I wish I had some of that nappy cream Vera uses on you, I'd rub it –'

'How do you know about that?' Stephanie demanded.

'I watched you yesterday afternoon,' Hermione admitted happily as she went back to spanking Stephanie's bottom. 'I thought you were up to no good, and it's easy to climb from my balcony on to yours. But aren't you two naughty? You really do deserve this, Stiffy, don't you? Come on, stick it up, I want to see your bottom hole.'

'Hermione!' Stephanie gasped.

'I only want to see if I can make it open and close, the way it does when the aunts do you,' Hermione giggled. 'Come on, stick it up. Let me see.'

'I will not!' Stephanie answered in outrage.

'Stick ... your ... bottom ... up ...' Hermione demanded, punctuating each word with a hard smack to her sister's bottom. 'I ... want ... to ... see ... your ... bottom ... hole ... Come on, Stiffy. You let Vera ... and she put her finger in ... and a daffodil.'

Hermione had changed the rhythm of her spanking, peppering Stephanie's bottom with little stinging smacks of her fingertips each time she spoke. Stephanie began to struggle again, her mouth set in a hard, obstinate line, the tears welling up in her eyes as she fought to stop herself. But Hermione tightened her grip once more and spanked all the harder.

'I'll use my hairbrush, Stiffy!' Hermione threatened.

'Pig!' Stephanie wailed, her resolve not to make it any worse for herself finally breaking.

'A pig, am I?' Hermione. 'Right.'

The spanking stopped, and Stephanie felt her sister's body shift beneath her. She gave a frantic lurch, but Hermione clung on while digging in her bag and a moment later something smooth, hard, cold, and infinitely more painful than her sister's hand landed across Stephanie's bottom. A piercing screech rang out across the empty field as the smack hit home, and a second as Stephanie began to kick and wriggle once more.

'Just stick up that bottom and it will stop,' Hermione promised, using a tone of voice so infuriatingly superior that Stephanie lost the last of her self-control.

A second later she was beating her fists on the ground and her sister's legs, kicking wildly in the air and bawling her head off as she went into a spanking tantrum.

'You don't fool me,' Hermione said, spanking all the harder. 'Remember, I know all the tricks. Now stick your bottom up!'

Something inside Stephanie seemed to snap and she did it, stuck her bottom high to let her cheeks spread and show off the rude little hole her sister wanted to see, the ring already pulsing in her pain. Hermione gave a peal of laughter, but the spanking had stopped. Stephanie kept her bottom high, the tears streaming down her cheeks and her mouth working furiously as her anus was inspected by her giggling sister.

'All right, you're done,' Hermione finally announced, 'but don't you ever try to spank me again.'

'I won't . . . I promise,' Stephanie sobbed. 'Just let me up, please.'

'One more thing, just to be sure you don't forget,' Hermione said.

Stephanie twisted around as her sister's voice gave way to a curious sucking noise. Hermione had the handle of the hairbrush in her mouth, and Stephanie immediately began to struggle again, because she knew exactly where it was going.

'Oh, no, you don't!' Hermione said firmly. 'I have a long memory, Stiffy, and at least you're not going to get caught by Great-aunt Victoria while the brush is up your bottom.'

As she spoke she pushed the handle of the hairbrush between Stephanie's bottom cheeks. Stephanie was struggling furiously, but the spit-wet tip of the handle was already in the mouth of her bottom hole, and her cries and pleas changed to a gasp of shock as she was penetrated. Hermione pushed the handle in deep, giggling as Stephanie's ring squeezed the bumpy silver shaft.

'Now, what was it Myrtle Finch-Farmiloe used to do?' she said in mock forgetfulness. 'Oh yes . . .'

'No!' Stephanie squealed, but instead of the next expected humiliation being inflicted on her bottom she found herself being tumbled to the ground.

'Quick, get up!' Hermione urged. 'Somebody's coming!'

Stephanie had landed on the hairbrush, and it took her a moment to rearrange her senses before she scrambled hastily to her feet. She tugged her dress down to cover her bottom, but there was no time to remove the hairbrush from her anus, let alone close her union suit. A curious procession was approaching across the field beyond the stile at a brisk march, a double column of young men, all identically clad in khaki shirts, baggy shorts of an indeterminate brown, knee-length khaki socks, wide-brimmed hats and heavy boots. As the group drew closer Stephanie realised that several of them were girls. She had already recognised the man at the front as Claude Attwater.

Only the low wall had saved her from being seen, and she threw Hermione a dirty look before hurriedly composing herself. Her hat had fallen off during their first struggle and she retrieved it, hoping that Claude Attwater and the others would assume that was why she had popped up, as if out of nowhere. He had recognised them anyway, and raised his own hat.

'Good afternoon, Mr Attwater,' Stephanie and Hermione said, almost in chorus.

'Column, halt!' Attwater commanded, raising a hand.

The group came smartly to attention, spoilt somewhat by the last boy in the left-hand column, who had not being paying attention and had walked into the girl in front of him.

'Good afternoon, Miss Stephanie, Miss Hermione,' Attwater responded. 'Out for a healthy walk, I see? Nothing like fresh air for building the constitution, and exercise is everything. Exercise and discipline, those are the maxims we live by in the Brown Shorts, and you, of course, could never be accused of going short of discipline.'

A distinct smirk crossed his face as he spoke, and Stephanie found herself blushing, wondering if he'd somehow seen or worked out what had been going on, although it seemed more likely that he was referring to the spanking she'd had from her Aunt Lettice.

'These are your famous Brown Shorts, then?' she enquired carefully.

'They are indeed,' he answered with pride. 'What you see here, Miss Stephanie, is the nucleus of a great movement. You should join us. It is a fine life, with stimulation for both mind and body, and rest assured, we are the future for this country, the heralds of a new dawn. Here is a pamphlet on the subject.'

He held out a brightly coloured object, the front of which showed a drawing of himself smiling in a fashion that made him look more fatuous than ever. Stephanie took it, wondering how to decline his invitation with sufficient tact to ensure that the long-term result wasn't a spanking from her Aunt Gertrude. Hermione gave a gentle tug on her arm while Stephanie wondered whether it was better to claim to be a communist or feign an allergy to ant bites.

'Excuse me,' she ventured instead, and allowed herself to be drawn aside.

'We should join,' Hermione whispered.

'Join?' Stephanie retorted. 'Don't be a loony!'

'No, don't you see?' Hermione insisted. 'If we join his beastly organisation we get uniforms, which are ever so much better than dresses when it comes to sneaking around after dark, while if we are seen but manage to make a run for it, everything will be blamed on the Brown Shorts.'

'That's true,' Stephanie admitted, 'but if we're Brown Shorts too . . .'

'We must have an alibi,' Hermione responded.

'For the middle of the night?'

'I'll think of something.'

'I'm not sure . . .'

'Mr Attwater,' Hermione announced loudly, not waiting for Stephanie to finish. 'We are prepared to give your organisation a trial. How do we sign up?'

'Excellent!' he responded. 'And a wise choice. There is a small ceremony, when you receive your uniforms, but for the present we plan to march to the top of Hare Tor and back to my house in Sourton. You should come along.'

Stephanie sat down rather gingerly as a faint pop announced the withdrawal of the cork from the lunch-time bottle of Chablis. It had been a long while since her spanking, and her cheeks had recovered, but the long march across Dartmoor with her sister's hairbrush stuck up her bottom had left her anus so sore than even the liberal application of Wilberforce's patent 'Sootho' had failed to stop the stinging. It had only added to the sensation of having to keep her cheeks clenched in order to prevent an accident that could easily compete for a spot in her top three most embarrassing moments.

'Trout?' Sir Richard Truscott queried, sniffing the air.

'With nut butter and new potatoes, Sir Richard, sir,' Mrs Catchpole confirmed, 'and there's a nice carrot and herb pie for them as is fussy little madams.'

Aunt Lettice stiffened, and Stephanie was forced to stifle a giggle. Mrs Catchpole took no notice of either, but began to serve.

'Plenty of sauce, Lucy,' Sir Richard instructed as Mrs Catchpole began to serve. 'Splendid, splendid, nothing like a stiff gallop to work up an appetite, eh? But what's this Gertie tells me about you joining the Brown Shorts, Stiffy? And you too, H.? I thought you both had more sense.'

'It will do them both a power of good,' Gertrude put in.

'You always say we should experience different facets of life, Grandpapa,' Hermione answered him.

'Traipsing across the moor dressed up like a boy?' he queried. 'Well, it's up to you, and I dare say you'll soon grow out of it.'

He addressed himself to the trout, as did the others, leaving a silence broken only by the sounds of determined mastication and a faint plop as Mrs Catchpole manoeuvred a slab of orange and green substance on to Aunt Lettice's plate.

'The Emperor weighed in at ninety-five exactly this morning,' Sir Richard remarked after a while, 'but Drake's beast is well over the hundred, damn him. Would you like to walk down to the sty with me after lunch, girls? Or would a drive be more to your taste? We might go to Launceston.'

'Hermione is practising piano with the Reverend Porthwell,' Victoria Truscott pointed out, 'and if you are going out in the car, you might give me a lift. Lord Salisbury is not at all well.'

'I'm not having your damn dog being ill all over my upholstery,' Sir Richard answered. 'Why can't the veterinarian come here?'

Stephanie was no longer listening, but had gone into a daydream in which Mrs Catchpole had lost all touch with reality and spanked Aunt Lettice for not eating her trout. Just possibly, she considered, it might be worth dropping a hint and seeing what happened. After all, Lucy Catchpole had been with the family for over forty years, and nothing would induce Sir Richard to sack her. There was a faint smile on her face as she imagined Lettice's slender buttocks exposed for spanking, and she let her mind dwell on the delicious fantasy as lunch continued.

Afterwards, she followed Hermione out on to the terrace, hoping for a proper reconciliation after the morning's spanking, which they hadn't had a chance to discuss, and a restoration of what she felt to be the proper order of things. It was only right and proper that she should be spanked by her mother, and perhaps occasionally by her grandmother. Great-aunt Victoria she could accept as an unavoidable disaster, like a volcano or typhoon, which in turn made the lesser aunts lesser disasters. Being done by Vera Clapshott really was a bit much, but there were compensations involving the application of Sootho. Even the thought of getting it from Myrtle Finch-Farmiloe made her want to grind her teeth, and yet she had never been able to rid herself entirely of the feeling that it was appropriate. Hermione was another matter.

Big sisters spanked little sisters, not the other way around. That was the natural order of things, and she burned with resentment at Hermione's behaviour. What Hermione needed was a long talking to, an even longer spanking and a cuddle to make her better, preferably in immediate succession. Unfortunately, one look at the sulky expression on Hermione's face as she stood picking the petals from a luckless primrose made Stephanie realise that it was a subject to approach with care. First she would have to make Hermione see the error of her ways, and meanwhile there was something else she wanted to know.

'What's this about you cramming with Porker?' she asked as she came up beside her sister.

'I failed my music exam,' Hermione complained, 'and Great-aunt Victoria says I have to do it again, which is completely silly, because I hate piano, and I have no intention of playing, ever, and I don't like Porker Porthwell at all.'

'He is a bit of a beast,' Stephanie agreed, 'but think how much money we'll be able to clean him out of. You can leak the Emperor's weight, as well, while you're there.'

Hermione managed a weak smile and carefully removed the final petal from the primrose, letting it flutter to the ground. Stephanie waited a moment, then spoke again.

'You were a bit of a beast too, spanking me like that.'

'You were going to spank me,' Hermione pointed out, 'and you needn't pretend you wouldn't have got me bare, or teased me, or been rude with me.'

'I wouldn't have stuck a hairbrush up your bottom!' Stephanie protested.

'You might,' Hermione said. 'You did that time Great-aunt Victoria caught us.'

Stephanie winced and took an instinctive glance back across her shoulder.

'That's as maybe,' she admitted, 'but it's not the same, is it?'

'Why not?' Hermione demanded.

'I'm older than you,' Stephanie pointed out.

'So what?'

'So . . . so you shouldn't spank me!' Stephanie was outraged that Hermione could possibly fail to comprehend such a basic fact. 'Do I go round spanking the aunts, or Mama?'

Hermione shrugged.

'Well, then,' Stephanie went on. 'I think it's only fair that you come up to my room later and I give you a jolly good spanking, and a nice cuddle afterwards to make you better. I don't want to quarrel.'

'Then don't spank me,' Hermione told her. 'And if you try, you'll be the one who gets it, Stiffy. But I'll give you a cuddle.'

Stephanie made a face. It was a hard offer to refuse, and yet she was determined to get back on top. Obviously she had been in London too long and lost the authority she had always enjoyed over her sister, but she was sure that once she had Hermione's bottom nice and hot she could reassert herself. It was just a question of finding the opportunity.

'All right,' she said, and held her arms open.

They came together, holding on to one another for a long moment before breaking apart with a gentle kiss. Inside the house, the grandfather clock in the drawing room chimed the half-hour.

'I'd better go,' Hermione said. 'I'll see you this evening.'

Stephanie watched her sister walk from the terrace with considerable irritation and no less curiosity. Hermione usually accepted such unpleasant things as piano lessons with at least moderate good grace, but today she seemed unusually sulky. Something was going on, just possibly something to do with Hermione's mysterious new philosophy about nudity, which was both intriguing and worrying. Strolling indoors as if in no great hurry, she sat down where she could watch the drive and pretended to read.

Hermione soon appeared, dressed in a pink frock, which was unusual for her, and looking more agitated than ever. She set off up the drive. Stephanie finished the story she was reading, then followed. Hermione did not take the Bridestowe Road but made for Bidlake, then turned north along the main road and across a field to the rear of the rectory. The faint tinkling of a badly played piano was audible as Stephanie stole into the rectory garden by the back gate and took up a position behind the screen of a yew hedge.

The music stopped but, having had to suffer in just the same way, although with a different tutor, Stephanie knew exactly where Hermione would be: in the music room at one end of the building, seated at the piano with her back to the main window. The ancient wisteria that cloaked much of the rear of the rectory allowed her to peer through the panes with little chance of being observed. Inside, her sister was indeed sitting at the piano, her face set in a stubborn scowl. Standing beside her was the Reverend Benjamin Porthwell, curate to Bridestowe Parish, with his cassock raised to reveal well polished black boots, dark socks held up by suspenders, plump, hairy legs unencumbered by underwear, and an erect penis.

Although it was only the third male organ Stephanie had set eyes on, she was fairly sure it was not a typical specimen. Freddie Drake's was handsome and virile. Lias Snell's was ugly, but still virile. Porker Porthwell's was grotesque, not at all virile, and oddly in contrast with his globular body. It was long and thin, with a small bright-red helmet and a skinny shaft, stretched so taut that thin purple veins could be seen. All of that would have been bad enough, but it paled into insignificance beside the fact that the organ was so severely twisted that the helmet almost faced backwards. Beneath it depended a pair of monstrous testicles, the outline of each clearly visible within a pink and almost completely hairless scrotum: altogether a peculiarly unpleasant set of male equipment.

The window was open, and his voice carried clearly to Stephanie as he spoke, high and piping, full of barely suppressed excitement.

'We agreed, didn't we, Miss Hermione. If you get it wrong you have to touch. Now take hold and pull up and down a little.'

Hermione made no move to comply, her sulky scowl only growing more intense. The curate hitched his cassock up a little higher, exposing a segment of rounded belly the colour and texture of lard. Hermione reached out, very gingerly, to tap his erection with a single, sudden motion. He wagged one plump finger at her, his voice firm and yet also wheedling as he spoke.

'Oh no, young lady. I'll need a little more than that, I'm afraid. Come along now, take hold and pull up and down, just a few times.'

Hermione bit her lip, extended a hand, then stopped.

'If . . . if we should be proud of what God gave us,' she said, 'and I should think it a privilege and a pleasure to touch your thingy, then why is it my punishment?'

'Ah ha, but it's not a privilege or a pleasure for you, is it?' he retorted, once more wagging his finger. 'If it was, we should have to find some alternative punishment, shouldn't we? The same goes for removing your clothes.'

Hermione frowned, then with sudden decision reached out to grasp his cock, which she gave a few inexpert tugs before hastily letting go. The curate gave a long sigh, checked his watch, then spoke again.

'Once more, and do try, or we'll just have to have those darling little titties out again, won't we?'

After wiping her hand on the piano seat, Hermione put her fingers to the piano keys, hesitated a moment, then began to play, producing a set of notes so discordant that Stephanie couldn't even identify the tune.

'Dress down. Titties out,' the curate demanded, sounding anything but disappointed.

Hermione obeyed, scowling furiously as she pulled her arms out of the shoulder straps of her dress and folded down the front. She was naked underneath, her puppyfat breasts lolling bare and round as she glanced up at the curate.

'Let that be a lesson to you,' he said, but as she turned back to the piano his fat pink tongue extended to moisten his lips. 'Try again, three times, and if you don't get it right, off comes that pretty dress.'

Again Hermione tried, her bare breasts quivering as she played, and if anything the attempt was worse than before. The curate drew a heavy sigh.

'I really don't think you are trying at all, Hermione. Perhaps having to sit bare bottom on your stool will help?'

'You said I had three goes,' Hermione pointed out.

The curate gave a sceptical grunt and stood back a little. He began to fiddle with his cock, keeping it erect with his eyes fixed on Hermione's bare breasts as she tried to play her piece again. She was no better than before, and he shook his head sadly. Once more she tried, so ineffectually that Stephanie was left wondering if the two of them were playing a game, and Hermione might actually want to be made to take her clothes off.

The expression on Hermione's face as she stood up suggested otherwise, and the way she lifted her dress and peeled it off looked genuinely reluctant. Yet she was naked underneath except for stockings and shoes, her chubby pink bottom quite bare as she settled it back on to the piano stool.

'Spankies next,' the curate announced eagerly. He had abandoned the effort to sound authoritative.

Hermione's fingers were shaking so badly as she tried to play her piece once more that it would almost certainly have been wrong anyway. As it was she made a hash of it, and the curate immediately bent down to plant a firm smack on the two meaty pink bulges sticking out over the edge of the piano stool. Hermione was left with a pink hand mark on her bottom and shaking harder than before, so that her next attempt was worse still. Again her bottom was smacked, and Stephanie saw that tears of frustration and shame had begun to trickle down her sister's face.

'I don't think you're even trying!' the curate declared. 'If you can't do better than that, I'll have to make you do you know what.'

He was now so close to Hermione that when she turned her tear-stained face up to deny the accusation his cock was just inches from her mouth. Stephanie grimaced at the thought of having the hideous thing so close to her own face, and began to wonder if she should intervene. Yet it was impossible to be sure of Hermione's true feelings, while there was also the morning's spanking to be taken into consideration. She decided to carry on watching, telling herself that her decision had nothing to do with the sharp thrill she had felt at the thought of seeing her sister take the fat curate's cock in her mouth, which seemed to be what he was expecting.

'Once more,' he demanded, masturbating himself shamelessly, his small, bright eyes flicking between her breasts and the reddened bottom meat bulging over the edge of the stool. 'And stick it out a little more.'

Hermione obeyed, adjusting herself so that her thighs were on the stool but her bottom cheeks pushed out behind, the tight star of her anus clearly visible between them. The curate, now red-faced and masturbating vigorously, nodded for her to begin. Hermione played and failed as miserably as before. As the last note faded he lost his temper with her, or seemed to, reaching down to aim a salvo of hard smacks at her cheeks.

'I've warned you before!' he declared. 'This time it goes in your mouth!'

'No!' Hermione answered him, with what Stephanie was sure was real revulsion. 'Not in my mouth!'

His response was to plant several more hard smacks on her bottom, making the flesh jiggle and redden even more.

'Take it in your hand then,' he demanded, 'and quickly.'

Hermione pulled a face, but did as she was told, taking hold of his erection. He stood back to his full height, lifting his cassock and the shirt beneath to reveal the full rotundity of his stomach, which had begun to quiver like an enormous pale jelly as Hermione masturbated him. Her breasts were also quivering, to the same motion, and her big pink nipples were stiff, despite the look of utter disgust on her face.

The look was mirrored by Stephanie. As Hermione pulled the curate's cock up and down, the head rotated, reminding Stephanie so forcefully of a patent corkscrew that she found herself looking to see if it had a left- or right-hand thread. She had just worked out that it was right-handed when he began to speak again, his voice low and guttural.

'One day I'll make you suck it. One day, Hermione, my angel, I'll make you suck it ... and when you are my wife ... I'll stick it right up that pretty cunt, every night, and in your mouth ... and up your cunt again ... and in your mouth ... and up your darling bottom ...'

He broke off with a grunt, projecting a gout of come into the air just as Hermione adjusted her position, so that her lolling breasts caught the full force of his ejaculation. She gave a shriek as jets of sticky white fluid splashed over her plump globes and spattered her tummy. The third eruption caught her in one eye and across her nose. She dropped his cock but he snatched it up, to milk the last of his come over her already dripping breasts.

'Filthy beast!' she managed as her spunk-smeared features screwed up in utter disgust. 'Why do you always have to do it in my face?'

'Because you look so pretty like that,' he told her, 'and you get so delightfully petulant about it. I save up all week, you know, just to make sure I have plenty.'

'Filthy beast,' Hermione repeated as she accepted a handkerchief and began to wipe the mess from her face.

In the bushes, Stephanie's knees were wide and her dress rucked up, one hand pushed into the slit of her union suit as she fiddled with her quim.

As she looked from her window in the Blue Room into the darkness of the Devon night, Stephanie was rapidly coming to appreciate the difference between plotting to steal a gigantic pig and actually doing so. She had not even started out, and already her heart was hammering. The hundred and one things that could go wrong were jostling for attention in her imagination, from the highly probable, such as being caught sneaking out by her Great-aunt Victoria, given a spanking and sent back to bed, to the highly improbable, such as being abducted by Elias Snell and sold into an Arabian harem. Nevertheless, she told herself, she was her father's daughter and a Truscott. She would go on.

It had been a peculiar day. Hermione had been sulky the previous evening, and Stephanie had not dared admit to having peeped at her with Benjamin Porthwell, despite feeling both sympathy and curiosity. It had been the same the next day, although there had been little opportunity for talk. Claude Attwater had come to collect them in the morning, bringing with him two Brown Shorts uniforms. Both were rather large, so Stephanie had spent the subsequent initiation ceremony and rally terrified that her shorts would fall down at some crucial moment. She had also discovered for the first time in her life how it felt to have rotten eggs thrown at her, although she had managed to dodge skilfully enough that none hit her.

By a lucky chance they had run into Freddie Drake on the way home and, after a little artful flirting and a great deal of playing on his guilt, Stephanie managed to extract twenty pounds from him. They had then called in at Bridestowe Rectory, and after a few minutes of somewhat embarrassed conversation with the Reverend Wallace Tredegar managed to get Porker Porthwell alone. The money had changed hands in return for a neatly written betting slip accepting twenty pounds for the Emperor to win the fat pigs class at odds of ten to one.

They had returned home in time for tea, well pleased with themselves, and spent the late afternoon going over their plan for the evening until every detail was honed to perfection. At her grandfather's insistence she had dressed for dinner, but she made the mistake of feeding Lord Salisbury a chop bone from her plate and ended up with her bare bottom flaunted to the room as she was given a brief but effective spanking by Great-aunt Victoria. Even now she felt a little tender behind, which kept her firmly in mind of what would happen to her if they were caught.

The Brown Shorts uniforms were in the huge wicker basket in which Mrs Catchpole and the maids collected items for the wash; that was just where Stephanie had told Vera to put them. The first step of the plan was to retrieve them and the last to put them back, thus establishing an alibi in the event of later accusations. So as she prepared to leave the Blue Room she was in nothing more than her nightie and shoes, which would also allow her to pretend, if she were caught going downstairs, that she had intended to raid the pantry.

Not that she had any intention of getting caught. Holding her door just ajar she waited and listened, then slipped out into the corridor and down the servants' stairs. The lower storey of the house was absolutely dark, but numerous real pantry raids had taught her every obstacle on the way, except the soft, squashy thing she ran into as she reached the doorway of the scullery.

'Stiffy!' Hermione hissed as Stephanie stepped back with her heart pounding. 'Watch where you're going!'

'Sorry, I didn't see you,' Stephanie whispered.

Hermione didn't bother to answer, and together they moved on into the scullery. A trace of light from a crescent moon turned the familiar room into a confusing pattern of shadows, but they quickly located the basket. Finding their uniforms was harder, especially the socks, and when Stephanie had tugged the baggy brown shorts up around her hips they immediately fell down again.

'I think you've got my shorts, H.,' she whispered, then froze.

Somewhere in the house a door had been opened and closed again. Footsteps sounded in the passage above, and without waiting to risk discovery the girls scampered to the far end of the room, where a door let them out into the night. It was cool, and Stephanie found herself shivering slightly, but neither dared turn back. A light in one of the bathrooms had come on, and a female figure stood silhouetted against the curtains.

'Aunt Lettice,' Hermione said quietly, 'but I don't think she heard us.'

While they waited for the light to go out Stephanie tucked the waistband of her shorts into itself, securing them loosely on her hips. When the gurgle of water announced the completion of Aunt Lettice's business they set off, first making for the outhouse where the apples were stored, then running light-footed across the lawn. Their eyes gradually adapted to the gloom. The lake was a puddle of liquid gunmetal beneath the black bulk of Burley Down, and the high wall just visible as a shadow among shadows. On the bridge Stephanie took her sister's hand for comfort, and they stayed close together as they left the grounds.

Utter blackness returned as they entered the tree-shrouded track along the bottom of Burley Down, and Stephanie felt Hermione's hand tighten on hers. A breeze had got up, rustling the leaves and filling her with fears she knew to be irrational to go with the very rational ones she already had, but she continued to put one determined foot in front of the other until they reached the main road. She heard the gentle chink of harness and caught the scents of horse and tobacco long before she saw the dray or the faint red glow of the drayman's pipe.

'Mr Snell?' she enquired.

'Who else do you think it might be?' he asked, chuckling.

'Not so loud, please,' she urged.

'Nobody to hear,' he assured her, 'not at this time of night. Now, how about you two have a little cuddle, and we'll be getting to work.'

Stephanie had been trying very hard not to think of what he had demanded for his help, and even now that she could put it off no longer she found herself prevaricating.

'All that would be better once we have the pig,' she said quietly as she lowered the bag of apples into the dray, 'and besides, what is the use of us . . . us touching each other if you are unable to see anything?'

'I've a lantern that'll show plenty.'

'What if somebody else sees?'

'We'll charge 'em sixpence.'

'This is no time for levity,' Stephanie hissed. 'Now, please, the pig first . . .'

'Cunt first, pig second and cunt for afters,' he insisted. 'That's what we agreed.'

'We'd better do as he says, Stiffy,' Hermione broke in. 'After all, he could do anything he wanted with us, out here.'

'I'm sure Mr Snell would not think of taking unfair advantage,' Stephanie lied as her quim went suddenly tight.

'Could be,' he remarked, 'and there's no better way to make sure I don't than to make sure I can't.'

'And we did agree,' Hermione added, 'so it wouldn't be entirely unreasonable if he was cross and made us . . . made us surrender. And if he drives up the track a little and we go in the back of the dray we couldn't possibly be seen.'

'H.!' Stephanie gasped. 'Really, you . . . oh, very well, Mr Snell, but must you always make such an utter beast of yourself?'

With a chuckle he went to the head of his lead horse, whispering to her as he pulled gently on her bridle. Stephanie and Hermione stepped quickly out of the way as the big dray was turned, and followed as Lias led his team back up the track. Stephanie's stomach was fluttering and there was a huge lump in her throat. She was barely able to take in what she was about to be made to do.

'Climb up on the wheel,' Lias suggested.

Too numb to fight any longer, Stephanie obeyed, raising her foot to a spoke only to have a huge hand cup her bottom and boost her up on to the side of the dray.

'Whatever are you wearing?' he asked. 'Sackcloth?'

'Shorts,' Stephanie answered as she clambered into the dray.

'Girls in shorts, whatever next?' he remarked. 'Still, I dare say shorts come down as easy as dresses come up. In you go, my love.'

He had boosted Hermione up as he spoke, but rather too hard, so that she lost her balance and tumbled in, bringing Stephanie down in a tangle of spread-eagled limbs.

'Hang on there, wait until I can see,' Lias demanded.

Holding back an answer with some difficulty, Stephanie untangled herself from her sister. The dray smelt of stale beer, and the rough wooden boards on which she was sat were distinctly sticky, except where a scattering of straw covered them. Lias climbed in, and when he opened the lantern a beam of dull yellow light revealed more straw, in bales. 'Straw,' he explained, 'for the pig.'

'How appropriate,' Stephanie remarked as he sat down on the nearest bale.

He ignored her, turned the lantern so that the part of the dray where she and Hermione were sat was illuminated, then began to unfasten his trousers. Stephanie watched with a resigned expression as his fat brown cock was pulled out one more time, along with his balls, which he began to stroke.

'Come along then, girls. No time like the present.'

'What ... what do you want us to do?' Stephanie asked weakly.

'Get out of those silly shorts, for a start,' he replied. 'You can keep the shirts on, but pull them up to show your titties.'

Hermione began to comply, but Lias shook his head.

'No, no, not like that,' he told them. 'Do each other. You turn your bottom to me, Hermione, and you, Stephanie, you pull your sister's shorts down, nice and slow.'

Hermione didn't look too happy but did as she was told, much as she had for the Reverend Porthwell, sticking out her bottom to make a plump ball of flesh, the waistband of the shorts slack around her waist. It was an extraordinarily rude pose and was going to become a great deal ruder if Stephanie pulled the shorts down, but it was also tempting, offering her an opportunity both to avoid disgracing herself and to take a badly needed revenge.

'Perhaps you'd like to watch me spank her?' she suggested to Lias as she took hold of the waistband of Hermione's shorts.

'Hey!' Hermione protested, twisting round, her shorts already half down, with such force that Stephanie was taken by surprise. Sprawled on her back in the sticky straw, she could only manage a squeak of alarm as her foot was grabbed and twisted, forcing her face down. An instant later Hermione was on her back, and Stephanie realised that her sister really was quite heavy.

'I warned you!' Hermione spat, and Stephanie's shorts were hauled down, baring her bottom to the night and to the interested eyes of Elias Snell. 'Now I'm going to do you!'

He was laughing, and laughed louder still as Stephanie's shock gave way to consternation and she began to thump her fists on the wooden platform of the dray and kick her feet.

'No!' she squealed. 'Not this! Not again! Hermione, please ... I beg you, not a spanking, not in front of him!'

'You were going to do me,' Hermione answered, and planted a hard smack on her sister's bottom.

Stephanie's skin was cold and the slap stung, but her answering howl held far more of humiliation than of pain.

'Shut up!' Hermione ordered. 'You wanted him to see a spanking, didn't you?'

'Yes, but not mine!' Stephanie wailed.

'I suppose your bottom's too precious for him to see?' Hermione snapped back, and began to spank her sister's wriggling bottom as hard as she could.

'Ow!' Stephanie squealed. 'Not so hard! Ow! Ow! Ow!'

'Will you shut up?' Hermione demanded. 'Somebody might hear you!'

'Then stop spanking me, you horrid beast!' Stephanie whined. 'Ow! Hey, no ... Hermione! N –'

Her protests turned to a weird gulping noise as one of the over-ripe apples from their bag was wedged firmly into her mouth, gagging her.

'Now that is comic!' Lias said with a laugh. 'Just like a pig ready to be served up with apple sauce and roast tatties. Only difference is, she ain't been stuffed!'

Stephanie twisted her head around to glare at him, but then her eyes widened as the spanking began once more. He'd been enjoying the show: his cock was rigid in his hand and he was wanking as he watched her bottom dance. She lost control, her fists drumming on the hard wooden boards, her feet waving wildly in the air, as the tears burst from her eyes. She was wriggling so desperately beneath her sister's weight that she was providing the drayman with a thoroughly rude show of her open bottom slit and the rear of her quim as he masturbated over her. Only her pulled-down shorts prevented her spreading her legs and making a yet more blatant display.

'There,' Hermione said suddenly, 'maybe that will teach you your lesson, Stephanie. Is that all right for you, Mr Snell?'

The spanking stopped. Lias Snell's answer was an incoherent grunt. An instant later Stephanie felt something hot and wet splash over her burning rear cheeks, and her face screwed up in disgust as she realised she'd had her bottom spunked on. Again he grunted and a second ejaculation spattered her cheeks and thighs, then something hard yet fleshy pressed against her smacked flesh: his cock. Her disgust rose higher as he wiped his spunk over her bottom. She clamped her jaw and the apple in her mouth suddenly gave way, exploding in a mess of half-rotten pulp and pips over the floor and in her face, leaving her spitting out bits as Hermione finally lifted her weight off her.

'You'll be needing my handkerchief,' Lias remarked, holding out a large grey rag that appeared to have been used several times. 'I brought a couple along, 'cause I figured they'd come in handy. Messy things, you girls, when you get excited.'

Stephanie didn't answer but took the dirty handkerchief, glaring at him as she wiped her bottom. Hermione was looking smug and recriminations were obviously pointless, so she contented herself with an angry silence until she was sure she'd removed every trace of spunk from both bottom cheeks. Pulling up her shorts, she turned to Lias.

'I hope you're satisfied! Now, are we going to steal this pig, or not?'

'Certain sure we are,' Lias answered as he stuffed his cock and balls back into the recesses of his clothing. 'And yes, that was a fine show, thank you, but you needn't think you've got away without a lick of each other's cunts, my girls.'

'Beast,' Stephanie answered, but quietly, while Hermione said nothing.

Lias had to turn the dray, a difficult manoeuvre, leaving Stephanie to contemplate the gross indignity she'd just had inflicted on her, and attempt to cope with her reaction. Her bottom was hot and, as always after a good spanking, no matter who from, that heat had gone to her quim. She was wet, and she couldn't stop thinking of Lias' big dark cock. He'd compared her to a roast pig and said she hadn't been stuffed. She knew what he'd meant too, not a sage-and-onion forcemeat but his big fat cock, rammed home up her virgin quim, her cunt as he called it, a far more suitable word for the mound of puffy, slippery flesh between her thighs.

Only the fear of discovery as they started down the main road deflected her mind from the awful, disturbing thought of having her virginity taken. The night was as dark and empty as ever, but her imagination populated the lonely country road with angry landowners, vengeful pigmen and stern, dutiful police constables. None of these materialised, and before long she caught the familiar waft of pig and managed to make out the squat black shape of Jan Wonnacott's cottage, with the sty beside it. The dray drew to a halt and she scrambled down, pulling the bag of apples behind her. Hermione followed, and spoke in a whisper as the dray pulled away once more.

'Sorry, Stiffy. I got a bit cross.'

A flood of possible retorts and demands to be allowed her revenge rolled through Stephanie's head, but what came out was the thought uppermost in her mind.

'You've made my bottom all hot!'

'Sorry,' Hermione repeated. 'Now where's this pig?'

'In his sty, I hope.'

They stole forward, Stephanie expecting the door of Jan Wonnacott's cottage to burst open at any instant. She was unsure whether the low, grumbling snores she could hear emanated from him or from the pig. A sudden snuffling noise as they reached the corner of the sty confirmed that the snorer was human, and an enquiring oink followed as she opened the door. The interior of the sty was dark, but there was no mistaking the location of the pig as a large, moist snout pressed against her leg. She jumped back, tripped over a stray mangel-wurzel and sat down in something that squashed unpleasantly against her bottom.

'I think I just sat in pig poo.'

'Stop fooling around, Stiffy, or we'll get caught!' Hermione hissed. 'Give me an apple, quick.'

Stephanie lifted herself carefully from the ground, only to discover that whatever she had sat in preferred to adhere to her shorts rather than to the floor. It was also quite heavy, and as she groped for the apple bag her shorts fell down, just as Singularis Porcus chose to nuzzle her again, so that this time his huge, rubbery snout pressed between the cheeks of her bottom, snuffling.

'Hey!' she squeaked. She stepped hurriedly forward, tripped over her shorts and went flat on her face.

'Will you stop playing the fool?' Hermione hissed.

'I can't help it!' Stephanie answered. 'Oh no, not that . . .'

Singularis Porcus had begun to snuffle at her legs, and for one awful moment she thought she was going to be mounted, only for him to pull away as Hermione spoke again.

'Here we are, boy, a nice juicy apple, just for you.'

A single squashy crunch signalled the consumption of the titbit as Stephanie scrambled to her feet and pulled her shorts up as fast as she could. Her seat was obviously dirty, but she would need a stick or something to clean herself up, while if she let go of her shorts they would fall down again. Realising she'd just have to stay dirty for the time being, she put a tuck in the shorts and gave a little wiggle to make sure they'd stay up. Hermione spoke again.

'Do you mind helping, please, Stephanie?'

'I'm busy!' Stephanie protested.

'What with?'

'I've messed my shorts!'

'You haven't! Stiffy, you big baby . . .'

'Not like that! I told you, I sat in pig poo.'

'Is that all? Don't be so precious. Take the apple bag, will you?'

Unable to find words to express her feelings, Stephanie accepted the apple bag. The pig snuffled closer, drawn by the tempting scent of decaying fruit. She backed away, as much in alarm as from any desire to get the monstrous creature out of the door. He followed, venting an irate snort as both girls backed hurriedly out into the road. Stephanie took an apple from the bag and watched him gobble it up, his full form now revealed in the weak moonlight that now paled the sky, seeming bright after the utter blackness of the sty.

There was no doubt that the judges at both Okehampton and Tavistock had made the correct decision in awarding last year's gold medal. Singularis Porcus was not only fatter than the Emperor but longer and taller at the shoulder. He was also black, and the moonlight reflecting from his tiny eyes gave him an unnerving quality, as if Sir Murgatroyd Drake, realising that he could never hope to win by fair means, had made a pact with Satan for the supply of a demonic pig of guaranteed prize-winning proportions.

Eager to placate the monster, Stephanie fed him three apples in quick succession. He snuffled them up eagerly and as the girls began to walk down the road he followed without protest. Ahead was the turning where Lias was supposed to be parked with the dray, as indeed he proved to be, with the tail boards folded down to make a ramp. Now able to see more or less what she was doing, Stephanie allowed the pig a sniff of a particularly large apple, then tossed it up into the dray. He followed, the boards creaking beneath his weight, up on to the dray. Stephanie threw in a few more apples, Lias and Hermione closed the tailboards, and the deed was done.

'Easy as winking,' Lias remarked.

'For you, maybe,' Stephanie answered.

He merely chuckled and climbed up on to the driver's seat, motioning to them to follow. The seat was broad enough for three but Stephanie remained standing, only to lose her balance as the dray jolted into motion. As her bottom made contact with the hard wooden seat the muck adhering to her shorts squashed up between her cheeks and against her quim, with only the material of her shorts between it and bare flesh.

'Bother!' she managed, and made to rise, but a wheel hit a rut and sat her firmly back down in the muck.

'Whiffs a bit, don't he?' Lias remarked.

'That's Stiffy,' Hermione replied with a lack of tact only possible in a little sister. 'She sat in pig poo.'

Stephanie didn't answer, her mind occupied with black thoughts concerning lecherous draymen, little sisters, Myrtle Finch-Farmiloe, but most of all pigs that didn't have the common decency to select a remote corner of the sty for a toilet. Nor was there any possibility of stopping to clean up, with the evidence of their theft snuffling up apples in the back of the dray, so she was forced to stay as she was until Lias turned into the deep, winding lane that led up over the southern flank of Burley Down, beside which a stream ran down the hill.

'Please may we stop?' she asked. 'I need to tidy myself up.'

'Best keep going,' he responded. 'Just take your shorts off.'

'What, sit bare bottom, next to you?' she demanded.

'Well, you'd have to anyway if your shorts were all wet, wouldn't you?' he answered. 'Catch your death of cold, you would, sitting in wet shorts.'

'He's seen it all anyway,' Hermione pointed out, giggling, 'and it's jolly dark.'

Stephanie hesitated, but the lane was considerably rougher than the road, making her bounce up and down on the seat so that every landing squashed what was under her a little deeper between her bottom cheeks. Muttering the rudest word she knew, she quickly lifted herself up and pushed her shorts down and off. The next jolt of the dray sat her back down again, now bare bottom in the pig's mess.

'Bother!' she spat. 'Bother and drat and damn and . . . and bugger!'

'Fine language, that is, coming from a young lady,' Lias remarked.

'Shut up and drive.'

She folded her arms and settled down to sulk, giving in to fate, which seemed to have decided to pick on her that night. Hermione and Lias began to talk, speaking in low, excited voices, both of them clearly pleased with the night's work, their differences forgotten in the comradeship of thieves. Gradually Stephanie too found her mood lightening, feelings of triumph and adventure crowding out her chagrin and disgust, despite her spanked bottom and the slipperiness of what she was sitting in.

Worry added to her feelings as they passed through Lydford, which was impossible to avoid, but the cottages were as dark and silent as the fields and hedges. Beyond, a broader lane took them to the main road between Okehampton and Tavistock, but that too was deserted, and at last the dray came to a halt beside the woods of Stukely Hall. Only then did Stephanie discover that her bottom was stuck to the seat, but the river was nearby, providing her at last with an opportunity to wash.

She left Lias and Hermione to deal with the pig and scrambled over the wall, her shorts in one hand as she felt her way in among the trees to the same shelf of rock where she and her sister had performed for the drayman. The water of the Lyd was bitterly cold but felt good on her hot, dirty bottom, so much so that she closed her eyes with a long sigh as she began to clean her cheeks. It was done, phase one of the operation complete, with the pig safely in the wood and the Okehampton show just two days away.

As she began to scrub at the seat of her shorts she was smiling, only to bite her lips as she remembered that the night's work was far from complete. A powerful shiver ran through her at the thought of what she was expected to do, but the events of the night had reduced her willpower to resist, and she knew that if he insisted on the full terms of his bargain she would find an excuse to give in. Even now he was coming through the trees, the lantern in his hand to show the way, with Hermione following. Beyond them, she could hear the pig eating apples.

'Shouldn't we move the dray?' she suggested in a weak attempt to postpone her fate.

'Don't you start with your excuses again, Miss

Stephanie,' Lias said, sitting down on the rock he'd chosen before. 'Nude, I want you, both of you.'

'We'd better,' Hermione said.

'You see to him then,' Stephanie responded as she climbed from the water. 'It's jolly well your turn, and besides, I'm all wet.'

'Cold too, I'd imagine,' Lias observed. 'Nothing like a bit of horseplay to warm you up, is there? So just you get on with it.'

Hermione had already peeled her shirt off and stood with her puppyfat breasts naked in the yellow lamplight. Lias had freed his cock and was tugging at it as his eyes flicked between the two girls, as if he was unable to choose between the joys of one sister's bottom and the other's breasts. Hermione glanced at the big wrinkly penis and made a face, expressing disgust and sympathy with Stephanie, but her behaviour told rather a different story as she cupped her breasts in her hands and ran her fingers over the big pink nipples. Her teats were already stiff in the cool March air.

'Nude, I think I said,' Lias demanded, 'and how about a little of that arty business you showed me before?'

After only an instant of hesitation Hermione turned her back to him, still holding her breasts as she made a swan's neck of her back, sticking her bottom out in an enticing globe. She began to wiggle, a slow, sensuous motion, but just enough to make her shorts slide down her hips, showing first the swell of her bottom, then the crease between her cheeks, before they fell down. Now bare except for her knee-length khaki socks and the sensible black shoes she'd chosen for the expedition, she gave a final wiggle of her bottom and turned to her sister.

'Come on, Stiffy,' she urged. 'It will be all right.'

Stephanie wasn't at all sure if it would, but she found herself unable to resist. She peeled her shirt up and, with her tummy fluttering and her throat so full she could barely breathe, stepped forward into the puddle of brightness cast by the lantern beam. Trembling, she took her sister in her arms, horribly ashamed, but unable to deny the little pulses of pleasure running through her body.

'I suppose we must,' she said, and kissed Hermione's cheek.

Hermione returned a peck no less shy, and another, a little closer to Stephanie's mouth. Their arms were around each other, tight, and Stephanie gingerly began to stroke her sister's back and neck. She could feel her resistance melting and the need to touch growing stronger. The heavy slapping of Lias masturbating had faded to a background noise. Her lips opened and they were kissing properly, their tongues entwined, their mouths joined, first gently, then with greater pressure as both surrendered to their feelings.

Stephanie's hands moved lower, to cup the heavy, smooth cheeks of her sister's bottom, no longer pretending but lost to very real passion. Hermione responded in kind, sliding her hands down Stephanie's back and on to her cheeks to stroke the soft flesh. Their breasts pressed together, hard nipples against each other's flesh, their embrace now as urgent as their kiss.

Lias had become a mere distraction as they sank together on to the smooth rock, immediately lying head to toe which they had long ago discovered was the best way to bring each other off. Hermione got straight down to business, opening Stephanie's thighs over her face and applying her mouth between them as she pulled her own legs up and open to offer her sex. Stephanie gave a quick glance to where Lias was now pulling furiously on a full-fledged erection, then poked out her tongue and touched flesh. She was doing it, licking her own sister's quim in full view of a man as he masturbated over her. Nor could she pretend they were doing it only for him. Hermione's tongue was busy among the folds of Stephanie's sex, too eager for it to be pretence, and it felt far too good to resist. Abandoning herself to pleasure, Stephanie began to lick properly, her face buried deep between Hermione's plump, smooth thighs, her mouth full of ripe, girlish cunt, her tongue busy in the virgin hole and between the sleek lips.

She slipped her hands under Hermione's bottom, holding the plump cheeks and spreading them to show off the tight little star between, knowing that her sister liked it tickled while she was brought off. Lias could see and gave an urgent grunt, making Stephanie think he had come, until he spoke, his voice hoarse with lust.

'Lick her arse,' he demanded, 'lick it clean, you dirty little angel.'

Stephanie felt a touch of annoyance at the interruption and slowed down, hoping he would come and leave her to enjoy Hermione properly, but then her eyes opened wide in astonishment. Her sister had obeyed the filthy demand, lifting her head and poking her tongue between Stephanie's cheeks. She gasped as Hermione's tongue found her anus, a noise that turned into a helpless sigh of pleasure as her sister began to lick and probe at the little hole.

'That's my girl,' Lias grunted, 'my dirty, dirty little girl, licking your sister's arsehole clean while I pull the pudding.'

He gave another grunt, and again Stephanie thought he was going to come, but a glance showed that he was still wanking. It was more restraint than she herself was capable of showing. Hermione's tongue was well in, and she'd put a knuckle to Stephanie's cunt, rubbing the tiny bump from side to side. Stephanie sat up a little, her mouth falling open with a weak sob as the muscles of her thighs and bottom began to go into contraction, her quim too, while her bottom hole was pulsing on her sister's tongue. The orgasm hit her and she was screaming out her ecstasy and wriggling her bottom in Hermione's face, lost to everything but the exquisite sensation of having her anus licked as she was masturbated.

Wave after wave of sensation flooded through her, until she thought she would faint, but she had barely finished before she was being rolled on to her back and her own face was sat on. Eager to return the favour, she took a single gulp of air and began to lick in her sister's slit, enjoying the musky feminine taste and the feel of the plump young bottom cheeks spread in her face. Hermione gave an encouraging wiggle and Stephanie transferred her attention to her sister's anus, probing at the tiny, puckered hole with the tip of her tongue.

'That's right,' Lias grunted, 'clean her up ... taste what she does in the dunny, you dirty strumpet you ...'

Stephanie barely heard, much too busy with her sister's bottom. Hermione had sat up, queened full on Stephanie's face, her cheeks spread to give her sister full access to her bottom hole and to show Lias what was happening, her own fingers busy in her cunt slit. He came close, and Stephanie caught the smell of his cock as he thrust it at them. Hermione grabbed it, tugging hard at the shaft even as she rubbed herself, while Stephanie cocked her thighs open and stuck her hands between, masturbating shamelessly as she licked her sister's bottom. She knew Lias could see her cunt, open and wet. Surely her virgin hole would be too much of a temptation for his raging erection? He'd fuck her, he had to, and with her sister's weight on her face she'd have no chance to resist, the perfect excuse to surrender.

She was about to beg for it, all common sense and decency lost in her need for an engorged penis up her cunt hole, but suddenly it was too late, as a jet of spunk erupted over her belly and breasts. Hermione had started to come at the same moment, and sat down firmly in Stephanie's face, smothering her. Still Stephanie struggled to lick, pushing her tongue in up her sister's bottom as far as it would go and holding it

112

deep until at last Hermione dismounted to collapse exhausted on the rock.

Lias had moved away too, but Stephanie wasn't finished, her thighs still cocked wide as she masturbated, while with her free hand she rubbed his spunk on to her straining nipples and smeared it over her breasts and belly. Moments later she came, her second orgasm nearly as strong as the first, leaving her too weak to do anything but lie panting on the rock, her limbs spread and her lips parted, with the taste of her sister's cunt and bottom hole still thick in her mouth.

When she managed to pull herself up on to one elbow she realised that Lias had not been the only one to watch her perform with her sister. Singularis Porcus stood peering out from among the trees, his immense, heavily creased face set in what looked uncomfortably like lecherous amusement. She put one hand over her breasts and the other over her quim, then immediately felt silly, telling herself that it was ridiculous to be shy about a pig seeing her in the nude, especially after what she'd just done. Yet, despite the sure knowledge that she had disgraced herself beyond all hope of redemption, even if she were to be caned, naked and in front of an audience, every day for the rest of her life, she found herself unable to work up a decent sense of embarrassment.

Five

The embarrassment came the following morning as she lay in bed, slowly allowing herself to believe that the events of the night before had been real and not some appalling dream. She could remember every moment, from standing by the window as she plucked up the courage to go through with it, to slipping back between the welcome sheets as the first hint of dawn illuminated the ridge of Dartmoor beyond that same window.

The operation had been a success, of that there was no doubt, and yet she was left wondering at her own behaviour, and attempting to put the most embarrassing moments of her life into their new order. Being spanked in front of Lias Snell by Hermione definitely deserved a place in the top ten, perhaps fifth or sixth, closely followed by having to ride at least two miles on a dray with her bare bottom in cold pig dung; but being made to lick her own sister's bottom hole for a man to masturbate over put both to shame. Possibly, she considered, it was even a contender for fourth place, ahead of being caught by her great-aunt inserting the handle of a hairbrush up Hermione's bottom; or even third, because although what she thought of as the black bottom incident had been hideously public, it had been nothing like as intimate.

A glance at the clock showed that it was past ten, and she forced herself to sit up, well aware that laziness might be considered sufficient excuse to warm her bottom, especially by her great-aunt. At that moment the door opened and her stomach gave a lurch, but it was only Vera, holding a tray.

'Good morning, Miss Stephanie,' the maid said brightly. 'I've brought you your breakfast, a bowl of American cereal, some bacon and eggs, toast and a nice glass of milk.'

'Thank you,' Stephanie answered, although there was something about the maid's tone of voice she didn't altogether like.

'I thought you'd be hungry,' Vera continued as she placed the tray on the bedside table, 'after a busy night.'

Stephanie froze.

'Busy night?'

'A very busy night, I should imagine,' Vera said, smiling. 'Out with Mr Drake, I imagine?'

Stephanie relaxed a trifle and pretended to be busy fluffing up her pillows against the headboard. She was hoping that Vera was just guessing.

'And how did those peculiar shorts you were wearing get all wet?' the maid went on. 'Fell in the river, did you? Because I can't imagine you'd want to keep them on if you went for a midnight bathe, not with Mr Drake?'

'I . . . I got them dirty,' Stephanie admitted. 'I had to wash them.'

Vera gave her a knowing look.

'So you were out with Mr Drake? Be careful what you say, Miss Stephanie.'

'No . . . yes, yes I was,' Stephanie said.

'And him engaged to Miss Finch-Farmiloe,' Vera said with a shake of her head. 'Well, I never. You know I shall have to spank you, of course?'

'I suppose so,' Stephanie answered sulkily.

'Kneel up on the bed then,' the maid instructed.

Stephanie obeyed, grimacing furiously as she adopted the rude, humiliating position, on all fours with her face pressed down on the bed and her bottom lifted. She was in a proper nightie, but it was quickly lifted, exposing her bare bottom. Vera took a moment to stroke Stephanie's cheeks, slipped a finger between to tickle, then began to spank. It was harder than usual, and Stephanie bit her lip in an effort not to cry out. She closed her eyes too, wondering if the maid was going to take advantage of her once the spanking was done. It had to come soon, she was sure, and chagrin mixed with desire at the thought of being made to lick the maid's quim.

'You've been a very bad girl,' Vera said suddenly, 'but at least you're sensible.'

The spanking had stopped as she spoke, and Stephanie gasped as the maid's fingers found her sex lips, opening them to inspect the virgin hole between.

'Intact, yes,' Vera stated. 'Does he make you take him in your hand, or do you suck him?'

'I ... I suck him,' Stephanie admitted, blushing scarlet.

'Well, at least that's better than being made to take it up your bottom,' the maid went on. 'Men are such beasts, aren't they?'

'Yes, sometimes,' Stephanie agreed.

She wanted to add that women could be just as bad, but it didn't seem advisable in her current position. Vera had begun to spank her again, but with the other hand, while the first was still between Stephanie's thighs, stroking her quim.

'I never have anything to do with them, myself,' Vera went on. 'Girls are ever so much nicer, don't you agree?'

Stephanie made a face, not wanting to admit the pleasure she was getting from having her sex manipulated, and determined that, if she was going to lick her maid's quim, she would be made to do it and not surrender voluntarily. She got a series of hard slaps for her impudence, but her bottom was beginning to warm up and Vera's fingers were now rubbing in just the right place. A sigh escaped her lips as both rubbing and

116

spanking grew firmer still, and a moment later she'd begun to come. Vera gave a soft, knowing chuckle as she brought Stephanie off, but said nothing until the last ecstatic shivers had died away.

'There, that was nice, wasn't it?' she said. 'Not much of a punishment, perhaps, which you really do deserve, but nice. Now, why don't you return the favour?'

'How do you mean?' Stephanie asked, although she was sure she knew.

'Don't you think I've been naughty too?' Vera responded. 'I think I have, and I think I deserve a good spanking.'

It was not at all what Stephanie had been expecting, and she could only gape in astonishment. The maid had sat down on the bed, and there was none of the usual formality in her voice.

'Don't you think so?' Vera asked, almost pleading. 'After all, what do you think your Mama would do if she knew I fiddle with your cunt? I'd get spanked then, maybe given the cane, so why don't you do it? I'm sure you'd like your revenge too, wouldn't you? Come on, Miss Stephanie, put me across your knee and spank my naughty bottom, please?'

'Um . . .' Stephanie began, still struggling with her emotions, but the desire for revenge came out on top. 'Right, I will.'

She twisted around, throwing her legs over the side of the bed to make a lap. Vera came across not just willingly but enthusiastically, scrambling into position and sticking up her bottom to make a round ball beneath her black maid's uniform. Stephanie applied a gentle slap to the taut black bombazine.

'Bare, please, Miss Stephanie,' Vera sighed. 'I'm sure I deserve to be made bare, and spanked hard –'

'I know how to give a spanking, Vera,' Stephanie interrupted. 'Now be quiet.'

'Yes, Miss Stephanie,' Vera answered, her voice a whisper.

Not wanting to hurry the operation, Stephanie took her time in lifting the maid's dress, exposing first a cotton petticoat and then a pair of old-fashioned split-seam drawers of a sort she herself hadn't worn since the end of the war. There were no buttons, so she simply dug her thumbs in at either side and hauled them wide, exposing Vera's trim but distinctly womanly bottom to the air.

After a moment spent admiring the view, she began to spank, and with every slap of her hand on the soft, resilient meat of her maid's bottom her sense of satisfaction grew. It was wonderful to have somebody to punish instead of always getting it herself, and as Vera's bottom became slowly rosy, Stephanie promised herself that spanking was going to become a regular occurrence for the maid.

Vera's full, cheeky peach was a rich pink all over before Stephanie remembered that she had been asked to return the favour, which presumably meant masturbating her now sobbing maid as well as spanking her. It had to be done, both for revenge and to play fair. From the drawer of her bedside table she extracted the Sootho, and grinned as she placed a large blob on each hot bottom cheek. Vera let out a soft whimper when she realised what was to be done to her, but stuck her bottom up to offer her quim. Stephanie laid a firm slap across the reddened cheeks.

'You are a . . . a bad girl, Vera,' she said.

'A slut, Miss Stephanie,' Vera answered. 'I'm a slut . . . a strumpet.'

'Strumpet, that's a good word,' Stephanie agreed, remembering that it was what Lias had called her. She began to rub the nappy cream into Vera's bottom. 'Yes, you're a strumpet, and I think I shall spank you while I make you come.'

'Yes, please,' Vera sighed, and gasped as Stephanie began.

The maid's quim was moist even before Stephanie slapped on the cream. Nor was she a virgin, whatever she had said about not letting men near her, unless something other than a cock had been inserted in a hole that took two of Stephanie's fingers easily. She was also very rude about it all, moaning and wriggling her bottom as she was simultaneously spanked and masturbated, lacking even the decency to pretend she didn't like what was being done to her.

'You really are a strumpet, aren't you?' Stephanie said with a laugh, spanking harder still. 'A dirty little strumpet. I shall spank you often, Vera, and when I have spanked you I shall make you stand in the corner with your red bottom showing to the room. How would you feel about that? You liked it when I was made to, didn't you? But how would it feel for you, perhaps with my little sister watching? Yes, that is what I shall do. I shall spank you in front of my little sister, bare bottom, just as you are now. Maybe I'll even let her spank you too . . .'

Stephanie broke off. Vera was coming, writhing against Stephanie's hand and gasping out her passion, shiver after shiver running through her flesh, while her bottom bounced and quivered to the furious slaps. Cruel delight filled Stephanie as she brought Vera off, and she was still grinning when the maid slumped panting on to the floor.

The smile remained on Stephanie's face as she washed, threw on a light dress without bothering about underwear, slapped her school boater on her head and made her way downstairs. Spanking Vera had been immensely satisfying and had even helped to remove the shame of her behaviour the night before, leaving only the nervous thrill of knowing that the giant pig was now safely ensconced in the woods – a feeling magnified a dozen times when she caught the sound of voices from the breakfast room, her grandfather's and that of Sir Murgatroyd Drake.

'Good morning, Grandpapa,' she said as she entered. 'Good morning, Sir Murgatroyd.'

Her grandfather made a polite response. Sir Murgatroyd Drake ignored her, his face much the same colour as Stephanie and Vera's bottoms had been a half-hour before, his moustache quivering with rage as he addressed Sir Richard, who had been reading the morning paper and had lowered it only slightly to address his visitor.

'You, sir, are despicable, a disgrace to the county and to the Empire!' Sir Murgatroyd stormed, thrusting out an accusing finger.

'Whatever is the matter?' Sir Richard responded calmly. 'Sit down. Help yourself to a fried egg. Or perhaps some kedgeree?'

'I do not want a fried egg,' Sir Murgatroyd snapped, 'nor any kedgeree, and you know perfectly well what is the matter, you pig thief . . . you swine rustler, you . . .'

'You don't mean to say somebody has pinched your pig?' Sir Richard broke in, his puzzled tone giving way to open amusement, which caused Sir Murgatroyd's face to darken from smacked-bottom red to the shade of old burgundy.

'As you know perfectly well!' he roared. 'I . . . I shall have you expelled from your clubs!'

'I don't have any,' Sir Richard pointed out.

'Thrown off the hunt committee!' Sir Murgatroyd thundered.

'I own the kennels, and most of the horses.'

'Disbarred from the Tamar Valley and West Devon Association of Pig Breeders!'

'I doubt it, not if it means the Porker's out of the running for the show, and besides, I'm not sure why you should assume I stole your rotten pig. You'll probably find it was the work of some public-spirited group dedicated to good causes. You know, like the chaps who provide soup to the poor of Exeter and Plymouth.'

'What would they want with my pig?' Sir Murgatroyd demanded.

'Bacon? Ham? Chops? Trotters in vinegar even,' Sir Richard suggested as the colour of Sir Murgatroyd's face continued to darken, from a somewhat younger burgundy through ripe fig to a rich mulberry purple. 'There would be enough to feed a whole platoon of paupers, I should think. Are you sure you won't have some breakfast? We have devilled ham, and some excellent kidneys.'

'I do not wish breakfast!' Sir Murgatroyd answered. 'I came here to demand the return of my prize pig, and if he is not forthcoming, to call you out!'

'I do not have your pig, and therefore I am not in a position to return it,' Sir Richard responded. 'As to calling me out, aren't you a little behind the times? Nobody's fought a duel in these parts for years, and besides, as a magistrate, shouldn't you be setting a good example?'

'There are times when a gentleman has no choice,' Sir Murgatroyd replied, his voice now cold and his face once more of a smacked-bottom hue.

'Perhaps true,' Sir Richard admitted, 'but this is not, I feel, such an occasion. Nevertheless, if you insist, I can hardly refuse, so if you still feel the same way when you've calmed down a little, send your second round and he can arrange matters with, let me see ... Stiffy, do you fancy being my second in a duel? It might be rather fun.'

'Me?' Stephanie queried.

'Your granddaughter!?' Sir Murgatroyd demanded. 'Are you trying to make a mockery of me?'

'Not at all,' Sir Richard replied. 'If she is to have the vote, she can stand as second in a duel. We will expect your challenge.'

'You shall have it!' Sir Murgatroyd promised. He turned on his heel and left.

'What a frightful temper,' Sir Richard remarked, putting down his paper. 'Are you about to have breakfast, or would you care to stroll down for a look at the Emperor? If that buffoon's animal really has been stolen, then I fancy we're in the running for a gold medal.'

'I'll come with you,' Stephanie offered, realising that there would be no better time to extract a loan from him, 'but you're not really going to fight Sir Murgatroyd, are you?'

'I very much doubt it,' he said as they stepped out on to the terrace, 'but yes, if I have to.'

'He's very much younger than you,' Stephanie pointed out in genuine concern.

'Fifteen years, I believe,' he answered with some asperity, 'and while I'm not in the habit of smacking your bottom, young Stiffy, any more impudence and I might change my mind.'

'Sorry,' Stephanie said quickly, 'but still, a duel . . .'

'I could hardly refuse,' he said. 'The ancestors would be spinning in their graves. But you are forgetting that as the challenged party I will have choice of weapons.'

He gave a wry chuckle and they walked on in silence for a space, down the long slope of the lawn. When they reached the lake she decided to act.

'Grandpapa,' she said, 'do you remember that I asked if you could advance me twenty pounds until my allowance came through?'

'Ten, I believe you asked for,' he said with a chuckle.

'Ten then,' she said, 'if you'd like to reconsider, that is, although twenty would be nice.'

'I believe my sister is watching from the house,' he replied, 'so if you don't want that little bottom of yours reddened up after all, I suggest we wait until we're safely in the Emperor's sty.'

'Does that mean I click?' she asked. 'Even though I'm in disgrace?'

'Why not?' he responded. 'Damn it, I'm the head of the family. Why should I worry about what Vicky thinks, let alone my daughter-in-law? But you be careful, young lady.'

'I will,' Stephanie promised earnestly. 'Thank you, Grandpapa.'

They had reached the sty, and the money changed hands under the incurious eyes of Cyril Wonnacott, who was mixing the Emperor's morning feed. Wary of her great-aunt, Stephanie waited until what she considered a decent interval had elapsed before leaving the sty and walking nonchalantly back to the house. An idea had occurred to her, and she went straight to Hermione's room.

'Got it!' she announced, waving the four large, white five-pound notes she had received. 'Do you suppose if we ran over to Bridestowe we could get it on the Emperor before Porker hears the news?'

'Probably,' Hermione admitted, 'but he's bound to be suspicious.'

'No,' Stephanie explained. 'He'll just think we heard first. There's no reason to suspect we pinched the pig.'

'He'd be jolly cross,' Hermione said, with a smile that immediately gave way to a grimace.

'Never mind that,' Stephanie said. 'Would he pay up, that's the thing?'

'He'd have to,' Hermione answered.

'Four hundred pounds?'

'It would clean him out, just about,' Hermione said with considerable satisfaction, 'but he'd have to pay, or everyone would start demanding their money back and he'd be in real trouble. Besides, we could threaten to tell old Tredegar.'

'That's true,' Stephanie agreed, 'and speaking of telling old Tredegar . . . no, never mind.'

'What?' Hermione demanded.

'Nothing, nothing,' Stephanie said hastily, having remembered that revealing that she knew what Porker Porthwell had made Hermione do would mean admitting to peeping. 'Shall I go then?'

'If you like,' Hermione answered, and there was no mistaking the gratitude in her voice.

* * *

Stephanie set off, using the stable entrance to avoid any stalking aunts and hurrying for Bridestowe. As she went she tried to decide whether she should accost the curate with what she knew and demand that he stop it, or whether Hermione deserved it for her refusal to accept a sisterly spanking. There was really no choice. Hermione was family and Porker Porthwell was not. By the time she reached the rectory Stephanie had steeled herself for a disagreeable interview.

As before, the door was opened by the Reverend Wallace Tredegar, and it took a while before Stephanie could speak to the curate alone. However, no mention was made of the stolen pig, which would shortly be the gossip of the entire district, and she was confident of broaching the topic of adding to her bet.

'How are the odds on the Emperor?' she asked as they walked out on to the lawn from which she had watched her sister masturbate him.

'I can get you in at twelve to one,' he replied, abandoning his pious curate's voice for the oily tones of a turf accountant.

'Here's twenty pounds,' Stephanie said, slipping the note between his chubby fingers, 'to take the gold medal.'

He took the money without hesitation and ducked behind a yew hedge to write out her receipt. For a moment she worried that he was just a little too confident, but pushed the concern aside. Gathering her courage, she looked up at his imposing bulk and addressed him in her sternest tone.

'There's another thing I wish to talk about. You will stop bothering my sister, or I shall know what to do about it.'

For an instant he looked surprised, then answered her.

'Your sister is a dirty trollop, and she enjoys every minute of what we do together.'

'How dare you!' she gasped. 'How dare you call her a . . . a . . .'

'A dirty trollop,' he filled in as words failed her, 'which is what she is, whatever she may have told you.'

'She didn't tell me anything,' Stephanie retorted. 'I saw, the last time she came for a piano lesson.'

'Then you'll have seen how she deliberately tossed me into her mouth, and all over those fat little bouncers of hers,' he said, 'and you, Stiffy Truscott, shouldn't be peering in at people's windows.'

'Miss Truscott to you,' she snapped back, 'and you made her do that, you filthy beast!'

'I think not,' he answered. 'Last time, she let me do it over her bottom, after I'd spanked her. She even ate some off her finger, just to show off for me.'

'I don't believe you! She hates you!'

He shrugged, then answered in a thoughtful, almost philosophical tone.

'It is a curious thing, human desire. Perhaps she does hate me, in her own little way, but she loves being my trollop. Did you watch her rub her cunt after she'd finished with me?'

'No,' Stephanie replied, 'and I don't believe it either.'

'Oh, she did,' he assured her. 'She sat on the stool with her legs wide open, showing me everything and rubbing my spunk into her bouncers while she diddled herself, and when she came . . . ouch!'

His description of Hermione's behaviour ended abruptly as Stephanie's shoe made contact with his shin. But as she fled from the rectory garden she was far from sure that he'd been lying.

Rather than return to the house, Stephanie walked up towards the main road with the intention of catching a train for Postbridge. The two-seater would be ready, and she was itching to get back behind the wheel, although rather less keen on the prospect of teaching Hermione to drive. Then she heard her name called. Recognising the voice of Claude Attwater, she said a rude word under her breath before turning around and forcing a smile.

125

'Hello, Claude. I was just on my way to the station.'

'I'll walk with you then,' he offered, extending his arm. 'You will of course be at the rally at the Okehampton Show?'

'Um . . . yes,' she agreed.

'Excellent. I am expecting a good audience, and intend to speak on social decay and the dangers inherent in Bolshevism.'

He paused, then spoke again.

'A beautiful day, isn't it?'

'Rather dull, I thought,' Stephanie replied, glancing up at a sky the colour of lead.

'So it is,' he agreed. 'I hadn't noticed, and the reason I hadn't noticed, Miss Truscott . . . Stephanie . . . I may call you Stephanie, I trust?'

'If you like,' she answered cautiously, somewhat alarmed by his tone of voice.

'Stephanie,' he went on, 'every day is beautiful to me and always will be, so long as you, my darling, are upon this earth. Your face lights up the dullest day, the blackest night, the darkest coal bunker. I worship the ground you tread on, Stephanie, and so it is with both ardour and pride that I ask you to accept the honour of becoming my wife, and thus honour me in turn.'

He had got down on one knee in the middle of the road, causing considerable inconvenience to an oncoming bicycle.

'Um . . . er . . .' Stephanie faltered, too flustered to make a coherent response to the proposal. 'Mr Attwater, please . . .'

'I love you, Stephanie,' he repeated, taking her hand and beginning to kiss it as a metallic clatter signalled the failure of the bicyclist to remain on his machine.

'No, you don't.'

'I do,' he insisted. 'I adore you, Stephanie, as no man has ever adored a woman before.'

'No, you don't. You're only saying that because you saw my Aunt Lettice spank me, aren't you?' she answered, and immediately regretted it, blushing crimson at her own words.

'No, no,' he assured her, rather too hastily, she thought, 'that is not the case at all. I will grant that I am not immune to your physical charms, only a statue would not be, and that I am pleased to discover that you take a correct attitude to domestic discipline, but my love for you is pure and true, unsullied by base carnality . . . well, not as such, anyway. And think, Stephanie, I am destined to be a man of importance, and you will be my helpmate, and one day a great lady.'

'Look, Mr Attwater, I –'

'What can the matter be? We are in agreement on political matters. We share the same religion. My family is above reproach, while I have seven thousand a year.'

'Please, at least let me think about it,' she said desperately.

'Why, of course, of course,' he replied. 'How foolish of me to expect a delicate creature such as yourself to provide an immediate response, and yet –'

'That's my train,' she said, cutting him off as to her immense relief she saw a plume of greyish steam rising above the trees. 'I really must hurry.'

'You take my heart with you,' he answered.

'I do beg your pardon,' Stephanie remarked to the large pair of boots that were all that remained visible of the unfortunate cyclist, who had ended up in a ditch. Then she made a dash for the station.

As she threw herself into a seat on the train she caught her breath and began to see the amusing side of his proposal, but at the same time she felt immensely embarrassed. Whatever he said, his sudden love for her was clearly the result of having seen her upended and bare behind, and yet she had found his manner too comic to be taken seriously. Nevertheless, good manners demanded that she make a polite refusal, and as the train headed south she began to compose a suitable response in her mind.

By the time she reached Postbridge she had decided exactly what she would say and was rather pleased with her effort, which would be demure, as kind as was possible in the circumstances, but absolutely final. She even rehearsed a few of the lines out loud, stopping only when a passing yokel threw her a curious look, by which time she had reached the garage.

'Afternoon, Miss Truscott,' the mechanic greeted her, touching an oily hand to an equally oily cap. 'Here she is, good as new.'

As he spoke he pulled open one side of the wide doors that closed off the repair shop. Within was her car, easily identifiable by the STF 1 registration plate, a choice that had earned her a spanking of record-breaking duration from her great-aunt. Every dent had been removed, the chrome glinted in the sunlight, the paintwork shone, but there was one major failing.

'It's yellow,' she said.

'Buttercup,' he corrected her. 'Very popular colour, buttercup.'

'But it's supposed to be red,' Stephanie pointed out.

'Couldn't get red, Miss,' he answered, and sucked a little air in between his teeth, 'not without ordering specially from Bristol, and that would have meant waiting another week, and you did say you wanted it urgent.'

Stephanie gave a vague nod, barely aware of his words as she tried to work out how she could explain away a bright yellow car when she was supposed to have a red one. Not that owning a yellow car was a spankable offence in itself, but her explanation would definitely have to avoid all mention of dents and scratches.

'I suppose I'd better take it,' she sighed.

'Very popular colour, buttercup,' he repeated.

'So is red,' she answered, 'especially with my aunts.'

He accepted the comment at face value and she paid the bill and set off. For all her concerns, it still felt wonderful to be behind the wheel again, with the wind in her face, as she put her foot to the floor on the gentle rise west of Postbridge. She was careful to slow for the Hairy Hands bridge but opened up beyond, thrilling to the speed and freedom she had adored since her grandfather had first taught her to drive. For the full length of the moor road nothing else mattered, but as she crossed the flank of Black Down she found herself wondering if she should check on the pig.

She parked beside the gates of Stukely Hall and walked back down the road and in at the gate to the wood. There was no immediate sign of the Porker, although he had already reduced the interior of the makeshift sty to mud and his thick, musky scent hung heavy in the air. Outside, the wood was quiet, bathed in gold-green sunlight filtering down through the young leaves, while the first of the year's bluebells had begun to open. Tempted by the solitude and the sensation of being bare under her dress, she quickly peeled off and kicked her shoes away, to be naked but for her school boater. It felt deliciously naughty, and also free, the air cool on her skin, making her want to stretch and wriggle for sheer delight in her nakedness.

She began to walk up through the wood, wondering if it would be nice to play with herself, perhaps sitting on the ledge where she and Hermione had licked each other's quims and bottom holes, or simply spread naked among the bluebells with her fingers busy between her open thighs. More than once she had been made to go nude but for her boater by Myrtle, and she was just telling herself that she would come over something other than those memories when a loud grunt made her turn in alarm.

Singularis Porcus stood behind her, peering at her naked body from eyes sunk in the heavy folds of his porcine face. It was the first time she had seen him in full daylight; he looked even more impressive than he had in the dark, and rather more alarming. There was a definite glint in his eyes of something evil, an interest either lustful or gustatory, perhaps both. Not wishing to find out, she hurriedly pulled her dress back on, found her shoes and left.

Amazed at her boldness in stealing the monster, she walked back to her car. Above all things she wished to avoid Claude Attwater, who was quite likely to be lurking at Driscoll's, while there was also the problem of the car being buttercup yellow. For a long while she stood in the lane considering her options, but she had had no lunch and it was already late afternoon. Tea was beginning to call to her, and the previous day Mrs Catchpole had hinted that there might be a ginger cake, something Stephanie was particularly fond of. Finally she told herself that it would be easy enough to park the car out of sight and at least postpone explanations, while she could ask Hermione to chaperone her and thus avoid any further embarrassing protestations of love from Claude Attwater.

Ten minutes later she was approaching the gates of Driscoll's. She turned in, praying that no aunts were lurking along the drive. None were in evidence, and she drove on to the stables, where Gurney and Annaferd were rubbing down a trio of horses. That almost certainly meant that Great-aunt Victoria had been out riding, probably with Aunts Gertrude and Lettice, and that her brief pause in the roadway outside Stukely Hall had been just long enough to prevent a meeting. Luck seemed to be on her side. She parked the car in the long building that had been converted into garages, between the end of the wall and her grandfather's far larger vehicle. After washing her face at the pump and adjusting her hair, she went indoors. The family were about to sit down to tea, and to her vast relief Claude Attwater was not among the company. There was, however, a ginger cake, a large, moist-looking specimen decorated with pieces of candied peel. As she took her place she allowed herself to relax and begin the important estimation of how large a slice she could get away with without risking an accusation of greed.

'Manners, Stephanie,' Victoria Truscott stated. 'Bread and butter first.'

Stephanie had not realised that her appreciation of the ginger cake had been so obvious, and quickly turned her attention to the thin slices of bread and butter that family etiquette demanded be consumed first.

'Wherever have you been, dear?' her great-aunt continued.

'I went to Postbridge to collect my car,' Stephanie explained, sure that nobody would decide to go and inspect it with the prospect of tea in front of them.

Having selected two slices of bread and butter while Mrs Catchpole poured out tea, Stephanie ate in silence for a while. Hermione was already applying her fork to a large slice of ginger cake, and, when the time arrived to take her own, Stephanie was careful to ensure that it was of identical size. Great-aunt Victoria was talking to Aunt Lettice at the time, and other than a brief glance of disapproval from Aunt Gertrude there was no reaction. Now well pleased with herself, she gave the slice a liberal coating of butter and tucked in, at which point the doorbell rang. Catchpole appeared a moment later to announce the visitor.

'Mr Frederick Drake.'

'Hello, Freddie,' Hermione chirped up before Stephanie could decide on a more measured greeting, but when she turned in her chair she saw that he was far from his normal amiable self.

'I, ah . . . terribly sorry,' he stammered. 'I didn't realise you were in the middle of tea. Shall I wait?'

'No, no, sit down,' Sir Richard said affably. 'I expect you've come to arrange the duel?'

'Um . . . er . . . yes,' Freddie managed. 'I mean to say, father's in the most frightful temper about his pig, and he seems to have got it into his head that you stole it . . . silly idea, of course, but there it is. I understand that Stiffy . . . er, Stephanie is your second?'

'What is all this?' Victoria Truscott demanded.

'Didn't I mention it?' her brother answered her. 'Apparently some fellows have stolen Murgatroyd's pig, and he thinks I did it –'

'I know about the pig, Richard,' she cut him off, 'but a duel? And with Stephanie acting as your second?'

'She was convenient to hand,' Sir Richard explained. 'But a duel?'

'Why not? It will liven things up a little.'

'I forbid it, absolutely!'

'I'll do as I damn well please.'

'I expect you will, but you are to have no part in it, Stephanie. Is that clear?'

'Yes, Auntie,' Stephanie replied promptly.

'If you insist on such foolishness,' Victoria continued to her brother, 'Gurney must act as your second, although frankly I have never heard anything quite so preposterous in my entire life. Do sit down, Mr Drake. Will you have some tea?'

'Rather,' Freddie answered, seating himself. 'So er . . . you'd rather I spoke to your man Gurney?'

'I would rather the whole ridiculous idea was abandoned,' she told him. 'It will be the talk of the district.'

'The district could do with something to talk about, once the show is over,' Sir Richard responded, 'and surely you see that I can't refuse?'

'I see no such thing,' Victoria snapped back, 'and as for asking Stephanie to act as second, it's improper.'

'We're fighting a duel, not visiting a brothel,' Sir Richard countered.

'Richard!' his sister responded, but he merely shrugged.

An embarrassed silence descended on the table, finally broken by Freddie Drake.

'I just missed you on the way over, as it happens, Stiffy. You were turning in at the gate as I was coming up the lane. I do like your new car. Same model, but a spiffing colour.'

'Do you have a new car, Stephanie?' Sir Richard asked.

'Her father always did spoil her,' Aunt Lettice remarked.

Just as Freddie spoke Stephanie had inserted a large piece of ginger cake into her mouth, eager to buy precious seconds in which to decide on the safest answer. Unfortunately in her haste she had somewhat overestimated the capacity of her mouth, leaving her with bulging cheeks and able to breathe only through her nose.

'Really, Stephanie,' Aunt Gertrude commented. 'Your manners are dreadful.'

'She always was a little piggy-wig,' Mrs Catchpole remarked, ruffling Stephanie's hair.

Everybody was looking at her. She struggled to swallow at least part of her mouthful, made herself cough and projected a mixture of mucus and gingerbread crumbs on to her plate.

'Stephanie!' Great-aunt Victoria snapped.

She managed a muffled apology, still trying to decide if it was better to tell the truth and take her medicine, pretend the car was new and postpone the inevitable, or attempt to bluff it out. Taking the first choice would mean a spanking or the cane, very possibly in front of Freddie, which was unthinkable. The second choice would mean extra punishment for trying to evade her fate, but probably in private, which was better. The third was a gamble, and a chance too sweet to ignore.

'Excuse me,' she gasped as she swallowed the last of her ginger cake. 'I think a crumb went down the wrong way. I don't have a new car, Freddie, don't be silly.'

'Oh, you had her repainted, did you?' he responded. 'It's a jolly colour, all the rage too, bright yellow.'

'It's buttercup yellow,' Stephanie said, with sudden inspiration. 'Those silly men at the garage in Princetown thought I wanted it completely repainted, when I'd only run out of petrol.'

She finished with a light laugh, praying her story would be accepted.

'Completely repainted?' Aunt Gertrude demanded.

'Wasn't that frightfully expensive?' Aunt Lettice queried.

'I had just enough left from my allowance,' Stephanie said hastily.

'They made you pay?' said Great-aunt Victoria. 'That is outrageous! I shall drive up with you first thing tomorrow, and demand a full refund.'

'No, no, really,' Stephanie said quickly, 'it's quite all right. I rather like yellow . . .'

'That is quite beside the point,' her great-aunt snapped. 'It is plain that these people have sought to exploit your innocence and good nature by pretending to have misunderstood you. I, you may be assured, will not be so easily misled. It really is outrageous, the way tradesmen behave today . . .'

'It's the show tomorrow,' Sir Richard pointed out, interrupting what was threatening to become a lengthy speech.

'The day after, then,' Freddie put in ingratiatingly, 'and I'll jolly well come with you to lend a bit of support.'

Stephanie threw a panic-stricken glance to where the French windows stood open to the air and freedom, at least temporary freedom. The choice before her was now even worse: confessing the truth, or at least an approximation thereof, or an appalling scene at the garage. To choose the second was to court disaster, maybe a public spanking, delivered in the middle of the road in front of not only Freddie but the mechanics and, with her luck, a large crowd of interested onlookers, who always seemed to appear at such times. It had to be the first choice.

'Um . . . actually that won't be necessary,' she said weakly. 'I didn't want to tell you, because it was a bit expensive, but, you see, I rather fell in love with that yellow colour, so I ordered the repainting.'

Silence descended over the table as she finished. She

hung her head, studying the mess on her plate as she waited for her sentence. Aunt Lettice spoke first.

'How extravagant.'

'How very untruthful,' added Aunt Gertrude.

'Fetch me my cane, would you, Hermione dear?' Great-aunt Victoria asked.

'Oh, no, not the cane, please,' Stephanie babbled, half rising in panic and fear. 'I don't deserve the cane!'

'On the contrary,' her great-aunt informed her. 'You have lied repeatedly, and I strongly suspect that you are still lying. Well?'

'I'm not lying, not any more!' Stephanie blustered, only for her will to break at the realisation that her great-aunt might know something more. 'Oh, all right. I pranged the car. Some stupid man in a dray got in my way on the Cherrybrook bridge and I ended up in the drink. I had some scratches and a dented fender, a crack somewhere too. That's all, I promise.'

Stephanie slumped in her seat. Hermione threw her a pitying look as she left the room, but did as she was told, returning almost immediately with the long, whalebone cane that was reserved only for the most serious infractions.

'Do you admit you deserve the cane?' Great-aunt Victoria asked as she took hold of the wicked-looking implement.

'I suppose so,' Stephanie admitted sulkily, knowing full well that to remonstrate would only make it worse.

'I er ... I suppose I'd better make myself scarce?' Freddie suggested.

'Not at all, Mr Drake,' Victoria Truscott responded. 'I always feel that in matters of domestic discipline the object lesson is best delivered in front of an audience. Stephanie, go and stand by the clock. I shall give you six strokes.'

Stephanie stood up, trembling so violently that she had to clench her fists in a vain effort to hide her emotions from Freddie. He looked uncomfortable, but made no further move to leave nor to look away when she took her position as ordered, with her back to the tea table. Great-aunt Victoria took a sip of tea and a dainty forkful of ginger cake before herself rising and crossing the room to stand behind Stephanie.

'Raise your dress, Stephanie,' she ordered.

Stephanie had known from the start that there would be no possibility of being caned on the seat of her dress, but still she hesitated, the humiliation boiling in her head at the thought of revealing herself to Freddie for so ignominious a reason, and painfully aware that going bare under her dress was likely to make things worse for her. Yet it took only a faint cough from her great-aunt to make her hurriedly reach for the hem of her dress and lift it to the level of her waist to show off her bare bottom.

'No underwear, Stephanie?' her great-aunt demanded. 'Really, I despair of you ever growing up to be a lady. It is most indecent. Perhaps two extra strokes will help? Touch your toes.'

Stephanie had already begun to colour, and blushed darker still at the remark, but she was unable to find the courage to point out to her great-aunt that she would be more indecent still once she was touching her toes, since that would inevitably make her cheeks open and show off her quim. To make matters worse, she had nothing on her top either, so as she bent down she would have to be very careful to catch her dress between her tummy and her thighs, so that she would not add the exposure of her breasts to the display she was making of herself.

'Eight strokes,' Great-aunt Victoria confirmed.

Stephanie bent to touch her toes, her bare bottom on full show, painfully aware that her position exposed her anus, along with a rear view of her virgin quim. She could see Freddie, blushing with embarrassment and pretending not to watch, but clearly fascinated. Hermione had no such qualms, mouth and eyes both wide in spellbound horror, while both aunts showed a quiet satisfaction. Only her grandfather wasn't looking, apparently because he was more interested in a magazine article on the care of the pig.

'Four for lying,' Victoria Truscott declared, and brought the cane down across Stephanie's bottom.

The instant the long strip of whalebone landed, even her burning embarrassment was driven out of Stephanie's head, to be replaced by a searing pain and then a great wave of self-pity. She began to cry even as the cane was again lifted over her naked bottom cheeks, but her tears found no sympathy.

'There is no need to snivel, Stephanie,' her great-aunt told her. 'You brought this upon yourself, as well you know. One stroke.'

'Yes, Auntie,' Stephanie sobbed.

She bit her lip in an effort to hold her emotions in, but as the second stroke slashed down across her flesh she screamed out, unable to hold back, despite her desperate need not to be a baby about it in front of Freddie.

'Do try and take it like a lady, Stephanie,' Aunt Gertrude remarked casually.

'Two strokes,' Great-aunt Victoria said. 'I do apologise for her behaviour, Mr Drake. She has never had any real fortitude. Fingers to your toes, Stephanie.'

Stephanie obeyed but moved a little too much, so that her dress fell down round her head, revealing her upside-down breasts to the audience but mercifully covering her miserable, tear-stained face. She was now stark naked from her ankles to her neck, every private detail of her body on blatant exhibition, but nobody came to adjust her dress or even commented. A naked, beaten girl was commonplace in that household, and Freddie was much too well-mannered to intervene in a domestic punishment.

No longer able to see, Stephanie could only wait in an agony of anticipation for the third stroke, which seemed to be an inordinately long time coming. The faint sound of a teacup being returned to its saucer told her that her great-aunt had paused to take refreshment, but just seconds later the cane landed across her bottom with full force, taking her by surprise. She stumbled forward, a scream of pain bursting from her lips, lost her balance and went down on all fours, her bottom flaunted to the room in what was, if anything, an even ruder position than before.

'Do get up, Stephanie,' Victoria Truscott sighed. 'Must you always make such a drama of a simple punishment?'

'I'm sorry, Auntie,' Stephanie managed, scrambling hastily back into the correct position. 'I wasn't ready.'

'Well, are you ready now?'

'Yes, Auntie.'

'I'm very glad to hear it. Three strokes, and four.'

On the last word the cane bit into Stephanie's flesh, setting her dancing on her toes and babbling stupidly. Even when she managed to get her fingers to her toes again she was shaking uncontrollably, while the four welts on her bottom burned like fire. She could feel herself breaking down, and managed to hold her rude pose only by telling herself over and over that she was at the halfway mark.

'And two for extravagance,' Great-aunt Victoria said.

As the cane was laid gently across Stephanie's bottom cheeks something inside her snapped.

'But . . . but I wasn't extravagant!' she babbled. 'I had to get her repainted because I'd crashed! I had to! No more, please, Auntie, no more –'

Her words turned to a scream as the cane lashed down across her bottom, once more setting her jumping and wriggling, but clutching her bottom too, indifferent to the display she was making, her cheeks held as wide as they would go.

'You are making an exhibition of yourself, Stephanie,' Aunt Gertrude remarked.

'A most vulgar exhibition,' Aunt Lettice agreed.

'Five strokes,' Great-aunt Victoria stated. 'Take your hands away from your bottom, Stephanie.'

Tears running from her eyes and snot from her nose, Stephanie forced herself back into the correct position. With three strokes to go she was praying it would be done quickly, because she knew that if she was made to wait between each she would break completely. So, it seemed, did her great-aunt, who first laid the cane across the tuck of Stephanie's bottom cheeks, lower than before. Realising that she was to be caned across the line of her cunt, Stephanie's will snapped.

'No, please, not there!' she wailed, jumping up and once more grabbing her bottom. 'Please, Auntie, that's enough. I'm sorry . . . I'm really sorry! I've never tell a lie again, I promise, I promise!'

'Touch your toes, Stephanie,' Victoria commanded, only to be interrupted by a cough from Sir Richard.

'I think she's had enough, Vicky,' he remarked, lifting his eyes from the pig magazine.

'I awarded her eight strokes,' Victoria answered, 'and eight strokes it shall be.'

'Make the last three taps then,' he instructed. 'Unless you'd care for a dose across your own backside.'

Stephanie's dress had fallen back around her upper body, and she was able to see the speechless outrage on her great-aunt's face, but it was lost on Sir Richard, who was studying a picture of an impressively large saddle-back boar.

'I . . .' Victoria began, only to think better of whatever protest she had been about to make. 'Very well. Take your hands away, Stephanie, and stick out your bottom.'

Stephanie obeyed, still shaking badly as she made a target of herself, but when the cane came down it was a mere tap, not even hard enough to raise a line. Two more followed, a trifle harder, but easy to take.

'Eight strokes,' Victoria stated. 'You may go.'

Stephanie ran, tripped over her drawers and went down on her knees, her well-beaten bottom flaunted to the room one last time, before scrambling to her feet and fleeing. Her dress was still up, so she was effectively stark naked as she dashed up the stairs and into her room, where she threw herself on the bed and gave way to a full-blown tantrum.

Six

The day of the Okehampton show dawned with a cool breeze and a hint of rain in the air, but Stephanie had no interest in the weather, preferring to use her mirror to make a rueful inspection of the five neat red lines that decorated her bottom. It had been done well, she had to admit, the lines parallel and exactly straight, all five on the flesh of her buttocks, leaving her thighs and hips unmarked. Not that the expertise with which the punishment had been applied was much consolation, any more than the knowledge that her great-aunt had gained the expertise from years of practice upon her nieces' bottoms. The welts stung and would show for weeks, although she was hoping not to have anybody inspect her; and the embarrassment of having it done with Freddie watching exceeded even that of him rubbing his cock in her bottom slit. Moreover, as a final but strictly private humiliation, at some point in the dark, lonely hours of the night she had given in to the heat in her bottom and the sensation of lying face down with the covers off to spare her bruises and masturbated.

'Only five?' Vera's voice sounded from the door, and Stephanie spun around, dropping her nightie to cover her bottom. 'From the fuss you made I thought she'd given you two dozen at least. Even Mr Catchpole thought twelve, and he's known you –'

'It was in front of Freddie Drake,' Stephanie broke

in, 'and jolly hard, with a whalebone cane. I do wish you'd knock before you come in.'

'That's nothing I've not seen before,' Vera answered. 'I hope you put some Sootho on?'

'Plenty, thank you,' Stephanie answered, but chose not to admit exactly where she'd applied it.

'I'll rub in a little more later,' Vera offered, 'and perhaps we can give each other a little treat?'

She winked, and Stephanie found herself smiling in return despite herself. It had been the maid's evening off the night before, and as Stephanie had rubbed the Sootho into her bottom she'd been wishing Vera was there to kiss her better, the first time, and to do rather more the second.

'What will you be wearing for the show?' Vera asked. 'Your blue dress is the prettiest, and if you put your woollens on underneath you won't be cold at all.'

'She needs her Brown Shorts uniform,' Hermione said, entering as casually as had the maid. 'We've got to do the rally, Stiffy.'

'I don't see why . . .' Stephanie began, and went quiet, aware that they needed to keep up the pretence at least until the stolen pig was safely in London. 'Oh, very well.'

Hermione had the uniform, and threw it down on Stephanie's bed.

'Let's see your bottie, then,' she demanded.

Stephanie drew a sigh, but it seemed to be the time for her to have her bottom inspected, so she turned round once more and lifted her nightie to display the neat set of welts on her cheeks. Both her sister and Vera spent a moment contemplating Stephanie's cane marks, before Hermione gave her verdict.

'Ouch!'

'Ouch is about right,' Stephanie answered with feeling. 'Why didn't you come up and give me a cuddle?'

'They wouldn't let me. Great-aunt Victoria was furious because of Grandpapa making her let you off three strokes, and she said you had to stay on your own all evening to make up for it, and go without supper.'

'I noticed,' Stephanie answered. 'I'm starving.'

'See you downstairs then,' Hermione said, and turned to leave. Just then, Stephanie realised that the shorts on the bed were the large ones she had worn on the pig-stealing expedition.

'You've pinched my shorts again,' she said.

'I'm not wearing those,' Hermione answered. 'You sat in pig poo.'

'They've been cleaned, twice. Please, H., these ones are ridiculously large for me.'

'They're too large for me too, but these ones fit quite nicely, so at least one of us will be all right.'

'Yes, you! Give me my shorts back, Hermione!'

'No. Just use a safety pin or something.'

'Hermione!'

Her sister merely laughed and fled down the passage, leaving Stephanie with no option but to pull on the outsize shorts and wait while Vera put a stitch in each side to make sure they stayed up. By the time the maid was finished the shorts felt safe but she looked distinctly odd, as if she'd pinched her much larger brother's football outfit for a joke. It was no way to appear at the Okehampton Show, especially as Freddie, Myrtle and several other friends would be there, but when she reflected that Hermione would look equally ridiculous, she was able to leave the Blue Room with nothing worse than a feeling of resignation.

Breakfast the morning after a punishment was always an embarrassing affair, and more so than ever on this occasion, because even in her best silk drawers every movement reminded Stephanie of the five cane cuts across her bottom. The family were indifferent, not out of tact but because what had been done to her was entirely ordinary.

There were at least no further recriminations, and she helped herself to toast and marmalade, coffee, bacon, eggs and two types of sausage, until she felt pleasantly full. Most of the others had finished by then, leaving her and Hermione alone under the approving, matronly eye of Mrs Catchpole, who insisted that they each drink a large glass of milk before leaving the table. By the time they got out to the car Stephanie's tummy was bulging so badly that she was grateful for the shapeless khaki shirt and outsize shorts.

The rain had stopped and a breeze was beginning to break up the clouds rolling in over Cornwall, so that, as they drove, the lanes were sparkling wet from intermittent sunshine, with huge puddles that sent up impressive splashes as the wheels hit them. Just outside the town they reached the end of a long queue of drays and other vehicles. They abandoned the car by a gate, and again Stephanie was glad of her Brown Shorts uniform as they found their way to the field where the show was being held.

'Let's look at the pigs,' she suggested, 'I want to be sure we're on to a good thing.'

'Grandpapa's bound to be there,' Hermione agreed. 'With any luck he might give us some spending money.'

They began to walk down the field towards the stock pens, where horses, cattle, sheep and, most importantly, pigs were gathered in neatly fenced-off squares, each surrounded by a group of interested bystanders. Elsewhere on the field was a huge white marquee for refreshments, the last thing Stephanie currently wanted, a bandstand, assorted stalls, a large podium hung with bunting from which the speeches were to be made and the winners announced, and another, smaller podium from which flew a set of brown pennons and a larger flag with the emblem that Claude Attwater had chosen picked out in gold. Claude himself was visible, along with several other Brown Shorts, and signalled to the two girls, who pretended not to have noticed.

'He can't expect us to be there all day,' Stephanie said.

'I expect he wants us to hand out leaflets or something,' Hermione suggested. 'Look, there's Porker.'

Stephanie looked where her sister was pointing and saw a group of people, among whom the Reverend Benjamin Porthwell's large, round head protruded as if it were a balloon held by a small child in the throng. He appeared to be doing a brisk trade, but looked nervous, repeatedly glancing guiltily round the field.

'He's jolly scared old Tredegar'll find out what he's up to, isn't he?' Stephanie remarked. 'If he got caught, do you suppose he'd be defrocked?'

'Yuck,' Hermione laughed, 'what a horrible thought! There's Freddie too.'

Stephanie felt her heart skip, then sink. Freddie was indeed visible, walking towards them from the group gathered around the curate, and fixed to his arm in an unpleasantly possessive manner was Myrtle Finch-Farmiloe. Stephanie grimaced, then forced a smile, determined to hold her own. Freddie had seen her, and gave a cheerful wave. Myrtle made a remark to her companion; the words were inaudible but her subsequent laugh was enough to send the blood to Stephanie's cheeks. Two men were also approaching, Roly Bassinger and Eggy White, both London friends, increasing Stephanie's determination not to let Myrtle annoy her.

'Hello, Stiffy,' Freddie said as they drew close, his voice betraying just a trace of awkwardness.

'Whatever are you wearing?' Myrtle laughed. 'You look like a boy!'

'A very pretty boy,' Roland Bassinger put in.

'We're Brown Shorts,' Stephanie explained.

'You don't mean to say you've joined that ass Attwater?' Eggy White demanded. 'Oh, I say, Stiffy!'

'Only for the time being,' Stephanie hurried to explain.

'But you don't believe all that rot he talks, surely?' Eggy insisted.

'No, of course not,' she assured him.

'What?' Roly Bassinger queried. 'Do you mean you're trying to subvert them from within?'

'Something like that,' Stephanie admitted. 'I'll be able to explain in a week or two.'

'Ignore her,' Myrtle advised. 'She's just trying to be mysterious. Now tell me, Stiffy, I hear you're in disgrace, and that your mother had to spank you.'

Stephanie felt her face start to burn, unable to deny the accusation but equally unable to admit it was true. Hermione came to her defence.

'She was trying to get a policeman's helmet for the Gaspers election, and she'd have done it if Freddie hadn't been playing about.'

'I say, baby sis has found a voice!' Myrtle declared in mock astonishment. 'You were always such a mouse at Teigngrace, Hermione, but I suppose that's better than being a clown like your sister. I couldn't possibly tell you some of the things she used to do, boys, it would be quite indecent! Stiffy, that is. Little H. wouldn't say boo to a goose, and she used to blush ever so prettily at bathtime.'

'That's hardly surprising with you about ...' Stephanie retorted, only to trail off as she realised that any revelations would be far more embarrassing to her and to her sister than to Myrtle.

All three men were listening with polite interest, hoping for more, which Myrtle happily provided.

'Of course, Stiffy's still a complete clown. Do you remember that time she was dancing the black bottom at the Kit Kat Club, Roly? It was simply frightful. She had this awful dress on, like a cream puff, with great big bows down the back. Every time she came close to his table, Puffy Froplinson would tug a bow open, and she didn't even notice until her dress fell down! But the funniest thing, she didn't have a stitch on underneath. It was a scream!'

'That was not funny,' Stephanie said, doing her best to sound cold and haughty but only managing self-pity.

'Oh, it was,' Myrtle insisted, 'an absolute hoot. And why ever weren't you wearing any drawers, or those frightful American combinations your mother puts you in?'

'They spoil the line of my dress,' Stephanie managed. 'I prefer to look elegant.'

'You looked a prize chump,' Myrtle assured her. 'Imagine, starkers, in the middle of the Kit Kat, and then she tripped over her own feet. You've never seen such a disgraceful exhibition!'

'I tripped over my dress,' Stephanie struggled to explain, 'and it wasn't awful. It was from Paris, the very latest . . .'

'Paris is so prewar, don't you think?' Myrtle interrupted. 'But what was I saying? Oh, yes, you're in disgrace, aren't you, so can we assume you'll be standing down from the election?'

'Absolutely not,' Stephanie replied. 'I will be there on the night, and I fully expect to become the new secretary.'

'Take my advice and give it a miss,' Myrtle responded. 'You haven't a hope anyway, and you'll save yourself an awful lot of embarrassment and pain. Do you know what her ghastly aunts will do to her if she leaves Devon, boys? They'll whack her bare bottom with a cane, quite possibly in the drawing room, and they don't mind at all who sees. Perhaps we should get up a party to watch?'

She finished with a silvery laugh. Stephanie's face was burning, and her eyes had begun to fill with tears, but at least it was plain that Freddie hadn't told Myrtle about her caning on the previous afternoon, and despite his failure to support her she found herself feeling pathetically grateful.

'You're an absolute beast, Myrtle!' Hermione put in. 'How would you feel if Stephanie and I made jokes about you getting your discipline?'

'But I don't, do I?' Myrtle replied with a laugh. 'As Stiffy knows, I have never been spanked and I never will be. Even at Teigngrace I was exempt. It's only you peculiar country types who go in for that sort of thing nowadays, and it's dreadfully vulgar, of course, but also rather funny.'

'Maybe,' Hermione said, 'I should put you over my knee right now and teach you how it feels, because if anybody ever, ever needed a jolly good spanking, Myrtle, it's you!'

'How dare . . .' Myrtle began, but stopped, drawing closer to Freddie as Hermione took a step forward.

'Ladies, please,' Roland Bassinger said, although he was plainly having difficulty keeping the laughter out of his voice.

'Not here, girls,' Freddie agreed. 'I mean, damn it, we chaps really ought to be setting an example, don't you think?'

'Absolutely,' Myrtle agreed, 'but you'd hardly expect a Truscott to appreciate that. They're in trade, after all.'

'We are not!' Stephanie retorted.

'You own mines, don't you?' Myrtle answered.

'Grandpapa has sold his interests,' Stephanie responded, 'largely to your father, as it happens.'

'Oh,' Myrtle said, briefly discomfited, only to rally. 'Well, when you've lost all your money I dare say I'll have a place for a maid – not a lady's maid, of course, but in the scullery, or perhaps between stairs. Anyway, must rush, they're judging the pigs in a minute. Oh, and Hermione darling, there's a class for the best piglet this year. I'm sure if you run you could just make it, and who knows, you might take a prize!'

She finished with a peal of laughter, leaving Hermione as red-faced and angry as her sister. Freddie gave Stephanie an apologetic look but allowed himself to be led away, the other two men following and discussing the current odds. Stephanie and Hermione waited a moment, then came on behind.

'I should have done it,' Hermione said. 'I should have spanked the horrid beast.'

'She's jolly strong,' Stephanie said doubtfully, 'and I don't suppose the boys would let you, not in front of everybody. Anyway, the aunts are over there, and you'd only get in worse trouble yourself.'

'It would be well worth it,' Hermione answered. 'Anyway, with any luck her money isn't on the Emperor.'

'It's bound to be,' Stephanie countered, 'but not at the odds we got, so she'll be jolly green when she finds out how much we've won.'

'Four hundred and forty pounds,' Hermione breathed. 'Four hundred and eighty with our stake back.'

'I'll have to pay Freddie back his twenty, I suppose,' Stephanie said, 'but still.'

They had reached the pig pens, where the judges were already assessing the rival entrants in the top class. A complicated system of gates and fencing allowed each of the formidable beasts to be guided on to a weighing platform. It was hard to see anything with the press of people, especially as even some of the children were taller than she was, but by pushing between a pair of lanky farmhands Stephanie managed to get to the front just as a large white sow was led on to the scales.

'Mr Beston's Taworthy Sally,' the chief judge announced, and paused to allow the fluctuating needle to settle. 'Sixty-seven stone, eight pound.'

There was a little polite clapping, but all eyes were on the gate at which Cyril Wonnacott stood with a braided leather lead attached to the Emperor's snout ring. Stephanie allowed a smile to spread across her face. Farmer Beston's pig was an impressive beast, but next to the Emperor she looked positively underfed. He bulged in every direction, and as he was led on to the scales they gave a protesting creak and the needle shot upwards, above the hundred-stone mark, only to return and quiver a fraction below.

'Sir Richard Truscott's Emperor of Driscoll's,' the

chief judge stated with a satisfying hint of awe in his voice. 'Ninety-six stone, four pound.'

Stephanie gave a quiet sigh. It had all been worth it, since the Emperor's weight was still four stone or more short of his rival's. Across the pens, she could see Sir Murgatroyd Drake, his face set hard in annoyance, and her grandfather, smiling complacently; also the Reverend Benjamin 'Porker' Porthwell, who was looking far from happy and making hasty calculations in his book. Again Stephanie smiled, thinking of the consternation and disgust on her sister's face as she tugged on the man's twisted erection.

A motion in the crowd drew her attention, and she turned to find Farmer Urferd approaching, with a length of what looked like ship's rope in his hand. Attached to the rope was a snout ring, and attached to the snout ring was a pig. Although gigantic pigs had figured quite prominently in Stephanie's recent life, she found her jaw dropping slowly open in astonishment and anxiety. It was a sow, not only so colossal that it might have been passed off as the Emperor's big sister and no questions asked, but quite clearly pregnant, and looking as if she might produce a full litter of twelve piglets and a runt at any instant.

Stephanie's hopes had plummeted as soon as she saw the monster, and dropped further still as the stewards were forced to pull back the fence to allow it to mount the scales. As with the Emperor, the broad iron plate creaked in protest as it took the beast's weight, and as with the Emperor the needle shot above the hundred-stone mark, but this time it stayed there. A murmur ran through the crowd, voices in both Devon and Cornwall accents in agreement, many a pig farmer exclaiming in envy, not a few more genteel voices groaning in despair.

'Mr Urferd's Mother-in-Law,' the chief judge announced, then waited for the laughter and witticisms to die down before he went on. 'One hundred and twelve stone, five pound, and a new county record.'

'National record, I wouldn't wonder,' one of the farmhands beside Stephanie remarked, part of a rising buzz of conversation that barely penetrated her senses.

She felt sick, not only because of the forty pounds she had lost and the effort it had taken to earn it, but at the smug expression on Porker Porthwell's face as he flicked through the pages of his notebook. With all the money on either Singularis Porcus or the Emperor he had clearly made a substantial profit.

Much of the pig show remained, but Stephanie had lost interest and pushed her way clear of the crowd to wander dazed in the now bright sunshine as the full extent of the disaster sank in. She now had no money to get to London, with or without Singularis Porcus, while she had publicly declared her intention of standing against Myrtle in the Gaspers election. She had to be there, and yet she had already touched both Freddie and her grandfather for substantial sums, leaving her with nobody who could be good for more than a few shillings, with the possible exception of Claude Attwater, but only if she accepted his proposal. It was an appalling thought, but she found her steps turning towards the podium where he was currently haranguing three small boys and an elderly but determined heckler.

She stopped some fifty yards away, telling herself that it was a simple matter of accepting him, touching him for enough to make the all-important journey to London, then finding some excuse to break the engagement once she'd got safely back. Unfortunately there would also be the stigma of having been engaged to Claude Attwater, which Myrtle for one would never allow her to forget. It also seemed entirely possible that he might extend his opinions on the virtues of domestic discipline to engagements, although a spanking would at least provide an easy excuse for breaking it off.

He had seen her anyway, and ended his speech with a dramatic gesture somewhat wasted on his audience.

151

Stephanie began to walk towards him, already imagining herself upended and squalling across his knee: a grossly undignified fate, and yet her life seemed to consist of a long series of grossly undignified fates, of which this would merely be the latest.

'Ah, Stephanie,' he greeted her. 'I'm glad to have your support. We are only fourteen today, but the potential audience is large.'

'There are plenty of people here, certainly,' Stephanie admitted, glancing at the crowds that surrounded the pens, the refreshment tent and the bandstand, although not the Brown Shorts podium.

'They will come, they will come,' Claude assured her, clapping his hands together confidently, 'and remember, even the mightiest oak starts out in life as an acorn.'

'That's true,' Stephanie admitted, and went silent, wondering what she should say, if anything.

'Once the pigs have been judged,' he went on, 'they will no doubt wish to hear what I have to say on the subject of female suffrage. Meanwhile, dare I ask if you have had time to consider my proposal?'

'Um ... yes,' she managed, only to break off with a sudden twinge of conscience for what she was about to do.

'Yes?' he responded, and fell to one knee, taking her hand in his and beginning to kiss it.

'Um ... er ...' Stephanie tried, realising her mistake too late. 'Um ...'

'No, no,' he said, 'do not speak, for there are no words that can do justice to this moment. You have made me the happiest man in the world, Miss Truscott, Stephanie, indeed, the happiest man who has ever lived.'

He went back to kissing her hand, leaving her to throw a nervous glance towards the pens. The crowd around the pigs had begun to break up, moving instead towards the podium where the prizes were to be announced. Hermione was coming towards them, conspicuous in her Brown Shorts uniform, and she could see Myrtle, who appeared to be in earnest conversation with one of the stallholders and several men in rough clothes.

Claude Attwater was still kissing Stephanie's hand, but finally relinquished it as Hermione approached. He was beaming as he stood back to his full height.

'You must be the first to hear the glad news, young lady,' he addressed Hermione. 'Stephanie has kindly consented to accept my hand in marriage. There, is that not good news? You will be my sister-in-law.'

'Oh, wonderful,' Hermione answered doubtfully, and cast a worried glance at Stephanie, who managed a shrug as Attwater turned back to the podium.

'This is an important day,' he stated, 'perhaps a turning point, for myself, the organisation and the country. Come, Brown Shorts, stand proud with me.'

He had spoken the last few words in his orator's voice, loud and exceptionally carrying. The small group of Brown Shorts were already standing at ease in front of the podium, and Stephanie made to join them, only for Claude to offer her his hand once he himself had climbed up.

'Today,' he said, 'and every day from now on, you shall stand beside me.'

Stephanie gingerly accepted his hand and mounted the podium, from which she had a clear view across the field. Claude had a megaphone, and began to call on the crowd to gather round, making her feel extremely conspicuous as curious glances were turned her way. Her aunts Lavinia and Edith had both seen her and looked distinctly disapproving. Myrtle was pointing in her direction and saying something to two extremely shabby-looking men, who were holding large brown paper bags. The bags bulged suspiciously.

'Er . . . Claude,' she said. 'I think they're planning to throw eggs again.'

'Let them,' he answered. 'We must stand aloof from such behaviour.'

Stephanie bit her lip as he went back to shouting through the megaphone. A crowd was beginning to gather, and an alarming proportion of those approaching held the brown paper bags, while Myrtle was now passing coins to the stallholder she had been talking to before. Behind her the open field stretched up to a distant hedge, beyond which was a steep, wooded slope and then open moor. Escape would have been easy, but to run was to admit defeat, and she stayed obstinately in place.

'People of Britain,' Claude declared, apparently content with the number of people now present, 'I stand before you today . . .'

He went into his speech, apparently oblivious to the nature of the crowd, which Stephanie found distinctly worrying. A high proportion of them were carrying bags of eggs, and they weren't paying much attention to the speech, but seemed to prefer to exchange jokes and whispered comments. Myrtle was approaching too, with her own bag of eggs, while Freddie followed behind her, looking far from comfortable.

'. . . furthermore,' Claude was saying, 'we intend to introduce a two-year period of domestic service for all women, in order that they may better appreciate their proper role in life, learn obedience and respect . . .'

Myrtle had leaned close to a man in a flat cap with a noticeably broken nose, not her usual choice of company. She whispered in his ear and he nodded, then grinned as he dipped a hand into his bag of eggs. Stephanie made ready to duck. Myrtle gave a cheerful wave. Stephanie stuck her tongue out in response, and ducked as the man with the broken nose let fly the first egg. It missed her anyway, but exploded against Claude Attwater's shirt front. He merely raised his voice, continuing his speech with barely a pause as a second egg hit his shoulder, splashing Stephanie's hat and face. A third caught his hat, knocking it off, and with that he abandoned his attempts to explain the virtues of male-only suffrage.

'Yes!' he yelled. 'That is the sort of behaviour I would expect from the undisciplined, the degenerate, those who disgrace our great nation. You, yes you, you're ready enough to throw an egg, but what if I was to toss a Mills bomb back? You'd be running, I'll be bound. And where were you during the war, eh? Eh?'

'I was thirteen when it ended, mate,' the man answered, and hurled another egg.

'Not at him, you idiot, at her!' Myrtle yelled, pointing at Stephanie, but the man took no notice.

'Well, er . . . in any event,' Claude continued. 'This sort of behaviour –'

He broke off as an egg came in from the side, catching him on the shoulder to spatter his face and Stephanie's hat. Myrtle yelled something and an egg exploded at Stephanie's feet, another against her leg, stinging her badly and soiling her shorts. She ducked down, shielding her face as the eggs began to come thick and fast, the crowd yelling insults and Myrtle screaming encouragement. An egg burst on her shoulder and she felt warm, slippery mess splash her cheek, and more, down her neck and in her hair as she twisted away from what had become a full-blown barrage.

Eggs hit her back and bottom, her hat was knocked off and, as she staggered sideways, her foot skidded in the mess on the slippery wooden boards. She went down, sprawling in the muck as eggs burst against the planking and against her body, soiling her clothes and skin and hair. Her feet and hands were sliding in the mess as she struggled to crawl away, only to glimpse Myrtle in the act of hurling an egg from just feet away. It caught her full in the face, filling her mouth with bits of shell and a revolting, rotten mess of yolk and white, to leave her coughing up filth and blowing eggy bubbles from her nose. Another struck her forehead, splashing into her eyes to leave her blind and frantic.

All around her people were screaming and yelling, with Myrtle's delighted high-pitched laughter rising

155

above it all. Unable to see, with her mouth full of decaying muck and her body bruised and filthy, she struggled to crawl away, only to find the back of the podium instead of the steps. She realised her mistake too late, and toppled over with a despairing scream, to land on her bottom in a puddle of mud and broken eggs. Finally out of the line of fire, she found herself wondering if this was anything like the way her father would have felt in Flanders. Then she thought of Hermione.

Pulling herself to her knees, she wiped the egg from her face as best she could and peered cautiously round the side of the podium. Hermione was well clear and comparatively clean, but Myrtle was coming towards the podium with a purposeful look on her face that Stephanie knew only too well. Panic hit her and she ran, unthinking, up the field and towards the moor. Myrtle gave a delighted whoop from behind her and she knew she was being chased.

Memories flooded into her head as she ran, of similar chases and what had happened to her once she'd been caught, and with every one came the feeling she'd tried so hard to escape, the desire to give in to her persecutor. Again and again that sense of inferiority had betrayed her, sometimes even leaving her apologising to Myrtle for attempting to avoid her fate, and feeling that what was being done to her was just, even as it was meted out. As she ran she knew that this occasion would be no exception, but that only made her push herself harder.

She reached the wall and scrambled over, with Myrtle well behind her, and began to push up through the woods. It was hard going, steep and on ground littered with branches and broken by rocks, but her masculine clothing made it easier, and when she finally reached the top there was no sign of Myrtle. She staggered on, gasping for air, but determined to reach the high, lonely moor, which rose grey and green ahead of her to the summit of High Willhays a thousand feet above.

* * *

At last she rested, high above the woods. The field where the show was being held was just one patch of green among several, distinguished only by the big marquee and the crowd, most of which now seemed to be milling around the Brown Shorts' podium. There was no sign of Myrtle, provoking an instinctive stab of disappointment which she angrily suppressed. She told herself that it wasn't going to happen, not this time, but as her tormentor's yellow dress became visible among the trees the sudden responsive pang was as much of excitement as of fear. In her hand, Myrtle held a large brown paper bag.

'Oh, no, not more eggs,' Stephanie sobbed, then yelled out with all the power of her lungs, 'Beast! I hate you!'

Myrtle had been scanning the slope of the moor, perhaps unable to see Stephanie, but now looked directly towards her and started up the slope. Stephanie moved on, but the egg had begun to dry in her hair and on her skin, while some had gone down her neck and her shorts, making her back, cleavage and bottom crease slippery, all of which was extremely uncomfortable. It was also making her clothes stiff, and she realised that if she didn't get it out of her heavy silk drawers quickly they would be ruined.

She wondered if Myrtle would prove unable to cope with the rough ground, or perhaps get lost. A sharp valley fell away to one side, where the Redaven Brook tumbled down from the moor in a succession of little pools, each surrounded by reeds and worn granite boulders. Running quickly ahead, she waited until Myrtle was invisible beyond the brow of a rise of land, then changed direction and made quickly for the brook.

The first pool she reached was ideal, broad and deep, with a small waterfall feeding it at one end and several water-worn boulders along one side. Jumping across at the top, she climbed down among the boulders to stand on the largest of them. She gave a nervous glance back up the slope. The egg felt utterly revolting, gluing her clothes to her skin, while the bits of broken shell scratched her. She was also streaked with sweat, her face filthy and her hair caked with dried egg and mud. To get clean she would have to strip naked, making her very vulnerable indeed, but nobody was about, except possibly Myrtle.

She sat down on a rock, grimacing as egg squashed up between her bottom cheeks and around her quim. Again she glanced up the slope, then began to pick bits of egg off her face. Her emotions were in turmoil, but she made no move to carry on, even when Myrtle finally appeared, silhouetted against the sky, only to turn away. Stephanie hesitated, biting her lip, but she couldn't hold herself back.

'Beast!' she yelled. 'Nasty beast!'

Myrtle turned back, gave a single, knowing nod and started down the slope. Stephanie sat as she was, fiddling with a piece of grass, her mouth set in a sulky pout and her gaze directed at her boots. At last Myrtle reached her, still fresh in her pretty summer dress and miraculously free of egg, but breathing quite heavily and with a bead of sweat running down one temple.

'You're going to pay for making me come all the way up here, Stephanie,' she announced. 'Why couldn't you stop in the wood?'

'I didn't want to,' Stephanie answered sulkily.

Myrtle gave a dismissive snort and sat down on a rock, placing her eggs by her side. For a moment they watched each other, Stephanie with her lower lip pushed out in a sullen pout, Myrtle calm. At length Myrtle spoke.

'Whatever is to be done with you, Stiffy?'

'I don't know,' Stephanie answered.

'Well, let's not waste these eggs, for a start,' Myrtle said. 'Stand up.'

'I thought it would be the eggs,' Stephanie answered

miserably as she obeyed. 'They really hurt, and you got me right in my mouth, and in my eye.'

'Good,' Myrtle said, getting to her feet.

Stephanie shut her eyes, trembling badly as she waited for the first egg, which she expected in her face again. Nothing happened, and she allowed herself a cautious peep from beneath one eyelid, to find Myrtle climbing cautiously around the pool.

'What are you going to do?' she asked.

'Shut up, and pull out the back of those ridiculous shorts.'

Again Stephanie obeyed, her mouth working in consternation as she stuck her thumbs into the waistband of her shorts and pulled open the pouch. Myrtle peered inside, her face set in fastidious distaste, but one corner of her mouth twitching towards a smile as she admired the mess plastered over Stephanie's bottom cheeks.

'What pretty drawers,' she remarked after a moment. 'Were they expensive?'

'Yes,' Stephanie admitted.

'What a pity.' She took an egg from her bag and dropped it down the back of Stephanie's shorts. It came to rest beneath the tuck of Stephanie's bottom, nestled between her shorts and her drawers, the less rounded end wedged between her cheeks. Myrtle added a second, which fell on top of the first, cracking the shell to release a trickle of warm, slimy white between Stephanie's thighs.

'Now open your drawers,' Myrtle ordered.

Pouting more furiously than ever, Stephanie obeyed, knowing perfectly well what Myrtle would see.

'You've been caned!' Myrtle announced in delight. 'Five strokes, and quite hard by the look of them. Why were you punished, and who by?'

'My Great-aunt Victoria,' Stephanie admitted, 'for pranging my two-seater.'

'You never could drive,' Myrtle said.

'I drive better than you,' Stephanie retorted, only for her voice to turn to a squeak as a hard smack was applied to the seat of her shorts, breaking both eggs against the turn of her bottom and squashing the contents up between her cheeks and down her thighs.

'Speak when you're spoken to,' Myrtle instructed, 'and don't be impertinent. Now let's see how many eggs will fit down your fancy drawers.'

Stephanie hung her head and surrendered to her degradation, with the back of her drawers and shorts held as wide as they would go. Myrtle began to drop the eggs in, the warm, round shapes pressing between Stephanie's bottom cheeks and quickly bulging out the seat of her drawers.

'These are much more fun than splitters,' Myrtle announced after a while. 'I wish you'd had them at Teigngrace, then I could have loaded them up and paraded you about so that everybody would think you'd gone to the loo in your drawers. Wouldn't that have been funny?'

'No,' Stephanie answered sullenly.

Myrtle merely laughed and dropped another egg down the back of Stephanie's still open drawers. It came to rest on top of the others, not touching her flesh at all but adding to the weight, which had grown so great that she'd had to take a tighter grip on the waistbands of shorts and drawers.

'You can let go now,' Myrtle said.

Stephanie relinquished her grip. Both her shorts and the drawers beneath immediately sagged so low that the top of her bottom slit showed, while the eggs made a huge bulge in the seat of her shorts, sticking well out and also hanging down, just as if she had soiled herself, but with an impossible quantity of dirt.

'You have no idea how comic you look, Stiffy! I wish I had my camera with me.'

Myrtle began to walk up and down, admiring the huge bulge in the seat of Stephanie's shorts and smiling

160

to herself, then dipped once more into her bag of eggs, drawing one out.

'Three left,' she said. 'Let me see . . . yes, face, titties and quim.'

'Not in me!' Stephanie blurted out in alarm.

'Tut, tut, Stiffy,' Myrtle answered, wagging a finger. 'I said not to talk, but don't worry, I'm not going to ruin your precious virginity. I'm not that cruel. Now open your mouth, wide.'

Stephanie did as she was told, allowing an egg to be inserted in her mouth, with part of it still sticking out. The sight set Myrtle laughing again, until suddenly she gave Stephanie a hard, open-handed slap across the face, bursting the egg and releasing a great gush of mess. Most of it went down Stephanie's cleavage, but a fair bit stayed in her mouth and some hung from her chin like a slimy yellow goatee, flecked with bits of shell. Myrtle gave a light chuckle, then reached out to scoop up the egg hanging from Stephanie's chin and plaster it over her face, leaving only her eyes unsoiled.

'Lift up your top, Stiffy,' Myrtle commanded. 'That's a good girl. No chemise or brassiere? You always were a little show-off, weren't you?'

Obeying without thinking twice, Stephanie lifted her shirt, exposing her pert, high breasts to Myrtle's amused gaze. Another egg was removed from the bag, squashed firmly into Stephanie's already slimy cleavage and rubbed well in over both breasts, bringing her nipples to erection and leaving her skin slippery and foul.

'Quim,' Myrtle said, holding up the final egg for Stephanie's inspection. 'I do hope it's a rotten one, a lot of them were.'

'Beast,' Stephanie answered, but stayed as she was, her shirt still held high, her legs a little apart to prevent the weight of eggs in her drawers from pulling them down along with her shorts. 'And . . . and please say cunt, not quim.'

'Cunt?' Myrtle echoed. 'What a perfectly horrid word,

161

but yes, why not? It suits you. All right, I shall squash the egg on your cunt.'

A whimper escaped Stephanie's mouth as Myrtle stepped close, holding up the egg. It was touched to her mouth, hard and round against her lips, and lower, between her breasts, and over her belly, to where the waistband of her shorts was stretched over her navel. She closed her eyes as Myrtle's hand burrowed in, the egg now cupped against Stephanie's flesh, on her lower belly, down to the gusset of her drawers, then in up one leg hole to press upon the swollen, slippery flesh of her quim.

'You're sopping, as usual,' Myrtle told her, and began to rub the egg between the lips of Stephanie's quim.

'Please, like that . . .' Stephanie sobbed, 'make me . . .'

'I shall,' Myrtle told her, 'but not until I've had my fun with you. Now hold still. Why do you always have to wriggle so much?'

The egg was now pressed firmly to her quim, and Stephanie's answer was another whimper, but she tried to resist the urge to rub herself on the hard surface, not in order to rescue her ruined dignity but because she had been told not to. Myrtle continued to rub, then suddenly let the egg slip lower, pressing it to the mouth of Stephanie's virgin hole.

'I wonder,' she said softly, her lips just an inch from Stephanie's. 'Which would break first, the egg or your maidenhead?'

'No, please, Myrtle,' Stephanie begged, but she lacked the willpower to try and pull away.

'I said I wouldn't, didn't I?' Myrtle assured her, rolling the egg up the groove of Stephanie's sex. 'And so . . .'

Stephanie cried out as the egg was abruptly crushed against her quim, bursting to spatter her flesh with slippery mess and bits of shell. Then her cry broke off as Myrtle's mouth found hers. She surrendered immediately, unable to resist the kiss even though it brought hotter shame than all the rest of the indignities she had been forced to endure. Myrtle was rubbing her and, as their tongues entwined, she thought she was going to be brought off. But then her tormentor suddenly jumped back.

'Not yet, Stiffy,' said Myrtle with a laugh. 'I haven't finished with you, not by a long way. All right, you can sit down.'

'Must I?' Stephanie asked.

'Yes.'

Stephanie made a face but obeyed, lowering herself gingerly on to a rock. She felt the eggs in her shorts touch the hard granite and press out to the sides, then, as her weight settled, one broke, and another. She gave in, setting her full weight upon the rock, her expression one of disgust as more eggs broke, smearing her bottom with mess and squashing up over her already filthy quim. Some had gone up between her bottom cheeks, squeezing out at the back, while bits soon began to fall out of her leg holes, to land on the ground with thick, wet plops. Myrtle was grinning with delight, and waited for a while before giving her next instruction.

'Stand up again. Let me see.'

Rising, Stephanie turned to show off her bottom, first sideways and then with it stuck out. Quite a lot of egg was on the ground or running down her thighs, but her drawers still felt heavy, and they and her shorts had pulled down further, leaving the upper half of her bottom slit showing.

'Disgusting!' Myrtle said happily. 'But your bulge is rather too saggy now. I preferred it when it stuck out.'

'You shouldn't have made me break the eggs, then,' Stephanie said.

'Perhaps not,' Myrtle admitted. 'Oh, well, there'll be another time. I'll feed you until your stomach is about to burst, then make you do it properly and take photographs of you with your drawers full of your dirt, which I'll send to all your friends and your bumptious little sister. She's quite the little brat now, isn't she? I don't suppose you've told her what you're really like?'

'No,' Stephanie confessed.

'Maybe I'll tell her myself,' Myrtle suggested, 'in a letter, along with the photograph, or I don't suppose she'd believe her precious big sister could be reduced to being my plaything. How would you like –'

She broke off, laughing, as a larger mass of broken egg detached itself from the mess in Stephanie's shorts and fell to the ground with a squelch.

'Please don't,' Stephanie begged.

'I'll do as I please,' Myrtle responded, 'but if you're a very, very good girl I might just let you off. Lie down on your back and keep that shirt up.'

Stephanie got down, sitting in the puddle of mess at her feet and lying back against a low bank of grass and moss. Her shirt had slipped down a little and she lifted it back, displaying her egg-stained breasts once more. She had guessed what was coming, and found herself unable to close her mouth, her jaw was trembling so much. Myrtle, after a quick glance to make sure they were truly alone, hoisted up her bright yellow dress. Beneath it she had on tight, frilly drawers and one of the new bras in a matching style, cut to flatten her breasts. She took both off, to stand naked but for her shoes, stockings and the yellow hat that went with her dress. Stephanie swallowed, her eyes fixed on to the low, furry mound between Myrtle's thighs.

'You first,' Myrtle said, her voice now thick with desire. 'In your drawers, but you're to let me see too.'

'All right,' Stephanie answered, and her legs parted, displaying the bulging, egg-soaked crotch of her shorts. Their legs were so loose that she could pull one aside, exposing the gusset of her ruined drawers to Myrtle's excited gaze. Her bladder was already tense, full from the coffee and milk she'd drunk at breakfast, but it still took an effort to let go. A low moan escaped her lips as she did, a little fountain of pee erupting into her drawers and quickly soaking through, to dribble down into the slimy mess between her cheeks and the rock beneath. She pushed, letting it squirt out, and abruptly jerked her drawers aside, showing off her filthy quim to Myrtle as the pee gushed freely, rising in a high yellow arc that spattered down into the pool.

She sobbed as she wet herself, her legs cocked as wide as they would go and her virgin cunt flaunted to her tormentor, who watched with eager fascination as the pee continued to gush out and spread into a broad, dark stain on the rock beneath Stephanie's bottom. Twice she closed her gusset while her pee was still flowing, deliberately soiling herself, and again when her stream finally died, to let the last of it trickle down into the bulging mess within her drawers. Arching her back, she began to play with her quim and breasts, her head turned to the side and her eyes shut as her pleasure rose, too far gone to even feel ashamed of herself as she began to masturbate.

'My turn,' Myrtle said. 'Look at me, Stiffy.'

Stephanie turned her head once more, her eyes wide as Myrtle stepped close. She was shaking so badly she could barely control the movement of her fingers over her filthy nipples and egg-smeared cunt.

'That's my girl,' Myrtle sighed as she straddled her and pushed out her belly. 'Open wide, Stiffy, and I'll do it in your mouth, the way you like it . . . here you are.'

Mouth as wide as it would go, one hand busy with her cunt and the other with a nipple, Stephanie leant up, offering herself as a receptacle for Myrtle's urine. It came, a golden spurt that splashed in Stephanie's face and ran down her neck, then more, full in her mouth, to bubble from the sides and run down her breasts.

'Drink it,' Myrtle gasped, 'drink it all up, Stiffy. Oh, I've missed this so much.'

Stephanie swallowed even as Myrtle spoke, deliberately filling her stomach with the hot, pungent urine, but letting the next mouthful spill out over her lower lip, not to waste it but to catch it in her hand and wet her breasts. More came, now a thick stream, and Stephanie closed her eyes and leant closer still, letting Myrtle's pee wash over her face. Again her mouth opened wide and again she swallowed what she was given, masturbating furiously as she was pissed on, her fingers working in the slime of her cunt as the orgasm began to rise in her head.

Myrtle moaned, pressing her sex to Stephanie's lips with the pee still coming. She was forced to swallow and it broke the rhythm of her masturbation, but she began to lick, with the piddle splashing in her face as her tongue worked among the folds of Myrtle's quim. At last the stream of pee began to die, allowing Stephanie to swallow a final mouthful and use her tongue properly, while her fingers once more found the right rhythm between her own slippery cunt lips. Myrtle pressed forward, her quim pushing hard against Stephanie's mouth, her gasps growing louder as they started to come, together. Her thighs squeezed in Stephanie's face, fresh fluid erupted from her pee-hole, and as she came she was begging to be licked harder and telling the girl she'd just degraded how much she loved her.

Seven

'She was absolutely horrible to me,' Stephanie declared. 'Look what she did!'

As she spoke she pulled up her dress, exposing her bare bottom. Hermione gave a low gasp and put her hand to her mouth.

'She put a load of eggs down my drawers and made me sit on them,' Stephanie explained, 'and other things. I hate her!'

She craned back to inspect her rear cheeks, not for the first time. They were covered in tiny red scratches from the eggshell, standing out from a more general pink but blending in with the harsh cane welts.

'Your poor bottom,' Hermione sighed. 'And she spanked you too?'

'No,' Stephanie answered with rising feeling as she let her dress drop. 'That was Aunt Lavinia and Aunt Edith. By the time Myrtle had finished with me I was utterly filthy, and she didn't help at all but just walked off. I had to wash, and that meant stripping off completely and going in the pool. It took ages to get all the egg out of my hair, never mind my clothes, and of course they were soaking wet afterwards, and you know how long these shorts take to dry. What was I supposed to do except lay everything out to dry?'

'Yes, but you couldn't tell the aunts what had really happened,' Hermione pointed out.

'Of course not,' Stephanie agreed, 'that would only have made it worse. Not that it could have been much worse. I didn't think they'd be looking for me, and I was getting bored just sitting there, so ... so I decided to diddle myself, and I was just getting started when who should turn up but the aunts! They spanked me so hard, turn and turn about, with me over one's lap while the other rested her hand. I lost count of how many times they swapped me over!'

'What did you tell them?'

'They didn't give me a chance. They knew about the eggs, so maybe if I'd just been in the nude I'd have got away with it, but they'd seen what I was doing. Then they made me bring Great-auntie a note saying what I'd done. You can imagine how embarrassing that was, and so that's why I got done at tea, in front of the vicar! It's so unfair!'

She pulled a face as she finished. Her bottom still smarted, and she put her hands back to rub her cheeks. She had returned just an hour before, following the painful events on the moor, at least the later half of which had happened exactly as she'd described them to Hermione. Her great-aunt Victoria had been furious about what had happened at the Brown Shorts rally as well, which had made the spanking both harder and more prolonged.

'There's one good thing,' Hermione said. 'Now we're not allowed to be in the Brown Shorts any more it'll make our alibi even better if we're spotted taking the pig to the station. But anyway, what are you doing getting engaged to that nut Attwater?'

'It all got a bit confused,' Stephanie said. 'I thought that if he was my fiancé I'd be able to touch him for enough to get to London, and he's more or less admitted that he intends to spank me when I'm his wife, and that probably means before, so it will be easy to break it off, but I had second thoughts, and he got the wrong end of the stick, and ...'

She trailed off with a despairing gesture.

'You didn't need to do that!' Hermione answered. 'To get money, all you have to do is hold Porker up.'

'What, rob him?'

'Yes, why not? He must be carrying hundreds!'

'But H . . .'

'Don't be wet, Stiffy.'

'It's not that, but what am I supposed to do? He'll recognise me, and besides, he's a sort of human gorilla. He'll just laugh at me.'

'Biff him on the head with something, from behind.'

'Biff him on the head? I can hardly reach his head.'

'Nonsense. Put a lump of granite in one of your socks. That'll see to him.'

'What if I don't knock him out? What if I kill him?'

'Make your mind up! Look, it's easy, you just give him a sort of medium tap, not too soft and not too hard. You see people do it in the films all the time.'

'What people?'

'Oh, you know, gangsters, hoodlums, bootleggers . . .'

'You've been spending too much time at the cinema, Hermione . . . How do you manage to sneak off to Plymouth? The aunts would never let you watch that sort of film.'

'Porker takes me to see educational films,' Hermione explained, 'or at least that's what we tell the aunts.'

'I bet you do,' Stephanie answered, 'so that's . . . that's what you've been up to.'

She had only just caught herself before revealing the full extent of her knowledge, and went on quickly.

'All right, if it's so easy, you do it.'

'You're the one who wants the money.'

'Don't you? I'll go halves, after expenses of course.'

Hermione paused for thought, then spoke again.

'It would be awkward if he called the police.'

'A little, yes!' Stephanie agreed. 'And Mama says she'll leave me in the jug if I get pinched again, for anything at all, never minding socking a curate with a lump of granite. What would that count as, anyway?'

'I think it's called robbery with an offensive weapon,'

Hermione said doubtfully, 'or something like that, but I don't suppose you get the option of a fine.'

'No,' Stephanie agreed, 'probably not. Look, H., why . . .'

She trailed off, wondering how to phrase her suggestion without giving herself away, then realised that it wasn't hard at all.

'He's jolly keen on you, isn't he?' she said. 'And I bet he'd like to make a beast of himself if you offered, maybe to suck his cock –'

'I couldn't!' Hermione broke in. 'That's disgusting!'

'Tug him off then.'

'Stiffy! I couldn't, not ever, not –'

'Why not?' Stephanie demanded. 'You were going to with Lias Snell, and he's a grubby old drayman, so why not Porker?'

'I just don't want to,' Hermione said, putting on her most sulky face. 'Why don't you do it? He's probably still at the show, so you could meet him in the lanes near Bridestowe, start talking to him, and suggest going in among the bushes, or . . .'

'He'd realise I was up to something,' Stephanie objected.

'He'd realise I was up to something too.'

'No, he wouldn't. He'd probably think . . . oh, for goodness sake, H., I know he makes you tug him off when you have piano lessons, and spanks you, and has all your clothes off, and . . .'

Hermione had gone crimson. Stephanie stopped and shrugged.

'Sorry, H. I watched,' she admitted. 'But I wasn't peeping, I . . . I just don't like him making you do dirty things, and . . . and I went to talk to him about it, and he laughed at me and said you liked it, and that afterwards you . . . you diddled yourself. Don't worry if it's true. I'm just the same. I . . . I like sucking Lias Snell's cock, but I hate it too. It's like that for you with Porker, isn't it?'

It had all come out in a rush, and she had only just stopped herself confessing the truth about Myrtle. Hermione said nothing, but she looked angry and embarrassed.

'Sorry I peeped,' Stephanie said quickly. 'Please don't be cross. Maybe . . . maybe you should spank me, but not now. I'm awfully sore behind, and . . .'

She stopped as Hermione shook her head.

'I'm not going to spank you, but you shouldn't have peeped.'

'Sorry. Do you want to tell me about it or not?'

Hermione nodded, and after a deep sigh she began to speak.

'He tricked me into it. When I first started going for piano lessons he was ever so stuffy, but perfectly proper. The aunts think he's wonderful, so when he suggested that he should take me into Plymouth to see an educational music film they let us go. He took me to see "The Jazz Singer", which has sound and everything, and I suppose is about music, but we both knew the aunts would disapprove, so it became our little secret. Next he took me to see "The General", which is jolly funny, and afterwards he stood me dinner and cocktails . . . several cocktails. On the drive back he parked up on Roborough Down and started telling me how much he loved me and trying to kiss me. I wouldn't, and he got in a tizzy, crying his eyes out and begging me to do all sorts of rude things. In the end I agreed to show him my top.'

'While he tugged his cock?'

'No, that came later. He's really sneaky, because he never actually said he'd tell the aunts what we'd been up to, but I knew he would . . .'

'No he wouldn't! You'd get caned, but he'd get thrown out of the church.'

'That's what I told myself,' Hermione answered, and Stephanie nodded understandingly as her sister carried on. 'Once I'd shown him my top there was no going back. Next he wanted to see my bottom, then have me in the altogether while I played piano. He made a little game of it, so I have to strip if I can't do my piece properly, and the third or fourth time he got his thingy out on me. Next he added spankings, and having to tug him.'

'I saw,' Stephanie said, 'all over your titties.'

'He's a dirty pig,' Hermione answered, making a face, 'and so sneaky. He said I had to diddle myself in front of him for a punishment, not all the way, but you know how it feels, and I'd got there before I could stop myself. Now I always do it. I have to.'

'I understand,' Stephanie said softly and put an arm around her sister's shoulders.

'Now he wants me to suck his thingy,' Hermione went on, 'and he says he'd like to stick it up my bottom, and do you know the worst thing? I think I'm going to let him. What am I going to do, Stiffy?'

'I don't know,' Stephanie answered, 'but I'm going to biff him with a lump of granite in a sock.'

As Stephanie stood in the hedge beside the narrow lane between Bridestowe and the Okehampton Road she was beginning to realise that were considerable drawbacks to the project. It was all very well to talk of biffing curates with weighted socks, but the Reverend Benjamin Porthwell was an exceptionally large curate, and once biffed would be impossible to move, forcing her to complete the deed in the middle of the road. Also, he had been at the show in a suit rather than a cassock, so the money would presumably be easy enough to find, but the thought of rifling his pockets while he lay unconscious and possibly bloody in the road made her hesitate.

Nevertheless, she had promised her sister, and a promise was a promise. She had also paused a while to admire the portrait of Devil John Truscott that hung in the hall. Devil John, she was sure, would not have hesitated for a moment. He would simply have biffed his curate, pinched the money and gone his way with a merry song on his lips. She planned to do the same.

She was at least well armed. The socks that went with her Brown Shorts uniform had proved ideal for the task, and as her own were still wet she had selected one of Hermione's. No suitable pieces of granite had been available, and walking up to the high moor had seemed an unnecessary detour, so she had chosen a half brick instead, which, while less aesthetically pleasing, would no doubt do the job.

Her position had been chosen carefully, concealed in a thick beech hedge on top of a high bank, from where she had a commanding view of the junction between the lane and the main road, some two hundred yards away. She could see who was coming and would know if anybody else was following close behind, so that unless someone approached from the Bridestowe direction she could at least be sure of not being caught red-handed. Nevertheless, the lane was busy with people returning from the Okehampton show, and she knew she would have to be both lucky and fast if she was to secure her prize.

A figure had appeared at the junction, causing her heart to give a little jump, but it was one of the local farmers, his suit brown rather than black, and his collar the right way around. She settled back on the conveniently horizontal branch she was using as a seat, only to rise again as another figure appeared, this time in a black suit and with his collar back to front, His bulk removed any possibility of mistaken identity. It was the Reverend Benjamin Porthwell.

The farmer was some twenty yards in the lead, and Stephanie reasoned that a man who spent his days doing active things with cows and sheep would probably move considerably faster than one who not only divided his time between the cure of his flock and seducing young girls but was markedly obese. Sure enough, by the time the farmer disappeared from view the gap had lengthened to a good twenty-five yards, and Stephanie braced herself for the attack.

It seemed to take an inordinate length of time for the farmer to reach her hiding place, and when she heard his voice, remarking on the availability of daffodils with which to decorate the church for Easter Sunday, she realised why. Rather than getting on with whatever important work awaited him back at his farm, he had chosen to pass the time in idle conversation with the curate, thwarting Stephanie's plan. Nor did he seem likely to hurry on his way, changing the topic of conversation from daffodils to the advanced state of the primroses in the hedge as the man strolled past her hiding place.

Despite a secret sense of relief, Stephanie said the rudest word she could think of under her breath. She knew she would have to follow, and, reasoning that it was hard to look nonchalant while holding a long khaki sock with a half brick in the toe, she reluctantly abandoned her weapon. As soon as the farmer's voice had faded she slipped down from the hedge, paused to brush leaves and a stray caterpillar from her dress and set off behind them, intent on catching up and including herself in the conversation.

As her last contact with the Reverend Benjamin Porthwell had been to kick him on the shin, a conversational opening seemed a little difficult, unless it was an apology. That could hardly be made in front of the farmer, but before she caught up with them he had turned down a smaller lane, presumably to his home. For one moment the curate had his back turned to Stephanie, with nobody in sight either way along the lane: the perfect moment to biff him, except that she no longer had her sock. Deprived of choice, she spoke to him.

'Good afternoon, Reverend. May I walk with you?'

He turned, looking somewhat wary as he recognised her.

'Good afternoon, Stephanie,' he said, 'if it's about your money . . .'

'No,' she said sadly, 'a bet's a bet, and I lost. I, um, I want to apologise for my behaviour the other day. It was very rude of me.'

'Yes, it was,' he answered, his tone changing instantly from worry to sanctimonious disapproval. 'Especially as I was right.'

'I know,' Stephanie admitted, deciding that it was no time to argue about the details of her sister's seduction. 'I spoke to Hermione.'

He didn't reply, and they walked on in silence for a little way. There was a conspicuous bulge in the left-hand side of his jacket, which suggested an inner pocket filled with a very substantial quantity of money. The opportunity to biff him was gone, and it was highly unlikely that there would be another, even if she dared take it, when he was sure to guess who the culprit was. Yet there was every chance of putting their second plan into operation, if only she could steel herself to the task. All she had to do was get his jacket off, and once they had been rude together he would be in no position to complain. It was nasty work, but it had to be done, and once more she thought of her ancestors in order to strengthen her resolve, although she was fairly sure that none of them had ever sucked a curate's penis in order to rob him.

Having decided to do it, the technique was simple.

'I was very naughty,' she said.

'Very naughty indeed,' he agreed.

'Perhaps I should be punished?' she suggested. 'I know you punish Hermione.'

'I do,' he admitted. 'Yes, perhaps a punishment would be in order, if you assure me that you think it appropriate.'

'I suppose so,' she said, and forced herself to add, 'but you will do it the way you do it to Hermione, won't you?'

'I knew it,' he said with a chuckle. 'You're just like your sister, you delicious little trollop!'

He reached out as he spoke, to squeeze Stephanie's bottom through her dress. She felt her tummy jump and her quim tighten at his touch. His hand was so large that it cupped one whole buttock, but pudgy and soft.

'What are you going to do with me?' she asked.

'I'm not sure,' he replied, still kneading her bottom. 'Perhaps a little spanking first? I understand your aunts frequently spank you?'

'Yes, three times just today, and the last one in front of your vicar.'

'Lucky man,' the curate answered, 'not that he'd appreciate it, dry old stick that he is, but I would have done. I've seen Hermione get it, several times, usually from your great-aunt Victoria, who seems to be a confirmed disciplinarian, and always on the bare bottom. I take it you get it on the bare bottom as well?'

'Yes,' Stephanie admitted, disgusted by the relish he put into the words 'bare' and 'bottom' but with a little shiver at each.

'Then I suppose I must do the same?'

'I suppose so.'

'You really are very like your sister,' he mused. 'Yes, I shall spank your bare bottom, across my knee I think, like the naughty little girl you are.'

Stephanie made a face, already imagining herself upended and squalling as she was turned red behind, and that only as a preliminary to having to attend to his grotesque penis.

They had reached the first houses of Bridestowe and there were several people about, so he went quiet, to Stephanie's relief, but offered his arm, which she felt obliged to take. She was steered down the street to a square red-brick house rather larger than its neighbours, which she recognised as belonging to a widow, Mrs Burridge.

'My rooms are on the top floor,' he explained. 'Quite private.'

She returned a nervous nod and allowed herself to be led through the gate and round the side of the house, where they entered by the scullery door and ascended what had once been a servants' staircase. His rooms were comfortable and masculine, a suite of bedroom and sitting room that might once have belonged to a butler. They smelt of dust, old leather and the curate himself, making Stephanie wrinkle her nose as she looked round.

The curate wasted no time with preliminaries but locked the door behind them and sat down in an over-stuffed leather armchair by the window, extending his knees to make a lap. Stephanie swallowed and glanced out of the window to the familiar skyline of Dartmoor, which now suggested an urgently needed freedom, but she found herself stepping forward. The chair and his abundant gut made getting over his lap difficult, forcing her to splay her legs and steady herself on the floor with one hand in order to keep herself in place.

'Could you move out a little more?' she asked. 'Otherwise I might fall off, and I feel pretty silly like this.'

'A girl about to be spanked ought to feel silly,' he told her. 'After all, it's a pretty silly position to be in, isn't it, over a man's knee with your bottom in the air? And don't worry, I'll hold you.'

His arm went round her waist as he spoke, while one large, podgy hand found the seat of her dress and kneaded her bottom through the thin material.

'You're not as plump behind as your sister, are you?' he remarked. 'But nicely rounded all the same. I shall enjoy spanking you, Stephanie. Now, let's have that pretty dress up, shall we? We'll see what you've got. Hmm, what pretty stockings, and such smooth thighs, nicely rounded too, but not as round as your bottom! What an adorable little peach you have, Stephanie. Oh, yes, I am going to enjoy spanking you.'

As he spoke he'd lifted her dress, exposing her stocking-tops, thighs and drawers in turn and remarking on each as they came bare. Now he began to fondle her bottom, stroking the seat of her drawers where the silk was pulled taut over her cheeks and tickling the two chubby crescents of flesh that stuck out below the leg holes. Stephanie bit her lip in rising consternation as she was molested and began to shake, already feeling the tears well up in her eyes.

'Just spank me, if you have to!' she sobbed.

He merely chuckled and continued with his exploration of her bottom, pulling the material of her drawers up between her cheeks so that the silk was tight against her quim and she was forced to lift her hips. A little shock of pleasure ran through her at the sensation, and she hung her head in shame. Most of her bottom was now sticking out of the leg holes of her drawers, making her wish she'd worn splitters or a union suit so that her exposure would have been less humiliating. The new style of drawers just seemed to encourage men to play with them.

'Shall I have you bare?' he remarked to himself. 'Or shall we begin with your drawers up? Yes, with your drawers up. They decorate your bottom rather nicely.'

As he spoke he began to spank her, but not the heavy, painful swats Stephanie was used to when she was punished. Instead he was doing little more than patting her bottom, using only the tips of his fingers, to create a mild stinging sensation more pleasant than otherwise. Evidently, to him, spanking had less to do with punishment than with the enjoyment of a girl's bottom.

'Pattacake, pattacake, baker's man,' he began to sing, 'smack me a bottom as quick as you can ... Were you ever spanked to that rhyme, Stephanie?'

'Yes,' she admitted, and the tears began to roll from her eyes at the memory of being held across Lucy Catchpole's knee and spanked while her husband looked on indulgently.

'Pattacake, pattacake, baker's man,' he repeated, spanking rather harder, and now across both cheeks, only to stop and tug her drawers tighter still into her slit.

The full expanse of her bottom was now bare, and her drawers pulled tight against her quim. He set to work on her bottom again, repeating the humiliating little ditty over and over as he spanked her, never hard enough to hurt, but just enough to bring a growing warmth to her cheeks, which she knew would have an inevitable result. Already her quim felt urgent and her nipples had begun to poke out. She wept bitterly as she realised that she would almost certainly end up surrendering to him, probably even masturbating in front of him.

'Getting warm, are we?' he said with a chuckle, and gave her bottom a wobble before starting again. 'Oh yes, Stephanie, I know what this does to you. I have plenty of practice with little tarts like you.'

'I suppose you do this to Hermione?'

'Several times. She gets ever so eager once her bottom's warm and rosy. And others – your friend Myrtle for instance.'

'Myrtle?' Stephanie exclaimed, twisting her head round. 'Myrtle Finch-Farmiloe? She doesn't get spanked. She's never been spanked!'

'Oh, but she has,' he answered, 'many a time, and a fine little trollop she is about it too.'

'You're lying!'

'Not at all,' he assured her, and planted another smack on her bottom, this time hard.

'Ouch!' Stephanie squeaked. 'You have to be lying. Myrtle never – ouch! Porker, that hurts!'

'What did you call me?'

'Um . . . sorry, I mean Rever – Ouch! Ouch! Ouch!'

He had laid into her bottom, his huge hand cupping both cheeks at once and slamming into the softness of her meat, hard enough to squash it flat with every smack. It was not only horribly painful but drove the breath from her body until she was squalling and gasping across his knee with her legs and arms all over the place. Even when one of her shoes flew off and caught him on the side of his head he continued, spanking her with furious energy until she had been reduced to a snivelling, tear-stained wreck, her limbs jerking at every slap, her head dizzy with pain. Finally it stopped and she was left panting and dishevelled, her body limp, her hair a mess, spittle hanging from her mouth and snot from her nose, her bottom a burning, agonised ball.

'Maybe that will teach you a little respect,' he remarked, and began to fondle her buttocks again as he continued. 'Do not call me that again. I am a man of the cloth, Stephanie, and lying is abhorrent to my nature. When I say I used to spank Myrtle Finch-Farmiloe I am telling the truth, no matter how fervently she denies it, as I know she does. Before I came here I was at St Mary Pimlico, where I used to make a little extra by tutoring pupils in the classics. Myrtle used to come to me, and a very poor student she was. It wasn't long before I had the little trollop across my knee with her bottom bare, and a delightful bottom she has too. How she used to squeal! Like a stuck pig, terribly undignified, but then you girls do tend to make a fuss over a little spanking.'

As he spoke he adjusted Stephanie's drawers so that they once again covered her bottom properly, only to stick his hand in up one leg hole and continue to fondle, his fingers well down in her slit, so close to her anus that it began to tickle.

'The trouble with young Myrtle,' he went on, 'is that if I spanked her at all hard she would lose control of her bladder and wet herself all over my leg. I used to have to do it in the bathroom across the landing from my old rooms, seated on the loo with my cassock pulled up. Still, it was always rather fun to make her mop her puddle up afterwards.'

He finished with a chuckle and the tip of his longest finger found Stephanie's anus, teasing the little hole, which immediately began to twitch, opening and closing at his touch. A surge of embarrassment hit her, stronger by far than what had come from being spanked or having her bottom cheeks molested, and she immediately began wriggling in his grip and begging him to stop.

'Very well,' he assured her, 'for the time being, at least. Now, it's about time we had these pretty little drawers down, isn't it?'

Stephanie shook her head but he took no notice, inserting two fat thumbs into the waistband of her drawers and sliding them gently down over her bottom. A sob broke from her lips as she came bare, for all that he had already made a thorough exploration of her bottom. Now it was showing, and not only her cheeks but her quim and the rude little hole he had just been investigating, all spread out on display, her precious drawers stretched taut between her open thighs. She tried to close her legs but received a slap on the back of each thigh for her pains, after which he hooked one foot around her ankle, trapping her in her rude position.

'You are a little wriggler, aren't you? Worse than Hermione, if perhaps not as bad as Myrtle. Now, do you think you've been spanked enough?'

'Yes,' Stephanie answered earnestly.

'Your bottom is certainly very red,' he admitted, laying one hand across her cheeks, 'and hot too. But still . . .'

He trailed off, and once more began to spank her, not as hard as before but with enough force to make her wiggle and kick with her free foot.

'Please, no,' she begged. 'I'm jolly hot, and I think that was a fair punishment, don't you?'

'Not entirely,' he answered, still spanking, 'but perhaps it's time for the second part. I'm going to make you take my penis in your mouth, Stephanie. I suspect that's the sort of punishment you had in mind at first, wasn't it?'

'Yes,' Stephanie admitted, and the spanking stopped.

It was a relief, her bottom now ablaze and feeling huge behind her, while for all her disgust at what she was going to be made to do there was no denying the wetness of her quim or how stiff her nipples had grown. Not that he seemed in any hurry, holding her firmly in place as he pulled her drawers a little further down, then abruptly spreading the tuck of her bottom. Stephanie gave a squeak of surprise and alarm as her quim was opened for inspection, and began to struggle as a finger probed her maidenhead.

'No, not that!' she squealed, now fighting in raw panic. 'No, don't you dare!'

'Do control yourself,' he chided, still probing at her virgin hole. 'I'm only checking to make sure you haven't been deflowered, which is surely part of my duty, as I am at least partly responsible for your moral well-being. Indeed, I make it a rule always to inspect my girls' cunts.'

'Beast! Pig!' Stephanie squawked.

Another salvo of hard spanks landed on her bottom, taking her mind away from how rude he was being with her. Then he suddenly let go of her, and in surprise she tumbled to the floor, legs akimbo and her quim flaunted more blatantly than ever. She quickly closed her legs, scrambled up into a kneeling position and would have risen, had the curate not spoken.

'There's no need to get up, my dear,' he assured her, 'but take off your dress, and anything you have underneath, the top part that is. I rather like you with your drawers around your knees.'

Stephanie gave a sullen nod and peeled her dress up and off. She hadn't bothered with a chemise or bra and was nude underneath, her breasts naked to his gaze. He gave a faint nod at the sight, clearly not particularly impressed, but his hand had gone to his fly in any case.

'Shall I help you undress?' she offered, as conscious of the bulge in his jacket as of the one in his trousers. 'Would you like that?'

182

'No, thank you,' he answered. 'Whatever you may consider my faults, I have no illusions about our relative pulchritude. You are beautiful, and so should be stripped at every opportunity. I am not, and so prefer to stay clothed.'

'Oh,' Stephanie answered, irritated and yet also grateful. 'Won't you even take your jacket off?'

'No, thank you,' he repeated. 'I prefer to be fully dressed, as I said, and it also emphasises your nakedness.'

Stephanie nodded, already well aware how humiliating it was to kneel at his feet in nothing but pulled-down drawers while he was fully dressed, but for the long, ugly cock and outsize scrotum he had just pulled from his trousers. If anything his genitals were more grotesque than she remembered, and her stomach twitched at the prospect of taking them in her mouth.

'Um . . . perhaps you'd like to tug yourself while I show off my bottom?' she offered. 'Hermione says you like that.'

'I do,' he admitted, 'but, as perhaps you know, she won't suck, and I could never make Myrtle do it either, or Florence, or Madeleine, or Roberta.'

'Roberta? Do you mean Bobbie Drake? Have you spanked Bobbie Drake?'

'Indeed I have, and a fine struggle the little minx put up before I could get her bottom bare, but to be candid, I didn't dare ask her to put me in her mouth for fear she might bite. This will be my first time.'

'Oh.'

He'd taken his cock in his hand and was stroking the already partly engorged shaft and rolling his foreskin back and forth so that a little more of his helmet appeared with every tug. Stephanie watched, unable to pull her eyes away, until the bulbous cock head was fully exposed, glistening and purple in the sunlight.

'Come along,' he demanded. 'Pop it in. You know this is what you wanted.'

183

Stephanie managed a weak nod, wondering what she could possibly offer to avoid having to suck his penis. Yet it was too late to back out, and if he grew angry her only chance would be gone. Closing her eyes tightly, she shuffled forwards, groping for his cock. Her gorge rose as she touched it, the twisted shaft was hot and unpleasantly moist, and it took all her willpower to make herself go down and open her mouth round the head.

'Good girl,' he said, taking her by the hair. 'That's not so bad, is it now?'

Her mouth full of cock, Stephanie was unable to give the answer she felt his question deserved. He tasted strongly male, and there was something about the way his cock twisted that made her want to be sick, but he had her firmly by the hair and there was nothing she could do but suck. As her lips and tongue began to work on him he gave a long, low moan and relaxed back into the chair, stroking her hair but still holding her head firmly down in his lap.

'You are a little trollop, aren't you?' he sighed. 'A lovely, dirty little trollop, just like all the others, only worse. I shall enjoy you, Stephanie. I shall enjoy having you over once a week to suck my penis and display that juicy little bottom for me. Perhaps I shall even have you and Hermione together, side by side for a double spanking ... stripped naked. You can dance for me. You can suck while she shows her darling little bouncers and her lovely plump bottom. Are you rude together? I'm sure you are, two little tarts like you, you're bound to be ...'

He trailed off with a grunt and Stephanie braced herself for a mouthful of come, imagining that the thought of her and Hermione together would have been too much for him. It didn't happen, but he tightened his grip on her head and began to fuck her mouth, his penis twisting in and out between her lips and his outsize balls squashing against her chin with every thrust. Her stomach lurched, and only by swallowing hard did she prevent herself from being sick all over him.

'Do that again,' he sighed. 'I'll come right down your throat.'

Stephanie shook her head, knowing that if he did she really would be sick.

'So you want something more, do you? You must be the filthiest girl I've ever met, Stephanie.'

He let go of her head and she pulled back gratefully, not sure what he expected but glad to have his cock out of her mouth.

'Stand up,' he ordered, leaning forward, 'and kneel in the chair.'

'You're not to take my virginity,' Stephanie said quickly, 'but ... but you can do it between my cheeks.'

'Your precious maidenhead is safe with me,' he assured her. 'Ah, yes, like that. What a glorious view!'

Stephanie had knelt in the chair, her knees wide and her bottom lifted to show off her cunt and anus and to make a cock slide of her slit. From there she had a clear view of the street outside, and of Dartmoor beyond. She realised with chagrin that passers-by would be able to see her face as he rubbed himself off between her cheeks. His upper body might also be visible, but she knew that everyone would assume she was being given discipline, none would guess the horrid truth.

'Hold your cheeks apart for me,' he demanded. 'I like to see what I'm doing.'

'You can see,' Stephanie pointed out, but reached back anyway. 'You're doing my bottom.'

She took hold of her cheeks and spread them, stretching her anus open to his view, and to his cock, which he promptly began to rub in her slit. Her face set in a look of bitter resignation, but despite her best efforts to tell herself that the sensation was disgusting, it made her want to push out her bottom. Now that his cock was no longer visible, and out of her mouth, it felt rather nice, the twisted shaft causing delicious sensations as he rubbed it up and down.

'Your bottom is a true joy, Stephanie, so small and yet so round, and not a trace of hair between your cheeks. You have a pretty bottom hole too, pink and neat, and puckered up like a little mouth. Is it virgin?'

'Never you mind!'

'Clearly not, although I can see you've not been used often, you're too tight. So which lucky man has had the privilege? Frederick Drake? Roland Bassinger, perhaps?'

'No,' Stephanie admitted sullenly. 'I've only been had once, accidentally.'

'Accidentally?' the curate queried, laughing. 'Nobody sticks his cock up a girl's bottom by accident, my dear. Tell me what happened.'

As he spoke he took hold of her hips. What she was saying was obviously making him increasingly excited, and her own feelings were getting hard to contain. Swallowing the lump of shame in her throat, she decided to reveal what had been the second most embarrassing incident in her life.

'It ... it was Gussie Fitzroy,' she said. 'I was being rude with myself ... playing with my bottom, in the bathroom, when nobody was about. I ... I was going to touch myself off, and it had just started to feel nice when he came in. I was on my knees, with my eyes shut, and he got on top of me before I could stop him, and ... and once he was on my back I couldn't get him off. I thought he was going to put it in my hole, that he'd take my virginity, so I put my hand back to guard myself, but he'd started to hump on my bottom, and ... and his cock caught in my hole and ... and I was so slippery it went right in, right up my bottom, and it felt so awfully shameful ... but so nice. Why don't you do it, Porker? Go on, do it to me, sodomise me, stick your horrid, twisty cock up my bottom hole, you filthy pig, you beast ... ow!'

He'd slapped her bottom, hard, but he'd also pushed his cock down, pressing the head to her anus. She stayed as she was, sobbing brokenly but with her cheeks held wide for her buggering. He pushed, but instead of sliding in up her rectum as Gussie Fitzroy had, he hurt her.

'Stop! Stop,' she gasped. 'I'm not slippery enough.'

The curate gave a grunt of annoyance and pressed closer, wedging his helmet a little further into Stephanie's now straining anal ring. He put a cupped hand under her face.

'Blow your nose,' he demanded.

'Blow my nose?' Stephanie queried, then realised what he intended to do. 'No! That's the most revolting thing I ever heard!'

'Not next to being sodomised by Gussie Fitzroy, it's not, and I wish to follow his example, so do it. You should be nice and snotty after making such a fuss over your spanking.'

'You filthy pig!' Stephanie exclaimed, and snorted as hard as she could.

'Thank you,' the curate replied, and slapped the handful of mucus between her bottom cheeks, smearing it over her anus and the head of his cock.

Stephanie shook her head in wonder, as much for her own behaviour as his, but kept her bottom wide as he pushed once more. Now well lubricated, her anus began to give, not easily, but stretching slowly round his helmet until she was panting and gasping against the back of the chair. Her tears returned, flowing down her cheeks in the sheer emotion of allowing him to push his penis up her bottom. At that instant it was what she wanted more than anything else.

She got it in abundance, his cock driving slowly in, past her gaping ring and up into her rectum, twisting her flesh as it went, until at last she felt the bulk of his scrotum press against her cunt. He gave a pleased groan and began to bugger her, moving his cock slowly in and out of her snot-soiled hole, every push making her juicier and easier. As her body began to rock back and forth she let go of her bottom in order to cling on to the back of the armchair, and he took over, gripping her by the hips with his thumbs holding her reddened cheeks apart so that he could watch her anus pull in and out on his shaft.

Stephanie closed her eyes, abandoning herself to the pleasure of her buggering, no longer ashamed at the sheer ecstasy of having a penis inside her. It was just as it had been with Gussie Fitzroy, with her grovelling on the bathroom floor, not merely content to have him on her back but rubbing herself while he used her. Now she was going to do the same. Her hand went to her sticky, swollen cunt and she began to rub, excited by the sensation of his cock corkscrewing in and out of her, but wanting more.

He was getting close too, grunting and puffing as he buggered her, and she rubbed harder, determined to hit her peak first, while he was still working himself in her rectum. Suddenly he let go of her hips and began to spank her. Immediately she felt her climax start, imagining how she looked, spanked and sodomised by the fat curate, her naked pink bottom stuck high with his cock in the hole up to his balls, with his hands and his great wobbling belly slapping on her naked cheeks as she masturbated in dirty, wanton pleasure at her own utter degradation.

'That's right, my little trollop,' he grunted, 'rub your cunt, rub your dirty little cunt until you come, you little trollop, Stephanie . . . my little trollop!'

Stephanie cried out as her orgasm overwhelmed her, and her anal ring tightened on his cock as it twisted in and out of the slippery hole with ever greater speed, only to be suddenly jammed deep. Her bottom hole was still in spasm, and she realised that she was milking his spunk into her rectum, a thought so filthy that she screamed again and hit a second, higher peak. The next moment he whipped his cock free, to jerk frantically on the shaft and send spurt after spurt of thick white come splashing over her hot bottom cheeks and into the still gaping hole between, which closed with a long, soft fart to expel what had just been done up it, all over her cunt and her busy fingers.

She was still coming, and began to rub it in, smearing the mess of spunk and her own juices between her cunt lips as her orgasm subsided in a series of decreasing peaks, to leave her weak and shaking in the chair, sore and filthy, but with a sense of peaceful satisfaction stronger than any she had known before. A long, happy sigh escaped her lips as the curate wiped his cock on her bottom. Then spoke.

'I expect you would appreciate some toilet paper?'

Stephanie nodded, telling herself that it was pointless to stand on her dignity when she had his spunk oozing out of her bottom hole. Not that she had any dignity left, kneeling spread-legged in the chair with her buggered bottom stuck out and her cunt slippery with their mingled mess, so she stayed as she was, feeling no more than a touch of resentment as he watched her wipe her bottom.

He had still not removed his jacket.

'Would you be very kind and make me a cup of tea?' she enquired as she finally climbed stiff-legged from the chair.

'I'd have thought a brandy would be more in order?'

'That would be kind,' she answered, turning to inspect her bottom in a convenient mirror.

She was clean but very red, her cheeks warm and the hole between loose and aching. Shame and embarrassment had begun to return, and as she pulled her drawers up from where they'd fallen round her ankles she struggled to convince herself that her surrender had been necessary. She knew it was a lie, but he was at least in a good mood, and surely there would be some way she could persuade him to take his jacket off and leave the room for long enough to allow her to investigate the inside pocket.

'Thank you,' she said as she accepted a large brandy. 'You are quite wrong, you know, about not going naked.'

'Why is that?' he asked.

'I would have preferred you naked, just now,' she lied.

'I think not,' he answered. He took a swallow of his brandy and turned to look out of the window.

Stephanie bit her lip, wondering how to persuade him, or whether it might be an idea to brain him with the decanter from which he'd just poured the brandy. After sodomising her he almost certainly wouldn't dare to complain. But before she could find the courage to go through with her scheme he had turned around again.

'I suppose I'd better pay you,' he sighed.

'Pay me!' Stephanie gasped in outrage. 'I may be a trollop, Reverend Porthwell, but I am not a . . . a lady of the night!'

'Good heavens, no,' he answered. 'I wasn't suggesting anything of the sort. I meant your winnings.'

'My winnings?'

'Yes. You wouldn't know, of course, because you left early, didn't you, after that frightful incident with Mr Attwater and the Brown Shorts. I cannot, incidentally, approve of you being a member of that organisation –'

'Never mind the Brown Shorts,' Stephanie interrupted. 'Hermione and I have resigned anyway. What about the fat pigs?'

'There was a stewards' enquiry,' he explained, extracting a thick bundle of notes from his jacket pocket, 'and Mother-in-Law was disqualified. Your grandfather argued that she was not one pig at all but several pigs, as she was obviously about to have a litter. Farmer Urferd has never been popular, and the judges agreed with Sir Richard, which means the Emperor won. That's four hundred and eighty pounds, isn't it?'

'Yes,' Stephanie managed weakly as her mind ran back over what she had just done, all of it completely unnecessary.

Eight

Stephanie relaxed back into her seat, staring idly out of the train window as the familiar Devon countryside moved past at ever increasing speed. Her mouth still tasted of Lias Snell's cock, but a buffet car was supposed to be joining the train at Exeter and she would be able to get a cup of tea. Otherwise, despite a strong sense of chagrin at being caned, piddled on, spanked so many times she'd lost count and finally sodomised during the course of an unexpectedly complicated Phase Two, she felt the operation was going well. Phase Three at least had begun smoothly.

She and Hermione had risen before dawn, this time with Vera's knowledge, although the maid thought the girls were going to meet Freddie Drake and Roly Bassinger. They had reached Stukely Hall without difficulty, met up with Lias and lured Singularis Porcus on to the dray with a large bag of apples. Hermione had stayed in the back with the pig, using an economy-size jar of Wilberforce's Bonny Blonde hair preparation to adjust his colour from black to piebald, while Stephanie sucked Lias' cock in the front, swallowing what came out to ensure that not too much attention was needed to her make-up once they reached Okehampton station.

The patent hair preparation had been less than fully successful, producing red patches rather than white, but in the bustle of loading the market train for London nobody had paid the least attention. Lias had dealt with the station officials, while Stephanie and Hermione changed from their Brown Shorts uniforms into dresses, and at precisely three minutes past seven the train had pulled away, with Stephanie aboard and Lias and Hermione waving from the platform.

With no stop until Crediton, well beyond the point at which anybody whose company might have proved awkward was likely to get in, Stephanie felt at ease. There was a long journey ahead, with nothing to do but eat, sleep and contemplate how best to present the pig at Gaspers. A dramatic entrance was essential, and it was probably best to bring him in through the back door once everybody was gathered in the reading room for the vote. That would require the collusion of the staff, but a few well-distributed ten-shilling notes would no doubt work wonders, and ten-shilling notes were something of which she now had an ample sufficiency.

Her mouth set briefly into a hard line at the memory of her buggering, only to soften as she recalled that she herself had ordered the curate to put his cock up her. Nor had her surrender been as unnecessary as she had first supposed, because without the rude conversation they had had while she was being spanked she would never have learnt an extremely significant piece of information – that Myrtle had received the same treatment.

At the time, with her bare bottom warming to the smacks and faced with the prospect of having to deal with the Reverend Benjamin Porthwell's hideous penis, the information had come as a shock but no more. Only that night, after the application of a generous amount to Sootho to her bottom by Vera, had the implications sunk in. She no longer felt in awe of Myrtle, the spell broken by the image of her lover, tormentor and arch-rival squealing and kicking across the fat curate's knee with piddle squirting from her open cunt. Nobody who had had that done to her could possibly be as superior as Myrtle pretended.

In future, she decided, things would be different. There would be no more abject surrender, no more submission of her will to Myrtle's desire. With luck there might even be revenge, and, as her mind started to dwell on the possibilities, for the first time in years her ideas seemed not only highly satisfying but appropriate. The only problem was thinking up something horrible enough to compensate for all the things Myrtle had done to her across the years: the spankings, the canings and strappings and sessions with the hairbrush or gymshoe, being piddled on, being made do to striptease and exercise in the nude, licking quims and kissing bottoms, being made to masturbate in front of an amused and interested audience, and, above all, the occasion that was the single most embarrassing incident of Stephanie's life.

By a combination of deceit, bribery and carefully calculated risk, Myrtle had arranged for Stephanie to be caned in front of the entire school. That would have been bad enough, although the Headmistress had awarded only three strokes across the seat of Stephanie's drawers, but Myrtle and her friends had had other plans. They had caught Stephanie in the toilets while she was preparing to face her ordeal, held her down, stripped off her drawers and smeared her anus with a mixture of one third Nut Brown boot polish and two thirds extra-hot mustard. Her frantic begging as she was led to the assembly hall had only made her tormentors laugh, and she had been obliged to climb on to the stage as she was. Four hundred and sixty-three girls, the entire staff and most of the servants had then watched as she was made to bend over a trestle and her dress lifted, to reveal not a pair of the modest and voluminous splitters that were standard wear at Teigngrace but her bare bottom, which she appeared to have neglected to wipe.

As she was caned, with her beaten bottom less painful than her burning anus, and her burning anus in turn less painful than the blazing humiliation in her head, something inside her had broken, destroying the last vestige of her will to resist the girl who was supposed to be her Protector. Afterwards, as she grovelled naked at Myrtle's feet in the showers, licking her quim and rubbing herself, she had achieved the first orgasm of her life, and had come over the memory perhaps a hundred times since; but that was not the point. Besides, no revenge would be fully satisfying unless it also brought Myrtle to orgasm, and in some thoroughly humiliating fashion; but nothing she could think of came close to what she felt would be justice.

The various possibilities and their attendant difficulties occupied her mind most of the way to Paddington, broken only by a period of concentration on her breakfast. All the solutions that occurred to her were either unsatisfying or impractical for some technical reason, such as landing herself with a long stretch in jail. At her journey's end she became distracted by the need to transport the one-hundred-stone pig from Paddington Station to Dover Street, Mayfair.

Her idea had been to hire a dray, a simple enough procedure in rural Devon, even if her method of paying had been somewhat unorthodox. In London it proved a rather different matter, as all the drays, wagons and lorries in Eastbourne Terrace and Praed Street appeared to be busy on specific errands. Finally, after being told somewhat sharply that Singularis Porcus was no longer welcome in the freight wagon where he'd spent the journey, she bought a bag of Cox's Orange Pippins at a convenient stall and a ball of rather pretty blue string from a stationers. Attaching the string to his nose ring and using the apples as bait, she led him from the train and out of the station.

Progress was slow, and also embarrassing, because while he was perfectly willing to follow her, he seemed to enjoy snuffling at her legs and bottom almost as much as he did the apples. She kept to the smaller streets, keenly aware that the local constabulary might be inclined to regard her behaviour as peculiar, and that, while she was fairly sure that no law specifically forbade leading a pig through the streets of London, the animal in question *was* stolen. He was also hungry, and by the time she had managed to cross the Bayswater Road a single apple remained from what had been a three-pound bag.

With no further apples on offer, the Porker redoubled his interest in Stephanie herself, turning her embarrassment into fear. While she was unsure of his exact intentions, they seemed to be more than merely friendly. At last, in desperation, she entered Hyde Park and selected a long twig, to the end of which she tied the apple. Mounting his back, which was so broad that she was forced to spread her legs as wide as they would go, she took a firm grip of the thick bristles growing along the top of his head and extended the twig so that the apple hung within a few inches of his snout.

The effect was as she had intended, in fact rather more than that. He set off so rapidly that she was nearly unseated and was forced to cling on with her calves and feet. His motion was not everything it might have been, his lively trotting making her bounce on his back in a highly disconcerting fashion and causing his bristles to rub against her quim. The sensation made her eyes pop and her face flush scarlet, but she dared not get off. The park seemed unreasonably crowded for a mild but cloudy spring day.

By the time she reached the junction of the North Ride and the Serpentine Road she realised that she was going to come; and just opposite the bandstand, where the musicians were playing a lively piece that encouraged the pig to both greater efforts and an improved rhythm, she did. It was a sharp, sudden orgasm, intensely shameful, and too strong to allow her to hold back the cry of ecstasy that broke from her lips. Just then, two of her mother's closest and most inquisitive friends reined in their horses at the end of Rotten Row.

Dizzy with erotic sensations, flushed hot with embarrassment and in a state of advanced panic, Stephanie dug her knees into the Porker's flanks and urged him to greater efforts. He responded magnificently, breaking from a trot into a canter and exiting the park at a pace she would never have thought possible for such a grotesquely obese animal. He also seemed to have an innate grasp of traffic etiquette, and proceeded down first Knightsbridge, then Piccadilly on the correct side of the road without overtaking in a dangerous manner or hitting anything. It was nevertheless with vast relief that she turned into Berkeley Street, steered him the last few yards into the mews that served the rear of Gaspers, and dismounted.

After a moment to compose herself, check her make-up and adjust her now distinctly sticky drawers, Stephanie knocked on what she had worked out must be the kitchen door of Gaspers. It was opened by a bulky woman with a florid face who was holding a large wooden spoon in one hand. Stephanie's bottom cheeks twitched instinctively despite the fact that the woman's expression, though puzzled, was respectful.

'Miss Truscott? Wouldn't you be better round the front, my dear?' she began, then stopped as the crash of a large bin drew her attention to Singularis Porcus, who clearly felt that three pounds of apples had been an inadequate breakfast. 'Whatever is that?'

'My pig,' Stephanie explained. 'May I bring him in?'

'Bring him in?'

'Yes, he's my trophy for the election this afternoon.'

'Your trophy?'

'Yes, I stole him in Devon and brought him up on the market train. Now –'

'You stole him?'

'Of course I stole him, Mrs Tubbs. You know the rules, I'm sure. Trophies have to stolen, or they don't count. And please could you stop repeating everything I say? It's most irritating.'

'Very good, Miss,' Mrs Tubbs answered doubtfully, 'but he's to stay in the yard until it's time for the election. I'm not having that thing in my kitchen.'

'As you please,' Stephanie agreed, 'and he seems happy enough. I'll collect him after lunch. Is Miss Finch-Farmiloe in?'

'No, Miss, but she's reserved a table for luncheon. Shall I add you to the party?'

'Yes, do,' Stephanie replied, making the best of her new-found confidence. 'And you're right. I should go in by the front door.'

Stephanie made her way to the smoking room and indulged in a leisurely cigar, something that was forbidden to her both at home and in Devon. There were plenty of people about and she did a little gentle canvassing, although she knew that the members could be divided into three roughly equal groups. The first included those girls who had been senior to her at Teigngrace – which a large minority of the club membership had attended – and their immediate friends. With a few exceptions who had themselves suffered from Myrtle's attentions, their votes would be lost to Stephanie. The second, rather smaller group were her own friends from Teigngrace, every one of whom was firmly on her side, if only because they shared her distaste for Myrtle. That left those girls who had not attended Teigngrace or formed any particular affiliations later; they would cast their votes according to the quality of the trophies presented by the rival candidates.

Her only concern was that Myrtle might be about to spring a horrid surprise on her – not the usual sort, but by providing a trophy even further out of the ordinary than the giant pig. Unfortunately Myrtle's allies would be sure not to tell Stephanie anything, while the other girls simply would not know, with the possible exception of Bobbie Drake. It was hard to gauge how Bobbie would react to the theft of her father's pig, so Stephanie determined not to mention the matter. She went looking for her and found her in the billiards room, potting cannons with casual ease in front of a group of admiring onlookers.

'So they let you in?' Stephanie asked. 'Extraordinary!'

Bobbie replied with a good-natured grin, turned her attention back to the table just long enough to bring off another perfect cannon, then returned her cue to the rack as she spoke.

'Freddie says you fluffed it trying to get a copper's helmet.'

'Yes,' Stephanie admitted. 'It was a good one too, a Sergeant.'

'Tough luck, and getting pinched too. So what have you got for us, or is it still under wraps?'

'Under wraps,' Stephanie confirmed. 'How about Myrtle?'

'I haven't seen her since she went down to Devon, and she didn't have anything then. She'll probably turn up with a barrel of cider.'

'That would go down well,' Stephanie joked, 'but I'd still win.'

'Good old Stiffy!' one of the other girls called out.

'The little brat hasn't a chance,' another remarked. 'Myrtle's sure to win.'

Stephanie gave what she hoped was a mysterious smile and took up the cue Bobbie had been using, only to miss completely with her first attempt at a cannon, sending a ball over the edge of the table and on to the foot of one of her own supporters. When Myrtle's friends had finished laughing and Stephanie's face had regained its normal peaches-and-cream complexion, she quizzed Bobbie again.

'So you have no idea what I'm up against?'

'Not at all, old thing,' Bobbie replied. 'Freddie doesn't know either. I suppose you know the silly ass has gone and got himself engaged to Myrtle?'

'Yes,' Stephanie replied bitterly, 'although not for long, if I can help it.'

'Stand aloof,' Bobbie advised. 'She's only doing it to spite you, and she'll soon get bored if you don't pay her any attention, but if you make a fuss she might actually go ahead and marry him.'

Stephanie made a face and attempted another shot, this time successfully, although with only Bobbie and a handful of her own friends watching it was something of a wasted effort.

Lunch was moderately successful. She took her place early, beside Bobbie, and Myrtle and her friends were satisfyingly discomfited, while other girls admired her cheek. She even managed to hold her own in conversation, at least most of the time, and to balance careful hints and mysterious silences about the nature of her trophy so skilfully that by the end of the meal Myrtle was clearly worried.

Feeling confident, Stephanie retired to the smoking room for a brandy and another cigar before making her way to the reading room. It was already full, the chairs lining three walls all taken and other girls standing at the back or seated in the windows. Three chairs stood behind a table along the fourth wall, where the outgoing Secretary, Clementina 'Britches' Ashburton, had already taken her place in the middle. Stephanie took her place on Clementina's right. They exchanged greetings, and Stephanie tried to forget the occasion when the older girl had birched her. Myrtle arrived moments later, no longer flustered but smug.

'Settle down, Ladies,' Clementina demanded, and banged on the table the base of the half-bottle of champagne she'd been enjoying. 'Settle down!'

The conversation died and a last titter was hastily stifled. Stephanie glanced round the room as Clementina went through the formalities. A count of heads to see who was there only confirmed what she'd known already, that the vote was in the hands of the unaligned girls.

'. . . and that's that,' Clementina concluded, 'so may the best girl win. Myrtle, you're up.'

As the senior girl, it was Myrtle's right to go first, and Stephanie struggled to look calm and composed as her rival got to her feet.

'I shan't bother with a speech,' Myrtle began, to an immediate ripple of clapping. 'You all know who I am, and that I'll make a jolly sight better Secretary than little Stiffy there, who can't even wipe her bottom properly.'

There was a ripple of laughter mixed with gasps of shock and outraged whispers, but Myrtle carried on blithely.

'I don't imagine she's up to much when it comes to trophies either. I suppose you've all heard how she got pinched trying to steal a policeman's helmet on Boat Race Day? Yes, I thought you would, but I don't suppose all of you know that afterwards her mother gave her a spanking and sent her down to Devon in disgrace?'

This time there was general laughter, even from some of the girls whom Stephanie counted as allies. Her face had flared red.

'She shouldn't even be here,' Myrtle continued, 'and when she gets back she'll be getting her bottom warmed again, by her ghastly aunts, bare, and in front of anybody who happens to be about. So you can see that she's just the sort of modern, independent girl we need for Secretary, I don't think.'

Stephanie's face was now crimson, while there wasn't a single girl in the room who wasn't either giggling or exchanging whispered remarks with her neighbours. She forced a smile and thought of the effect Singularis Porcus would have.

'But enough of her pathetic behaviour,' Myrtle went on. 'We've had some jolly good trophies, but I'm sure you'll all agree mine is the bee's knees, or maybe that should be the pig's wig.'

As she spoke she gestured to the door, which swung wide to reveal three of Myrtle's closest friends – and Singularis Porcus.

Stephanie's gasp of protest died in her throat as the assembled girls burst out laughing, cheering and clapping while the huge pig was manoeuvred into the room. Objecting would be useless and only make her failure all the more humiliating. Myrtle hadn't even broken the rules: the trophy had to be stolen, but there was nothing to say it couldn't be stolen from a rival. There was even a precedent, because Clementina herself had secured re-election by presenting a pair of sponge-bag trousers originally removed from an MP by her challenger.

All she could do was sit tight-lipped in anger as Myrtle soaked up applause and congratulations. She even found herself clapping. The crust of self-confidence she'd gained when she learnt that Myrtle got spanked had now cracked, and all her feelings of inferiority were welling up again. Only one girl wasn't joining in to praise Myrtle, Bobbie Drake, who pushed through the crowd to inspect the pig.

'That's my father's pig!' she exclaimed.

'Rather a coup, don't you think?' Myrtle responded.

'Maybe,' Bobbie answered, 'but I think you might have waited until after the Okehampton Show to pinch him, don't you?'

There was real anger in Bobbie's voice, and a sudden hope flared in Stephanie's brain.

'Excuse me,' she said to Clementina. 'I have to prepare my trophy.'

'As a matter of fact –' Myrtle was saying, but broke off as Stephanie came over to her.

'I need to explain,' Stephanie said.

'Yes, you do, don't you?' Myrtle responded, smugger than ever.

'Outside, please,' Stephanie said. 'It would spare embarrassment.'

Myrtle gave a derisive chuckle but followed Stephanie from the room, as did Bobbie. Stephanie's heart was hammering as she closed the reading room door behind her.

'In here,' she suggested, pushing into the now empty dining room.

'What's up?' Bobbie demanded.

'I need you to do something for me,' Stephanie meekly said as she reached up beneath her dress to lever her drawers down and off.

'What?' Bobbie asked, puzzled.

'She wants you to spank her, silly,' Myrtle laughed, 'because –'

'No,' Stephanie interrupted. 'Grab her, Bobbie, quick, please! I beg you, if we've ever been friends!'

Bobbie hesitated only an instant before gripping Myrtle from behind in a bear hug.

'Get off!' Myrtle squealed. 'Get off me, you great beast, you stupid gorilla, you –'

Her words were abruptly cut off as Stephanie's drawers were jammed firmly into her mouth and pushed deep, leaving her struggling furiously in Bobbie's grip, with no more chance of breaking free than if it had been a real gorilla that was holding her. Stephanie jumped back, avoiding Myrtle's efforts to kick her. Bobbie hauled Myrtle off the ground, leaving her legs waving in the air, but otherwise helpless.

Stephanie had been the victim of the same move all too often, and knew exactly what to do. Darting in, she grabbed one flailing leg, jerked Myrtle's stocking free of its suspender clip and hauled it down. Myrtle also knew exactly what was happening, and fought harder than ever to stop herself being tied, but there was nothing she could do. After just two failed attempts Stephanie managed to get the stocking around Myrtle's legs and pull it tight, trapping both at the ankles.

Still Myrtle fought, jerking her tied legs back and forth and mumbling furiously through her mouthful of sweaty silk, but Bobbie was too strong for her. She was forced, slowly but surely, down into a kneeling position and her arms pulled back behind her thighs. Using her own stockings, Stephanie bound Myrtle's wrists together and fastened them to the first stocking. Trussed up like a piglet ready for market, Myrtle was completely helpless, but she was still wriggling and doing her best to spit Stephanie's drawers out of her mouth. Stephanie wedged them deeper in before turning to Bobbie.

'Thank you,' she panted.

'Quite the fighter, isn't she?' Bobbie answered, and gave Myrtle a firm smack on her outthrust bottom. 'That's for the bruises on my legs, and this is for pinching Dada's pig.'

Myrtle's body jerked to a much harder smack, and her expression of pop-eyed fury became even more lurid. Stephanie laughed, reckless in her triumph, as she pulled one of the dinner trolleys from its place against the wall.

'Help me up with her, Bobbie,' she asked, taking hold of Myrtle's shoulders.

'What are you going to do?' Bobbie asked, only for a broad grin to spread across her face as she realised. 'I say, that's rather clever, Stiffy. She's your trophy, isn't she?'

'Yes,' Stephanie said, 'she is.'

Myrtle's writhing grew more furious still at the news, while the expression on her face suggested that she was about to have apoplexy. Stephanie spoke again as they lowered Myrtle on to the trolley.

'Do stop wriggling like that, or you'll fall off and hurt yourself. Now ... presentation. We must get it exactly right.'

'You should serve her up like a stuffed pig,' Bobbie suggested. 'It would be appropriate.'

'My thoughts exactly,' Stephanie agreed. 'Would you mind nipping into the kitchens for the biggest platter you can find, and perhaps a few vegetables? But first, could I trouble you for a stocking?'

'My pleasure,' Bobbie responded, and peeled the article off before leaving the room.

Stephanie used the stocking to tie her drawers into place in Myrtle's mouth, which reduced the frantic girl's protests to muffled grunting and the occasional snort.

'Very pig-like,' Stephanie commented. 'Now let me see . . .'

Ignoring Myrtle's continued efforts to make her feelings plain, Stephanie began to search the room for props. Lunch had been cleared away, but Mrs Tubbs had been putting fresh flowers out and had left a pair of scissors beside a vase of daffodils. Both had obvious uses.

The fury on Myrtle's face turned to panic as Stephanie approached her, holding the scissors up and grinning as she snipped the long steel blades together. Feeling far too pleased with herself to bother about either propriety or the likely consequences of her actions, she began to cut Myrtle's clothes off. It was a tricky job, made trickier by her victim's refusal to keep still, and she repeatedly had to break off to smack Myrtle's bottom. Nevertheless, by the time Bobbie returned she had removed Myrtle's dress, leaving the floor littered with scraps of deep red silk.

'Oh I say!' Bobbie declared, blushing faintly at the sight of Myrtle's bottom, which was covered only by a pair of fashionably brief drawers, into one side of which Stephanie had already slid the scissors. 'Not starkers, surely, Stiffy?'

'Starkers,' Stephanie confirmed, and squeezed the scissors shut.

Myrtle's drawers parted with a faint snap as the blades sliced through the silk. Already taut across her bottom and hips, they sprang apart, exposing her naked rear, the lips of her sex pouting between her thighs and the tight star of her anus blatantly displayed between her open cheeks. Stephanie laughed, indifferent to the demented tone in her own voice as she went on.

'What a sight! And before you suggest I have any mercy, Bobbie, remember how she had me caned in front of the whole school. I want to get my own back, Bobbie, so don't stop me.'

'She does look frightfully rude,' Bobbie said doubtfully.

'Not as rude as she will when I've finished with her. Help me get her on to the platter, would you?'

Bobbie hesitated for only a moment before helping Stephanie lift Myrtle on to the platter. Now far beyond the point of no return, Stephanie set to work preparing Myrtle as if she were to be served at table. A few more snips of the scissors allowed the already ruined drawers to be removed, followed by the remaining stocking, and finally the brand-new Caresse Crosby brassière, which needed tugging out from where Myrtle's breasts were squashed up against her legs. With Myrtle stark naked, Stephanie stepped back to consider.

'What do you think, Bobbie?' she asked. 'Do you think I should leave her trotters bare, or put her shoes back on, the way chefs put those little paper tops on a rack of lamb?'

'Shoes on, I think,' Bobbie responded, now getting into the spirit of things, 'and an apple in her mouth.'

'Oh, of course,' Stephanie agreed. 'It would be unthinkable to serve a roast pig without an apple, but that must be the final touch. Now, if you would care to arrange the vegetables, I think we can improve the display of her bottom.'

Myrtle had twisted her head round at Stephanie's words, her face full of consternation and then panic. From the long sideboard, Stephanie picked up a cruet set; pepper, salt, oil-and-vinegar-dressing and two types of mustard – one of them the brand that had been mixed with boot polish and applied to her anus before her caning in front of the Teigngrace assembly. She whistled to herself as she unscrewed the top of the pot, relaxing her lips from time to time to give a manic grin. Myrtle began to writhe again, so vigorously that Bobbie had to stop laying out potatoes and asparagus spears and hold her instead.

'Thank you, Bobbie dear,' Stephanie said, and dipped a finger into the mustard pot.

It came out thickly coated. The mustard was a satisfying dun brown and of the perfect texture for lubricating bottom holes. Stephanie opened Myrtle's quivering cheeks to improve her access and applied the mustard between, wiping it over her victim's now pulsing anus and then inserting a finger up to the second joint. Myrtle's bottom hole was tight and warm, which felt rather nice, and brought home to Stephanie that she was beginning to be aroused. She ignored the sensation, extracting her finger and giving a tut of mock distaste when Myrtle farted as her bottom hole closed.

'Disgusting!' she said with a laugh, and planted a firm smack across Myrtle's bottom.

Bobbie gave a doubtful smile and went back to arranging the vegetables, but Stephanie wasn't finished. She took the largest and yellowest of the daffodils from a nearby vase and poked the stem into Myrtle's now slippery anus, which opened obligingly to allow some six inches to be slid inside.

'Perfect!' Stephanie crowed. 'Or nearly so. An apple, please, Bobbie, and if you would be kind enough to wheel her in, I expect the girls are getting impatient.'

Stephanie took the large red apple Bobbie had chosen from a bowl on the sideboard. It was wax, but that didn't seem important, and as soon as the trolley was out in the main hall she began to undo the stocking she'd had knotted behind Myrtle's head.

'You have two choices,' she said as it came loose. 'The apple goes in your mouth or up your cunt.'

'Oh I say, Stiffy!' Bobbie protested.

'I mean it,' Stephanie insisted. 'So you'd better behave, Myrtle. Right, let's have those drawers out, shall we?'

'You're going to regret this!' Myrtle spat as Stephanie's drawers were pulled from her mouth.

'Maybe,' Stephanie admitted, 'but not today. Now open wide, unless you'd prefer to explain all this to Freddie on your wedding night?'

'Filthy beasts!' Myrtle hissed, but her mouth opened.

Stephanie wedged the apple well in between Myrtle's jaws, then pushed the door to the reading room wide and strode in, with Bobbie wheeling in the trolley behind her.

'Ladies,' said Stephanie, 'allow me to present my trophy, Miss Myrtle Finch-Farmiloe, stuffed and trussed in the manner of a roast pig, which I am sure you will all agree is highly suitable.'

Her words met with absolute silence, every girl in the room staring dumbstruck at Myrtle's naked body, with the daffodil in her bottom quivering gently in the air. The first to find her voice was Clementina.

'Good God!'

'Shall we vote?' Stephanie said calmly and took her seat, although her feelings were so heightened that she could barely take in her surroundings beyond the bound and humiliated figure of her arch-rival on the serving trolley.

'I, er . . . I move for a vote,' Clementina said, rallying herself.

'I object!' one of Myrtle's friends called out, stepping forward, only to find her way blocked by Bobbie.

'We'll do this properly,' Bobbie insisted.

'Absolutely,' Clementina agreed. 'What is the objection?'

'What is the objection?' the girl retorted. 'Look what the little beast's done to Myrtle!'

'I seem to recall Myrtle doing similar things to Stephanie on a number of occasions,' Clementina pointed out, to an immediate murmur of agreement. 'Not quite so inventive, perhaps, but all the same. Objection overruled.'

'The trophy has to be stolen, anyway,' the girl persisted. 'Myrtle's been kidnapped, not stolen.'

'That's true,' Clementina admitted. 'Stiffy?'

Stephanie gave a thoughtful nod before replying.

'Do you all agree that Myrtle's own trophy counts?'

There was a chorus of agreement, and glances to where Singularis Porcus was snuffling at a bookshelf, apparently considering whether a richly bound collection of the works of Charles Dickens would make a worthwhile snack.

'So you can steal a pig?' Stephanie demanded.

'Of course you can steal a pig!' Myrtle's friend answered. 'That's not –'

'Well then,' Stephanie interrupted, 'I don't see what the difficulty is. After all, anybody who's ever met Myrtle knows that she's a complete pig.'

Her remark was greeted by laughter, clapping and finally cheers. She sat back, smiling happily, sure she'd won even as Clementina called for a show of hands.

'Those in favour of Miss Myrtle Finch-Farmiloe as secretary?'

Eleven hands were raised and Stephanie's grin grew broader still. Clementina nodded and made an entry in the ledger book in front of her, then spoke again.

'Those in favour of Miss Stephanie Truscott as secretary?'

Twenty-three hands were raised, and Stephanie shut her eyes in pure bliss, basking in her triumph and the adulation of her friends as they clustered around her, a spell broken only by a terrified squawk from Myrtle. She had been squirming a little before, perhaps in reaction to the hot mustard smeared on her bottom hole, but was now wriggling frantically, and with good

208

reason. Singularis Porcus, tiring of Dickens, had decided to investigate the daffodil protruding from Myrtle's anus. A single bite had removed the head, a second the greater part of the stem, and he now appeared to be considering the merits of hot mustard as a condiment for what remained. Myrtle clearly disapproved.

'Get it off me!' she wailed. 'I'll be nice to you, Stiffy, I promise, but get it off me! Get it off me!'

Her voice had risen to a scream and she had bitten clean through the wax apple that had been in her mouth, so Stephanie decided to take pity. Rising, she pulled a bunch of flowers from a vase and used it to distract the pig's attention, then wheeled the trolley and Myrtle from the room, shutting the door behind her.

Never had she felt so supremely triumphant. Her head was singing with victory, and she was determined to take full advantage of the situation while she could. Wheeling Myrtle back into the dining room, she closed the door behind her, propped a chair beneath the handle and addressed her captive.

'Wasn't that kind of me?' she asked. 'And after you'd pinched my pig, you little rotter.'

'That was fair,' Myrtle said sulkily. 'Now could you untie me, please?'

'Presently,' Stephanie promised, 'but not until you've said thank you.'

'What for?' Myrtle demanded. 'Look, Stephanie, if you –'

'Now, now,' Stephanie interrupted, 'let's not have any of that, shall we? You're going to be a good girl, aren't you, and say thank you nicely, or I might have to find out if this cheeseboard makes a good paddle – not a rowing paddle, you understand, but a paddle for spanking naughty girls' bottoms.'

'You wouldn't dare!' Myrtle spat as Stephanie picked up the large wooden cheeseboard by its handle. 'Ow! All right, you would dare! Ow! You would, I said you would! Ow! Ow! Stephanie, that hurts! All right, you utter beast, thank you! Ow! Thank you, I said! Ow!'

'That's not what I meant by saying thank you,' Stephanie replied, putting down the cheeseboard. 'This is.'

She lifted the front of her dress, showing off her bare sex, just inches from her captive's face.

'Oh God!' Myrtle groaned, staring horror-struck at Stephanie's quim.

'Think of all the times you've made me do it,' Stephanie said.

'But . . . but you enjoy it!' Myrtle protested. 'You like to be made to do that sort of thing!'

'Maybe,' Stephanie admitted. 'Maybe you could too. Now lick!'

She moved closer, pushing her belly into Myrtle's face.

'Lick, you little beast!' she demanded, and reached for the cheeseboard.

'This isn't fair!' Myrtle whined. 'Please, Stiffy, I said thank you. No, not the cheeseboard, it hurts awfully! Ow! No, Stiffy . . . Ow! Ow!'

She began to buck and wriggle as the heavy cheeseboard smacked down on her bottom, but her pain and distress only made Stephanie more determined, and more excited. Taking Myrtle firmly by the hair, she pushed her belly further towards her and began to spank her. The meaty slaps rang in the empty room.

'Lick me, you little pig!' she screamed, and her voice faded to a sigh as Myrtle gave in, extending her tongue to lap tentatively between Stephanie's sex lips. 'That's right . . . just there. That's not so bad, is it? Not so bad at all . . .'

Myrtle didn't answer, but she seemed to have given in, licking obediently at Stephanie's out-thrust quim. Dropping the cheeseboard, Stephanie pulled herself closer, still holding Myrtle by the hair and still spanking, but now with her hand and punctuating the smacks with caresses on the beaten girl's hot bottom cheeks.

'That's nice,' she sighed, 'just like that. Now rub yourself while you do it, you little beast, or I'll pee in your mouth.'

Myrtle gave a violent shiver at Stephanie's words, but resisted, clenching her fists in her determination not to put her fingers to her sex, and to be seen not to do it.

'I will,' Stephanie warned. 'I'll pee in your mouth.'

She began to spank harder as she spoke, making Myrtle's bottom cheeks bounce and quiver, and spread to show off the smeared mustard between, and the few inches of daffodil stem still protruding from her anus. Holding Myrtle's head firmly in place, Stephanie slipped a hand between the warm red cheeks, to ease the stem free and replace it with her own finger. As she forced open the tight, slippery little ring, she was wishing she was a man so that she could sodomise Myrtle as she herself had been sodomised by Porker Porthwell. She could see Myrtle's quim too, which was wet with juice and squeezing softly in involuntary excitement, but her fists remained obstinately clenched.

'You may as well rub it,' Stephanie pointed out.

Myrtle responded with an angry shake of her head, but continued to lick, sending little pulses of pleasure through Stephanie's body. Unable to hold off any longer, Stephanie gave in to her pleasure, allowing her climax to rise as her eyes feasted on Myrtle's bound and helpless body, her finger easing out of her enemy's mustard-soiled anus, her cunt pressed hard forward. She cried out as the ecstasy hit her, cruel and triumphant, twisting her hand in Myrtle's hair and sticking her finger as far as it would go, deep into the hot, mushy cavity of Myrtle's rectum.

For all her delight in her revenge, it was only by biting hard on her lip that she managed to prevent herself crying out Myrtle's name, along with a flood of apologies, as her orgasm began to fade. When at last she pulled away, her legs were shaking so badly that she had trouble standing, but she was still determined to make Myrtle break.

'Now you,' she demanded. 'Do it, and for being so stubborn, you can suck my finger.'

She had pulled her finger out, brown and slippery with mustard and juices, and offered it to Myrtle, whose face was already soiled with Stephanie's own cream. Myrtle gave a single, sharp shake of her head.

'I'll pee on you, Myrtle,' Stephanie warned. 'I had most of a bottle of claret at lunch, as you saw.'

Again Myrtle shook her head.

'I mean it,' Stephanie said, pulling Myrtle's head back by the hair. 'If I let go, it'll go right in your face. Now rub off!'

Myrtle merely screwed her face up, obviously expecting it to be peed on at any moment.

'You asked for this,' Stephanie said, and let go.

Rich yellow piddle sprayed from Stephanie's cunt, full in Myrtle's face, splashing both of them and soiling the floor. At the same instant Myrtle's fingers uncoiled, her mouth opened and she eagerly swallowed Stephanie's pee as she masturbated herself. Stephanie burst out laughing, delighted by her conquest, indifferent to the hot piddle running down her legs and splashing over her dress. The sheer cruel joy she felt was almost as satisfying as an orgasm.

'That's the way!' she crowed. 'Drink it all up, you filthy little trollop! Drink up my pee-pee, Myrtle, drink it all up like the dirty little strumpet you are!'

She finished with a long peal of laughter, because as Myrtle swallowed she had started to come, her bottom cheeks squeezing and a long brown worm of mustard emerging from her anus as the muscular little ring went tight. At that instant somebody tried the door. Stephanie heard the scrape of the chair on the floor as it began to open, but she was in no mood to stop, and couldn't have held back her pee if she'd wanted to.

'Bugger off, will you!' she yelled. 'I'm pissing on my tart!'

The scraping noise stopped and Stephanie pulled herself close, holding her cunt to Myrtle's open mouth as she let the last of her pee out and giggling as she watched it dribble from the sides and run down her legs into the wide yellow puddle in which she was now standing. Myrtle had finished coming, but that didn't stop her from swallowing her final mouthful, and Stephanie realised that her triumph was complete.

Only then did she turn round to see what was happening with the door, to find it open, framing a woman who stood staring at her, speechless with horror – her mother.

Nine

Stephanie stepped from the train down to the platform of Okehampton station, her spirits still soaring from her victory. Admittedly, what had happened with Myrtle had taken second place among the most embarrassing moments of her life, ahead of the previous number two, her virgin buggering from Gussie Fitzroy, but behind being caned bare in front of the assembly at Teigngrace. Her subsequent spanking had been long and hard, delivered across her mother's knee with a leather strap and followed by an hour of standing in the corner of the dining room with her bare red bottom on display while her father and mother enjoyed a dinner of cold consommé, poached trout and jam roly-poly pudding with cream. Even that had done little to dampen her spirits, and the sheer joy of having at last conquered her rival sang in her head to the exclusion of all else, including her mother's lengthy and pointed lecture before she had been given another spanking for good measure and escorted to Paddington station that morning.

Getting off the train as it began to gather speed, returning to Gaspers in order to retrieve her pig, hiring a dray to take it to Paddington and boarding the very next train had been, she felt, a masterpiece of bold and decisive strategy. All that remained was to return Singularis Porcus to his sty, and with the blame laid firmly at Myrtle's door she stood every chance of getting away with the entire escapade. She didn't even have to

214

worry about being caught returning the pig, because she could explain that Myrtle had abandoned him in London, and thus paint herself as the honest and responsible party while getting Myrtle into yet deeper trouble. The only disappointment was that Myrtle's parents didn't believe in physical discipline, and despite extensive provocation it was hard to imagine Sir Murgatroyd Drake taking matters into his own hands. He would, however, undoubtedly refuse to countenance his son's marriage to a known swine rustler.

It still seemed best to stick as closely as possible to the original plan, another piece of advice she had picked up from her father's military reminiscences. The platform at Okehampton boasted a Ladies' convenience, where she changed back into her Brown Shorts uniform, which she had left tucked into the angle between roof and beams. A few adjustments to her hair, the removal of her make-up, and she might have been a rather pretty boy – so pretty, in fact, she considered, that anybody who saw her might begin to have doubts about Claude Attwater's private preferences.

Lias Snell was supposed to be meeting her from the train; unfortunately a later train, but even that failed to daunt her. One of the reasons they had chosen Okehampton station was that it stood closer to the edge of the moor than to the town, which allowed her to climb the flank of East Hill on the army road and head far out on the moor. A few passing soldiers gave her curious looks, and Singularis Porcus had begun his irritating habit of snuffling at her again, but she pressed on, determined to reach the woods by Stukely Hall, where she could house the pig and wait for Lias on the Okehampton Road.

After making arrangements with Lias, and probably being made to suck his penis once more, she would have to return to Driscoll's and face the consequences of going up to London while she was in disgrace. It would almost certainly be the cane, and if she arrived in time for dinner it would be given in the dining room, in front of the entire family, along with any guests who happened to be present. While hardly a pleasing prospect, it was something she had already accepted as inevitable; her unfortunate bottom might once more be a casualty, but there was also the prospect of having Vera apply a little Sootho afterwards.

Other difficulties remained, such as her engagement to Claude Attwater, but none of them insurmountable, and as she crossed the rise of Black Down she began to whistle one of the less respectable marching tunes she had picked up from her father, about a woman from somewhere called Armentières who had four chins and drank wine by the barrel. She was still whistling an hour later, and had managed to add another two verses, both ruder than the original, but when she reached the rocky outcrops of Sourton Tors she stopped in consternation.

The hills and fields she knew so well were spread out beneath her, as verdant and as beautiful as ever, with each familiar landmark as she could always picture it simply by closing her eyes – but with one irksome detail. Some way down the slope, where a lane crossed the railway by a bridge she had intended to take herself, stood the Reverend Benjamin Porthwell. She pursed her lips in vexation, knowing that, red patches or not, he was sure to identify the pig, realise what had happened and demand his money back on the grounds that she had effectively fixed the competition. Attempting to blame Myrtle would be impractical and, as she no longer had all the money, the least she could expect was to be taken back to his flat and sodomised.

Her bottom was in no condition for such rough treatment, although she had lubricated it that morning in order to ease the soreness, so he would no doubt slide up easily enough without having to resort to the singularly disgusting technique he had used before. That was beside the point. Having been taught to accept a cock up her bottom, she had intended to develop this new skill, but with Freddie Drake rather than Benjamin Porthwell.

It was not clear what he was doing, but he was definitely in the way and could not fail to see her if she started down the slope. All she could do was hide and wait until he had passed, but while she could easily have hidden among the rocks the same was not true of the pig. A stand of fresh spring vegetation, hawthorn and stunted rowan trees offered far better concealment, and she burrowed hastily in, towing Singularis Porcus behind her.

The foliage was not as high as she might have wanted, and she was forced to duck low to make sure she wouldn't be seen. A glimpse between the fronds showed that he was now coming up the hill, at a good pace for a man of his bulk. The pig had moved off in another direction, and she felt a touch of panic at the thought that he might have been seen, and that Porker was hurrying to investigate.

She froze, crouched low among the bushes, still peeping. There were several paths he might have chosen, but by ill luck he decided on one that passed only a few feet from her hiding place. He was sure to see her. A dip in the ground hid him from view for a moment and she dashed deeper in among the bushes, snagging her baggy shorts on a hawthorn branch. She jerked herself free, whereupon the stitch Vera had put in snapped, allowing her shorts to tumble down round her knees and send her headlong.

Sprawled on the ground, she needed a moment to recover from the shock of her fall. She heard the crash of a heavy body pushing through the bracken behind her and twisted round as she tried to rise, to find Porker Porthwell behind her, his eyes fixed on her bare bottom with evil intent.

'Oh no, not that! Not again!' she gasped. 'Get off!'

He took no notice, pushing her on to all fours again and mounting her, his sheer bulk forcing her body down and making escape impossible. She felt his cock pressing between her bottom cheeks and snatched back to guard her precious, virgin cunt hole even as her knees slid wide in helpless acceptance of penetration. His balls slapped on her hand as he began to rut in her bottom slit, bringing himself to erection with just a few urgent pushes, and with the last the tip of his cock slipped into the already slippery cavity of her anus.

Stephanie's mouth opened wide in a wordless belch as the full length of his twisted penis was rammed home up her bottom with one hard shove. Now buggered and with no choice anyway, she gave in completely, letting go of her cunt to steady herself. She was gasping and sobbing into the wet grass beneath her face, her eyes wide and her mouth agape, as the long, curly cock spiralled in and out of her bottom hole. Perhaps realising that she had given in, he made himself a little more comfortable on her back and began to bugger her with a steady, even rhythm, his corkscrew cock twisting her flesh with every push, while the huge, pendulous testicles swung against her cunt.

A bitter sob escaped her lips as she realised she was going to come before long, if he carried on like that, yet there was nothing she could do; she was unable to escape, and every smack of his huge balls against her quim drove her that little bit nearer to climax, despite the agonising shame in her head. She tried to wriggle forward, hoping to adjust herself so that his balls would stop hitting her puffy, well-spread cunt, sure that the motion of his cock in her rectum alone would not be enough to bring her off. It made no difference. Her body lay trapped and helpless, with no choice but to lie there and take it until he had finished himself off in her rectum.

'Please, no, not this!' she panted. 'Not like this . . . not with you up my bottom . . . oh God, no! I'm coming, you filthy beast . . .'

Her voice rose to a long, pitiful wail as she felt her muscles start to contract, her buggered anus squeezing on his erection and her cunt tightening hard, once, then again, and she was coming, in helpless, full-blown orgasm, shrieking out her ecstasy to the moor even as the hot tears of unbearable shame trickled down her face. Unable to stop herself, she reached back, grabbed his bloated scrotum and pulled it hard against her, rubbing the wrinkly flesh between her sex lips, making herself come again and again, indifferent to his grunts and squeals of pain as she crushed his balls against her hungry cunt. She was sure he'd already come up her bottom, because hot, sticky fluid was running down to lubricate both scrotum and cunt as she rubbed, but knowing that her rectum was full of his spunk only drove her ecstasy higher, as did the weird twisting sensation in her straining anus and even the feel of his bulbous gut pressing on her naked, upturned bottom.

She began to buck her bottom against him, her bruised cheeks squashing against the meaty bulk of his huge belly, still riding an orgasm that felt as if it would never end. He was still pumping into her too, his thrusts ever harder and deeper, his cock twice pulling free of her anus, only to be thrust back up the gaping, slippery hole. Then it did so a third time, but just as she stuck her bottom up, so that when he pushed again his cock went into the wrong hole. Stephanie screamed as she felt her hymen burst, but there was nothing she could do about it, with his long, twisted cock already ensconced deep in her cunt, save babble pitiful protests.

'You beast! You've had me, you beast! That was my maidenhead, you stupid pig, you stupid, stupid pig!'

He took no notice, unsurprisingly, and she was fucked where she lay, his cock pumping in and out, her body still responding with helpless little orgasmic jerks at every thrust. She could feel her virgin blood trickling down over her fingers, and her torn hymen stung dreadfully, but she kept her hand where it was, clutching at herself in helpless abandon as he pumped into her with ever greater speed. When a great mass of spunk exploded inside her cunt she realised that he hadn't come before, and that it was some other liquid that was still oozing from her bottom hole.

When it was finally over she collapsed. His cock pulled free, leaving a trail of spunk across one bottom cheek as he dismounted, while more bubbled from her deflowered cunt as it slowly closed. She stayed down, shaking and exhausted, her fingers still clutching rhythmically at her flesh, her legs splayed as wide as her half-lowered shorts would permit, too far gone to care what she was showing, until the sound of a voice brought her sharply back to her senses. It was her grandfather, calling her name, and when she twisted around she found him standing just yards away, dressed in stalker's tweeds and carrying an antique blunderbuss she recognised as one of a pair that normally formed part of a display on the drawing-room wall.

'Whatever are you doing, Grandpapa?' she managed.

'I might very well ask you the same question,' he retorted, his eyes bulging in astonishment as he viewed the state she was in.

She rolled over, hastily jerking up her shorts to hide her blood-smeared quim and her all too obviously buggered bottom hole, though it was too late for concealment. He was so close that he had to have seen everything.

'I um . . . he got on my back, I couldn't help it!' she babbled. 'Please don't tell anybody, Grandpapa, please!'

'It is hardly the sort of thing I would wish to advertise,' he replied, 'but I mean to say, he didn't, er . . . um . . . deflower you, did he? Yes, I rather fear he did.'

'Yes,' Stephanie sobbed.

'Don't cry, old thing,' he advised. 'Remember, you're a Truscott, and besides, it's not too late. You want to marry young Freddie Drake, don't you? Well, he's around here somewhere, and without wishing to be rude, he's not the brightest of fellows. Encourage him a little and he's sure to do the deed, which would rather kill two birds with one stone, don't you know.'

Stephanie responded with a blank stare, unable to take in what her grandfather was suggesting.

'Run along, then,' he advised. 'The sooner the better for this sort of thing. I think he's down by the railway.'

'But Grandpapa,' Stephanie began weakly, her head swirling with questions and objections. 'I've just been –'

'Precisely,' he interrupted, 'which will cause all sorts of awkwardness later unless you do the same with some more suitable candidate before you've um . . . dried up. Freddie Drake is the only sensible choice, for all my misgivings on the subject. Unless you'd rather marry Porker Porthwell, or that ass Attwater? He's somewhere about as well.'

'No,' Stephanie replied.

'Then go,' he insisted. 'Now, where's that damned curate?'

'Are you going to shoot him?' Stephanie asked, half in hope and half in concern.

'Good heavens, no,' her grandfather answered. 'The blunderbuss is for that fool Murgatroyd. We're fighting our duel, and Freddie's his second, if you remember?'

'Er . . . yes,' Stephanie admitted, 'but Grandpapa . . .'

'Not another word,' he insisted. 'Go and do what must be done.'

He moved off, crouching among the bushes, and Stephanie was left standing where she'd been fucked, with a mixture of fluids still trickling down the insides of her thighs. She felt dazed, but his advice made sense, and after a while she began to walk down the slope. There was no sign of Porker Porthwell, nor the pig, but before she'd gone a hundred yards she saw Freddie, buttoning his fly as he emerged from the shelter of a clump of gorse. It was rather hard to know what to say, and in the circumstances a slow, maidenly seduction was out of the question, so she simply waved.

'What ho, old thing,' he greeted her as they drew together. 'I say, those aunts of yours are in the most frightful bate, and –'

'Sh!' Stephanie pressed a finger to his lips while her other hand reached for his fly.

'I say!' he remarked as she hooked his cock from his half unbuttoned trousers. 'I say, Stiffy, steady on, old girl!'

Stephanie didn't reply, her mouth already full of cock. Freddie swallowed and quickly pulled her back in among the gorse bushes and out of sight, never once detaching her from his cock.

'You *are* eager!' he said, reaching down to stroke her hair as she sucked.

It was true. For all her muddled feelings, Stephanie was still strongly aroused. Being unexpectedly mounted by the Porker, sodomised and fucked by pure accident was hardly the way she'd imagined losing her virginity, but it had been done and there was no denying the results of being so thoroughly used. Her cunt was juicy and ready for cock, despite the sting of her newly broken hymen, and she was impatient to get him hard and put him inside her.

He obliged, quickly stiffening under the ministrations of her tongue, until she had a long, thick erection in her mouth. Determined not to let him see until he was inside her, she pushed him down, still sucking as he first sank to his knees and then fell supine on the grass. She mounted him, holding his cock as she pulled aside the leg hole of her shorts and guided him in. He gave a gasp of surprise as he felt his helmet push at her cunt, but made no effort to stop her. Her torn flesh still stung, and there was nothing false about her cry of pain as her cunt filled with cock for the second time in her life. He was bigger than the Porker anyway, and quite hard to get in, so she was satisfyingly tight round him when she began to bounce on his erection.

Freddie needed no further encouragement but took her by the hips and thrust vigorously. She pulled her

222

shirt up, and off, exposing her breasts to the warm spring sunshine and leaving her in nothing but shorts, socks and boots. It felt wonderful. Her pleasure quickly pushed aside the sharp pain. Her maidenhead was well and truly gone, her cunt fucked; the dirty words rang in her head as they pleasured each other, and before long she was rubbing herself on his trousers with every thrust, determined to come.

It took no time at all, her body tightening on his cock as his thrusts grew faster, and as her climax hit her she was wondering why she hadn't given in years before, so wonderful did it feel. She lost control, screaming out her pleasure as she rode him, her head burning with dirty images, all delightful: images of what she was doing, of the appalling shame and unbearable ecstasy of what had just been done to her, and of every exquisite moment she'd ever known, not excluding her suffering at Myrtle's hands, or her revenge.

As her cunt frantically contracted on Freddie's cock, he came too, filling her with spunk right at the peak of her orgasm. She collapsed on to him and their mouths met in an open kiss as he continued to pump into her, filling her up until the spunk was squashing from her gaping hole and spattering their clothes with every thrust. Even when they'd finished they stayed together, clinging to each other in the aftermath of an ecstasy that was far more than merely sexual. At last she broke away and rolled off, to lie panting in the grass, with the sky and the green and yellow of the flowering gorse spinning slowly above her head, until she forced herself to look at him. His cock was still hard, sticking up from his open fly, the thick pink shaft streaked white with his spunk and red with her virgin blood.

'I say, Stiffy,' he gasped. 'I know it's a frightful lot to ask, but I don't suppose you'd consider marrying a chap like me, would you? I mean to say, after –'

'Yes,' she cut him off. 'Gladly, but what about Myrtle?'

'Ah, yes,' he replied, just as the roar of a blunderbuss shattered the moorland calm.

Both of them jumped up, whereupon Stephanie's shorts immediately fell down and sent her sprawling face down in a cowpat that proved to have only the thinnest crust over a thick and squashy interior. With her eyes, nose and, worst of all, her mouth full of cow dung, even the possible fate of her grandfather took second place for a moment, until she'd managed to wipe her eyes and spit out the worst of the filth. Even then she was in no condition to follow Freddie, with her shorts round her knees and her face plastered in muck, but a stream ran down from the moor a little way away, and there she made a hasty toilet to both face and cunt.

By the time she'd finished and could see well enough to retrieve her shirt, a considerable number of people were converging at a point well up the slope of Sourton Tors. She recognised her grandfather, still holding the blunderbuss, and relief flooded through her. Sir Murgatroyd Drake was there too, his face, hair and upper body a hideous, pulpy red, but he was not only still standing but expostulating vigorously, his remarks on Sir Richard Truscott's parentage and personal habits clearly audible across a quarter-mile of moorland. Freddie was rather closer, apparently uncertain whether to help her or his father, while the Reverend Benjamin Porthwell was waddling slowly towards the others. She could also see Claude Attwater, Hermione, several servants and what appeared to be a full complement of aunts.

'Don't worry about me!' she gasped as Freddie returned to her side. 'What about your poor father?'

'He'll be all right,' Freddie assured her, 'they were loaded with raspberry jam. Sorry, I didn't realise you'd gone face first into a country pancake. Rotten luck, what?'

'Fairly typical, I'd say,' Stephanie replied with feeling. 'So he's not hurt?'

'Only his pride,' Freddie responded, 'but I'd better see to him, don't you know?'

'Yes,' Stephanie agreed, 'but I'd really rather not meet all my aunts just at the moment, so if you don't mind –'

She meant to continue, but her words were interrupted by a bellow from her Great-aunt Victoria.

'Stephanie!'

'Oh dear,' she said weakly.

Most of the group had begun to move down the hillside towards her, with the exception of her grandfather and Sir Murgatroyd Drake, who were still arguing. Stephanie considered flight, but it was obviously futile and would only postpone her fate, while no doubt a few extra cuts of the cane would be added for her attempt to evade justice. Against that was the large audience she'd have if they dealt with her on the spot, which would include the passengers of any passing trains, of which, with her recent luck, there were sure to be many. She was still lost in indecision when they reached her.

'Whatever have you been doing?' Victoria Truscott demanded.

'I fell in a cowpat,' Stephanie mumbled.

'She never could keep herself clean,' Aunt Edith remarked.

'She could never behave herself at all,' Aunt Gertrude agreed. 'She's an embarrassment to us all.'

'And what a scandal,' Aunt Lettice added, 'running off to London when she knows she's in disgrace.'

'An outrage,' Aunt Lavinia agreed.

'We shall have to punish her most severely,' Aunt Rosalie concluded, not even troubling to hide her relish at the prospect.

Stephanie sighed and hung her head, knowing that it was useless to protest, only to change her mind as yet another figure appeared, crossing the bridge over the railway. It was Myrtle Finch-Farmiloe.

225

'Um . . . I accept that I need to be beaten,' she said hastily, 'but wouldn't it be better to do it at home? After all, I'm . . . I'm sure I deserve the cane, and –'

'A switch cut from the hedge will do very well,' Great-aunt Victoria observed, 'and you needn't trouble to pretend that you're contrite. You never are, until afterwards.'

Stephanie made a face but didn't reply, not wanting to be seen to plead in front of Myrtle, who was now within earshot. However willingly Myrtle had licked the night before, she had clearly not accepted her fate as just – at least, not if her expression was anything to go by.

'I would like to speak to Stephanie, alone,' she demanded as she reached the group.

'You must wait your turn,' Victoria Truscott informed her haughtily. 'Stephanie is to be punished.'

'So she should be!' Myrtle responded with feeling.

'Perhaps so,' Claude Attwater stated, stepping forward, 'but as her fiancé I insist that it is I who perform this disagreeable but necessary task.'

'Her fiancé?' all six aunts demanded in chorus.

'That is the case,' he confirmed, 'and thus –'

'That is as maybe,' Victoria Truscott interrupted him, 'and I do not dispute your right to discipline her, but at this present moment my nieces and I will be applying whatever is necessary. Afterwards you may –'

'Perhaps,' the Reverend Porthwell broke in, 'in such a case a man of the cloth might be better suited to applying appropriate chastisement.'

'What she needs,' Mrs Catchpole supplied, 'is for her old nanny to warm her little bottie for her, that's what she needs.'

All of them began to speak at once, each arguing for his or her right to punish Stephanie, while she stood miserably to one side, attempting to pick pieces of drying cowpat out of her hair. Finally her Great-aunt Victoria's strident tones overcame the others.

'Ladies! Gentlemen! Please, this is a most unseemly

display. Stephanie needs to be punished; that at least is beyond dispute, and in matters of this sort I have always considered the best solution to be to take turns, in strict order of seniority, which, as my brother appears to be otherwise engaged, puts me first. Stephanie, take off that ridiculous outfit and come across my knee this instant.'

Nobody challenged Victoria's decision, and Stephanie moodily kicked off her boots, peeled her socks off, pulled her shirt up over her head and wriggled out of her shorts, to stand nude and trembling in front of them. Her great-aunt had already sat down on a convenient rock, making a lap, but Lucy Catchpole spoke up.

'Miss Victoria, if we are to smack her bottie in proper turn, by age, surely I should be first?'

'Very well,' Victoria agreed, looking slightly surprised.

'Just as it should be,' Lucy said, lowering her ample bottom on to a different rock. 'Come along, young lady, it's time big Mrs hand visited little Miss Bottie-Bot.'

Myrtle giggled. Stephanie came forward, blushing furiously and unable to control the pout of her lower lip as she arranged herself in spanking position across the old woman's knee, her bottom lifted to the open moor and her little tits pointing in the direction of the railway. Lucy's big hand settled across Stephanie's bottom, cupping both little cheeks, and the spanking began.

'Naughty, naughty, Stephie,' Lucy chided as she applied hard, even smacks to Stephanie's already wiggling bottom, 'running away up to London like that, and without telling a soul. Whatever were you thinking? So naughty!'

Again Myrtle giggled, sending the blood to Stephanie's cheeks, hotter than ever, and then hotter still as she caught the sound of an approaching train above the regular smack of Lucy Catchpole's hand on her bottom flesh. In sudden panic she tried to escape, but Lucy merely tightened her grip and began to spank harder still, setting Stephanie's legs kicking in her pain as the train appeared. It was an express, which meant that no fewer than ten well-filled passenger carriages were treated to a prime view of her spanking as they passed. There was an astonished, fascinated face at every window, from first class to third.

'Naughty Stephie, no wigglies!' Lucy Catchpole said sternly. 'You'll only get it harder, my girl.'

Stephanie bit her lip, struggling to keep her thighs together and hold back the tears that were threatening to spill from her eyes. But it was impossible: her head was full of shame and self-pity, and the pain of the heavy, rhythmic smacks upon her bottom was just too much to bear. As the tears began to trickle down her cheeks Myrtle gave a sharp, derisive laugh, then spoke up.

'What a baby she is!'

'True enough,' Lucy Catchpole agreed. 'Quite the cry-baby, aren't you, Stephie?'

Stephanie shook her head in angry, shamefaced denial, but with tears streaming from her eyes and snot beginning to drip from the tip of her nose, it was a pointless gesture. Myrtle laughed again, louder than before, and the spanking went on, slap after slap, until Stephanie's bottom was a hot red ball behind her. Then, an instant before the pain broke her completely, it stopped.

'That be enough from me, I dare say,' Lucy remarked, 'seeing as how there are others to take their turns.'

'Quite,' Victoria Truscott agreed. 'Stephanie, come here. Mr Attwater, pray be kind enough to cut a switch.'

Climbing unsteadily from her old nurse's lap, Stephanie shuffled the few feet to her great-aunt with her hands on her bottom. Her cheeks felt hot and hard, and she was already dizzy, but there was nothing to be done save submit to her fate. She laid herself across her great-aunt's lap and lifted her bottom without a fuss. The spanking began immediately, every bit as hard, but faster, and Great-aunt Victoria's long, bony fingers stung far more than Lucy's plump ones. At once Stephanie began kicking again, and crying more bitterly than ever, the tears and the mucus from her nose making long, glistening trails down her cow-dung-smeared face.

At last it stopped. Claude Attwater was still busy cutting switches down by the railway, so she was passed to her Aunt Lavinia. Again she was spanked, wriggling and tearful, her bottom now so hot the smacks barely hurt, but her burning sense of shame was as strong as ever. Lavinia passed her to Gertrude, and Gertrude to Edith, each taking out her feelings on Stephanie's blazing bottom, but through it all she kept her thighs firmly together, hiding her quim even as she bucked and squirmed with her bottom hole on show every time her cheeks opened to a smack or when her body bucked in her helpless wriggling.

Edith passed her to Lettice, and Lettice to Rosalie, who proved to have a hairbrush in her bag and once more managed to bring Stephanie back to a full realisation of how much a spanking could hurt. Yet the pain still took second place to her shame and consternation, because spankings were always given 'ladies first', and that meant the next knee she would be put over was Myrtle's.

'And let that be a lesson to you!' Aunt Rosalie said as she applied a final smack to Stephanie's cheeks. 'Whoever is that peculiar woman?'

'Probably some yokel come to take her turn with silly Stephanie,' Myrtle laughed.

Stephanie looked up, blinking away her tears, and saw a familiar dray crossing the railway bridge, only the driver was not Lias Snell, but a huge, red-faced woman she recognised as his wife. She swallowed hard, sure that everything was about to be revealed, in which case what she had just endured would be only a prelude to her proper punishment. Claude Attwater was also coming towards her, holding a bunch of supple, painful-looking switches. Mrs Snell reached them first.

'Myrtle Finch-Farmiloe?' she said as she climbed down from the dray.

'Yes,' Myrtle replied, puzzled but haughtier than ever.

'I'd like a word with you,' the huge woman replied, advancing.

'I am busy,' Myrtle began. 'I do not believe we have been introduced.'

'I'm Mrs Snell, Lias Snell's wife,' the woman answered.

Myrtle made to speak again, but broke off with a squeal of surprise as Mrs Snell grabbed her. 'What are you doing? Get off me! Get off me this instant, you ghastly woman!'

'Spanking your behind, that's what I'll be doing,' Mrs Snell answered, hauling Myrtle to her as she lowered herself on to the rock where Lucy Catchpole had spanked Stephanie.

Myrtle went wild, screaming and kicking as she was put into position, but she might as well have tried to resist a carthorse. Working with a slow, purposeful force, Mrs Snell upended the writhing girl across her lap, lifted her pretty green silk dress, took down the fashionable drawers beneath and applied herself to Myrtle's naked bottom. The result was an instant tantrum, with Myrtle howling her head off and thrashing her body in every direction. Within seconds her tits had fallen out of her dress and she was providing a rear view of virgin cunt and tightly puckered bottom hole, ruder even than what Stephanie was showing. Her audience watched in astonishment and considerable interest, no one making a move to help, not even Freddie Drake, who was gaping at her bouncing cheeks like a stupefied goldfish.

'Freddie!' she wailed, finally finding her voice. 'Help me!'

'Um . . . er . . . ,' Freddie stammered.

'You mind your business, young man, or you'll get a dose of the same yourself,' Mrs Snell warned.

'Er . . . um . . . , no, no, absolutely not,' Freddie went on. 'I wouldn't dream of interfering.'

'Freddie!' Myrtle repeated, louder and more desperate still. 'Stop her . . . Ow! Stop her now! Ow! Or our engagement is off! Ow! Ow! Ow!'

'I er . . . I don't think she wants me to,' Freddie replied weakly.

'Besides which,' Victoria Truscott put in, 'if this good woman sees fit to apply a punishment, it is no doubt deserved.'

A selection of nods and expressions of agreement greeted this statement and Myrtle's spanking continued. Stephanie took the opportunity to scramble up from Aunt Rosalie's lap and apply her hands to her own overheated bottom. Hermione stepped close, rather cautiously, kissed her and put a comforting arm around her waist. Their grandfather was now approaching with Sir Murgatroyd Drake, the one grinning, the other scowling furiously beneath a mask of raspberry jam.

'What the hell's going on here?' Sir Murgatroyd demanded, then broke off with a sharp cry as Singularis Porcus ambled out of the undergrowth. 'Good God, that's the Porker! Damn you, Truscott, what have you done to my pig?'

'I keep telling you,' Sir Richard responded. 'I haven't done anything to your damn pig.'

'It was Myrtle,' Stephanie put in, indicating her rival's still bouncing bottom. 'She stole him as her trophy for Gaspers. If you don't believe me, Sir Murgatroyd, ask Bobbie.'

'Bobbie?' he demanded. 'And who, pray, is Bobbie?'

'Your daughter Roberta,' Stephanie explained. 'She was there last night and will confirm everything I say, while Mrs Snell here can fill in the details.'

'That's the way of it,' Mrs Snell stated, never once breaking the rhythm of the smacks she was applying to

231

Myrtle's bottom. 'Seduced my Lias, she did, the dirty little brat, so as he'd lend her the use of his dray to cart your pig about country, she did, Sir Murgatroyd. Didn't you, you little hussy, you?'

Myrtle was far too busy squealing her lungs out to provide a coherent answer, but the question had plainly been rhetorical in any event, as Mrs Snell continued to spank just as hard as before. As Sir Murgatroyd began to question Mrs Snell, the Reverend Porthwell gave a polite cough, then spoke.

'I believe it is my turn with Stephanie?'

'Quite,' Victoria Truscott agreed. 'Stephanie.'

Stephanie made a face, but she knew better than to disobey. The curate sat down and patted his lap.

'Over you go,' he said jovially, 'face to face with Myrtle, so you can watch each other's spankings.'

Pouting furiously, but very glad to have escaped a session over Myrtle's knee, Stephanie got down across the curate's fat legs. He immediately applied his hand to her bottom with a loitering intimacy that stopped only at a meaningful cough from her great-aunt, at which he began to spank instead, aiming low under her cheeks to bring the heat straight back to her quim and more shame than ever to her head. His big hand was catching her thighs as well, which stung dreadfully and set her squealing, kicking and tossing her head, in exactly the same state as Myrtle opposite her.

Sir Murgatroyd Drake had accepted Mrs Snell's statement and, after a grudging apology to Sir Richard, stood watching Myrtle punished with an expression of stern satisfaction on his bewhiskered face. For a while nobody else spoke either, and the only sounds were the rhythmic smack of hands on bottom flesh, the girls' squeals and the snuffling of the pig. At length Victoria Truscott spoke up.

'A switch, please, Mr Attwater, if you would be so kind.'

Stephanie twisted around in fear, to find Claude Attwater passing not one but three long, whippy twigs to her great-aunt. For a moment she thought of begging him to intervene, but the expression of pompous self-righteousness on his face told her it would be futile.

'Hold her please, Reverend,' Victoria Truscott commanded. 'Firmly.'

The spanking stopped, and the curate's huge, podgy arm tightened around Stephanie's waist, trapping her. She began to wriggle with fear as her great-aunt swished the twigs through the air, but her anger showed in her voice as she spoke.

'If you think I'm marrying you, Claude Attwater, you —'

Then a squeal of pain rent the air as the triple switch lashed down across her bottom.

'We shall discuss the matter at a less emotional moment,' Claude Attwater remarked, stepping back a little to obtain the rudest possible view of Stephanie's rear.

'If you've some more of those,' Mrs Snell remarked, pausing in the application of her hand to Myrtle's bottom, which was now the same rich red as Stephanie's, 'I'm thinking this brat could do with a dose of the same as the other.'

'No!' Myrtle squealed, and gave a frantic lurch, but Mrs Snell merely tightened her grip.

As Stephanie looked up she met Myrtle's eyes, and to her astonishment found them full of sympathy.

'Sorry, Stiffy,' Myrtle said, her voice choked with tears.

Stephanie managed a weak smile. For all her pain and humiliation she felt a satisfaction beyond even that of revenge.

'I'm sorry too,' she said, as Mrs Snell spoke again.

'If one of you wouldn't mind? I can't hold this one properly and whip her at the same time.'

'I'll do it,' Hermione offered, taking the remaining three switches from Claude Attwater. 'Right, Myrtle, you've had this coming for years.'

'She's like that, I'm afraid,' Stephanie said, with a wan smile, then bit her lip as her great-aunt's switch was laid carefully across her bottom.

'Are you ready, Hermione?' Victoria Truscott enquired. 'Then let us begin.'

Both sets of switches landed across the girls' bottoms simultaneously, drawing twin screams from their lips, and the thrashing began. The pain was infinitely worse than being spanked, and Stephanie gave in at the very first stroke, squealing like a pig in distress and struggling in the curate's powerful grip. Myrtle was no better, wriggling in desperation as her prim little buttocks were introduced to the effect of a bundle of switches applied with every ounce of Hermione's strength. Her tits were bouncing and her legs wide, stretching her lowered drawers out between her thighs, until Hermione paused to pull them off and leave her target fully bare.

With the removal of her drawers Myrtle broke down completely, apologising over and over again for what she'd done and for anything else she could think of, including stealing the pig, and begging Hermione to stop. Stephanie had also given in, no longer even trying to escape. Her body jerked with the pain of the cuts, her head tossing at each impact and her kicking legs showing off her open, deflowered cunt to the moor and to those who had positioned themselves behind her in order to get the rudest possible view.

'I say, hang on a minute,' Claude Attwater said suddenly. 'Goodness gracious!'

'What is the matter, Mr Attwater?' Victoria Truscott demanded testily as she paused in Stephanie's thrashing.

Too far gone even to close her legs, Stephanie lay slumped across the curate's knees, her open thighs providing a clear view of her blood-smeared quim. Too late, she realised what had happened, but still tried to close her thighs, only to have them hauled apart again by her great-aunt.

'Stephanie?' Victoria Truscott demanded.

The remaining aunts, the servants, her grandfather, Sir Murgatroyd Drake and even Freddie himself all clustered behind Stephanie, inspecting her newly deflowered cunt. This culmination of events of the previous hour immediately took the number-one position in her list of life's embarrassing moments.

'Will you stop that, Hermione?' Victoria Truscott demanded. 'I can't hear myself think for Myrtle's squeals.'

Hermione stopped and she too came to see what the fuss was about, gasping as she realised. Mrs Snell also got up, tumbling Myrtle from her lap. Claude Attwater finally found his voice.

'Damn it, Stephanie, that's not cricket! I can't possibly marry you now.'

'Good,' Stephanie replied sullenly.

'And who, pray, is responsible?' Victoria demanded.

'I um ... er ... I rather think it was me,' Freddie admitted.

'What?' Sir Murgatroyd Drake roared, but his voice was lost beneath a babble of questions and accusations, everybody speaking simultaneously, until Sir Richard Truscott finally managed to make himself heard.

'Be quiet, all of you, damn it! Never mind who did what or who's got a thrashing coming to them, although, believe me, it will be anybody who tries to defy me, and that includes you, Vicky. It's perfectly obvious that Stiffy and Freddie will have to get married, and that's all there is to it.'

The curate had loosened his grip and Stephanie pulled herself up, to run straight into the arms of her beloved.

'I say,' he remarked, embracing the naked, hot-bottomed girl.

'Oh, Freddie!' she sighed. 'Kiss me!'

Freddie did so, once, and fled, pulling Stephanie behind him by the hand as his father began to raise his blunderbuss.

nexus

The leading publisher of fetish and adult fiction

TELL US WHAT YOU THINK!

Readers' ideas and opinions matter to us so please take a few minutes to fill in the questionnaire below.

1. Sex: Are you male ☐ female ☐ a couple ☐?

2. Age: Under 21 ☐ 21–30 ☐ 31–40 ☐ 41–50 ☐ 51–60 ☐ over 60 ☐

3. Where do you buy your Nexus books from?
☐ A chain book shop. If so, which one(s)?

_____

☐ An independent book shop. If so, which one(s)?

_____

☐ A used book shop/charity shop
☐ Online book store. If so, which one(s)?

_____

4. How did you find out about Nexus books?
☐ Browsing in a book shop
☐ A review in a magazine
☐ Online
☐ Recommendation
☐ Other _____

5. In terms of settings, which do you prefer? (Tick as many as you like.)
☐ Down to earth and as realistic as possible
☐ Historical settings. If so, which period do you prefer?

_____

☐ Fantasy settings – barbarian worlds
☐ Completely escapist/surreal fantasy

☐ Institutional or secret academy
☐ Futuristic/sci fi
☐ Escapist but still believable
☐ Any settings you dislike?

_____

☐ Where would you like to see an adult novel set?

_____

6. In terms of storylines, would you prefer:

☐ Simple stories that concentrate on adult interests?
☐ More plot and character-driven stories with less explicit adult activity?
☐ We value your ideas, so give us your opinion of this book:

_____

_____

_____

7. In terms of your adult interests, what do you like to read about? (Tick as many as you like.)

☐ Traditional corporal punishment (CP)
☐ Modern corporal punishment
☐ Spanking
☐ Restraint/bondage
☐ Rope bondage
☐ Latex/rubber
☐ Leather
☐ Female domination and male submission
☐ Female domination and female submission
☐ Male domination and female submission
☐ Willing captivity
☐ Uniforms
☐ Lingerie/underwear/hosiery/footwear (boots and high heels)
☐ Sex rituals
☐ Vanilla sex
☐ Swinging
☐ Cross-dressing/TV

☐ Enforced feminisation

☐ Others – tell us what you don't see enough of in adult fiction:

_____

_____

_____

8. Would you prefer books with a more specialised approach to your interests, i.e. a novel specifically about uniforms? If so, which subject(s) would you like to read a Nexus novel about?

_____

_____

_____

9. Would you like to read true stories in Nexus books? For instance, the true story of a submissive woman, or a male slave? Tell us which true revelations you would most like to read about:

_____

_____

_____

10. What do you like best about Nexus books?

_____

_____

11. What do you like least about Nexus books?

_____

_____

12. Which are your favourite titles?

_____

_____

13. Who are your favourite authors?

_____

_____

14. **Which covers do you prefer?** Those featuring:
(Tick as many as you like.)

☐ Fetish outfits
☐ More nudity
☐ Two models
☐ Unusual models or settings
☐ Classic erotic photography
☐ More contemporary images and poses
☐ A blank/non-erotic cover
☐ What would your ideal cover look like?

_____

15. **Describe your ideal Nexus novel in the space provided:**

_____

_____

_____

_____

16. **Which celebrity would feature in one of your Nexus-style fantasies? We'll post the best suggestions on our website – anonymously!**

_____

THANKS FOR YOUR TIME

Now simply write the title of this book in the space below and cut out the questionnaire pages. Post to: Nexus, Marketing Dept., Thames Wharf Studios, Rainville Rd, London W6 9HA

Book title: _____

nexus

NEXUS NEW BOOKS

To be published in June 2008

TRAIL OF SIN
Ray Gordon

When a young man addresses eighteen-year-old Alison as Ali, a name used only by her close friends, she believes it to be a case of mistaken identity. But later in a bar another young man greets her by the same name, saying that her dark hair doesn't suit her. Alison was adopted as a child and begins to think she may have a twin sister who has moved into her neighbourhood and is dating a string of men. Determined to get to the bottom of the mystery, she dies her hair blonde and adopts the other girl's identity. Alison is a shy girl but playing the role of her promiscuous sister plunges her into an underworld of seedy bars and depraved sex and the experience rouses her inner desires. Before long she is revelling in her new-found life of sexual abandon. When Alison finally meets her illusive counterpart, she makes a shocking discovery. Now she must decide her direction in life. Either she can revert to the refined young lady she once was or pursue her darker sexual needs.

£6.99   ISBN 978 0 352 341822

NEIGHBOURHOOD WATCH
Lisette Ashton

Cedar View looks like any other sleepy cul-de-sac in the heart of suburbia. Trees line the sides of the road. The gardens are neat and well maintained. But behind the tightly drawn curtains of each house the neighbours indulge their lewdest and bawdiest appetites. It's not just the dominatrix at number 5, the swingers at number 6 or the sadistically sinister couple at number 4 who have secrets. There's also the curious relationship between the Smiths, the open marriage of the Graftons, not to mention the strange goings-on at the home of Denise, a woman whose lust seems never to be sated. Everyone on Cedar View has a secret – and they're all about to be exposed.

£6.99   ISBN 978 0 352 34190 7

If you would like more information about Nexus titles, please visit our website at www.nexus-books.co.uk, or send a large stamped addressed envelope to:
  Nexus, Thames Wharf Studios,
  Rainville Road, London W6 9HA

NEXUS BOOKLIST

Information is correct at time of printing. To avoid disappointment, check availability before ordering. Go to www.nexus-books.co.uk.

All books are priced at £6.99 unless another price is given.

NEXUS

☐ ABANDONED ALICE	Adriana Arden	ISBN 978 0 352 33969 0
☐ ALICE IN CHAINS	Adriana Arden	ISBN 978 0 352 33908 9
☐ AMERICAN BLUE	Penny Birch	ISBN 978 0 352 34169 3
☐ AQUA DOMINATION	William Doughty	ISBN 978 0 352 34020 7
☐ THE ART OF CORRECTION	Tara Black	ISBN 978 0 352 33895 2
☐ THE ART OF SURRENDER	Madeline Bastinado	ISBN 978 0 352 34013 9
☐ BEASTLY BEHAVIOUR	Aishling Morgan	ISBN 978 0 352 34095 5
☐ BEING A GIRL	Chloë Thurlow	ISBN 978 0 352 34139 6
☐ BELINDA BARES UP	Yolanda Celbridge	ISBN 978 0 352 33926 3
☐ BIDDING TO SIN	Rosita Varón	ISBN 978 0 352 34063 4
☐ BLUSHING AT BOTH ENDS	Philip Kemp	ISBN 978 0 352 34107 5
☐ THE BOOK OF PUNISHMENT	Cat Scarlett	ISBN 978 0 352 33975 1
☐ BRUSH STROKES	Penny Birch	ISBN 978 0 352 34072 6
☐ CALLED TO THE WILD	Angel Blake	ISBN 978 0 352 34067 2
☐ CAPTIVES OF CHEYNER CLOSE	Adriana Arden	ISBN 978 0 352 34028 3
☐ CARNAL POSSESSION	Yvonne Strickland	ISBN 978 0 352 34062 7
☐ CITY MAID	Amelia Evangeline	ISBN 978 0 352 34096 2
☐ COLLEGE GIRLS	Cat Scarlett	ISBN 978 0 352 33942 3
☐ COMPANY OF SLAVES	Christina Shelly	ISBN 978 0 352 33887 7
☐ CONCEIT AND CONSEQUENCE	Aishling Morgan	ISBN 978 0 352 33965 2
☐ CORRECTIVE THERAPY	Jacqueline Masterson	ISBN 978 0 352 33917 1
☐ CORRUPTION	Virginia Crowley	ISBN 978 0 352 34073 3

NEXUS NON FICTION

-------- ✂ --------------------------------

Please send me the books I have ticked above.

Name   ....

Address   ....

            ....

            ....

            .... Post code ....

Send to: **Virgin Books Cash Sales, Thames Wharf Studios, Rainville Road, London W6 9HA**

US customers: for prices and details of how to order books for delivery by mail, call 888-330-8477.

Please enclose a cheque or postal order, made payable to **Nexus Books Ltd**, to the value of the books you have ordered plus postage and packing costs as follows:

UK and BFPO – £1.00 for the first book, 50p for each subsequent book.

Overseas (including Republic of Ireland) – £2.00 for the first book, £1.00 for each subsequent book.

If you would prefer to pay by VISA, ACCESS/MASTERCARD, AMEX, DINERS CLUB or SWITCH, please write your card number and expiry date here:

....

Please allow up to 28 days for delivery.

Signature ....

Our privacy policy

We will not disclose information you supply us to any other parties. We will not disclose any information which identifies you personally to any person without your express consent.

From time to time we may send out information about Nexus books and special offers. Please tick here if you do *not* wish to receive Nexus information.   ☐

-------- ✂ --------------------------------